VAMPIRE'S HEIR I

GREYMANTLE CHRONICLES

BOOK SIX

J DAVID BAXTER

Disclaimer:

This is a work of fiction. Any resemblance to action, events or persons, living or dead, is entirely coincidental.

Design and Production by Silver Paw Publishing.

Editing services by Dale McDowell.

Cover design by J David Baxter

Hardcover: 978-1-953708-27-4
Paperback: 978-1-953708-26-7
Ebook: 978-1-953708-25-0

For more on the Greymantle Chronicles series see:

Jdavidbaxter.com or GreymantleChronicles.com

This book is dedicated to:

My parents for fostering and enabling my life-long love of scifi and fantasy stories.

My oldest friend, Lawrence Verrett, without whom this particular world would never have evolved.

And especially to my wife for her support, patience, and invaluable assistance in getting this novel polished and completed.

CHAPTER 1
WORST BUFFET EVER!

NATE HAD TRIED to warn me...

I hadn't listened, though. Maybe because Nate had always been a jerk to me when he was a kid and made fun of my name, Chapman Daniel Hurley. I had tried to ignore it. Being several years older, it shouldn't have mattered to me. Unfortunately, I never liked my name, and I was self-conscious about it, which made Nate's teenage mocking a little too effective. That may be why the guy's statement about my garnet-set bronze pendant being magical seemed like some kind of strange roundabout jab. If only I could go back now and ask the jerk what he had meant and how he could have known.

Ugh... I'm getting ahead of myself.

Let me back up and start from the beginning of this terrible night.

This should have been one of the greatest nights of my life. My friend Barry and I were in Vegas, ostensibly to attend a Cybersecurity conference for which my employer was footing the bill. In truth, we were there to enjoy ourselves. I had never visited Sin City before and had heard all my life how much fun it could be. Its dining was legendary, with hundreds of great restaurants and dozens owned by celebrity chefs. Then, there was the gambling and the dream of hitting it rich. It might be a long shot, but I had nearly ten grand in the bank to spend or gamble away, thanks to that server build that Nate had commissioned a few weeks ago.

He was my friend Marcy's nephew, and he seemed to have matured a lot since his teen years, but what did I care if he was willing to throw his money around like that? I would have even put up with him mocking my name the way he had as a kid, using that annoying fake British accent. "Oiy, Mr. Chapman Hurley, sir, be a good Chap and fetch me a crumpet."

Never mind that we were both born and raised in Texas, and his fake accent was atrocious. I needed to put those thoughts out of my mind. The real question is how he had known my pendant was magic. I didn't believe in magic, so I ignored him. At first, he had just said, "It's pretty cool; looks magical." That hadn't been enough at the time to make me notice. Still, a minute later, he got a funny, serious look on his face and added, "Hey, be careful of that pendant; it really does look magic. Never know what something like that might do."

That had been all. Nate didn't elaborate, and I had dismissed his comment then, unsure what to make of it. I mean, who believes in magic in this day and age?

Well, I do now, but it's far too late for that to matter. What's done is done.

Crap, I'm still getting ahead of myself and not getting to the point.

The point is, I'm dead now. The magic pendant did its thing. Only, I'm still determining if I'm happy about that. I guess I should be happy. Obviously, I'm not actually dead, just undead.

That was quite a shock, and I'm still getting used to it. You see, I made the mistake of interfering with a robbery and got ganked for my troubles.

Barry and I had arrived in Vegas that afternoon. We had rented this little AirBnB just off the Strip. It was a nice neighborhood, or so we thought at the time. The house was built in the late 70s or early 80s and had a pool in the backyard. It wasn't anything to write home about, but I couldn't argue with the price of cheap.

We had settled in and unpacked and were about to head out to the casinos for dinner, planning to demolish some unsuspecting buffet and make them regret their 'all you can eat' policy. It was early, only about 8:15 or 8:30, but being the winter solstice, the sun was down, and the stars and moon were out. Not that you could see many stars with the light pollution in Vegas. Even so, the moon looked particularly cool, and I couldn't help but notice that it was shaped just like my pendant.

I might as well digress a bit more and describe the evil thing. I had purchased it at an estate sale in Dallas a few weeks before. Some old guy had kicked the bucket and didn't have any heirs or something. The agent at the sale had grumbled about his plane going down with his inheritors all on board, causing a mess of paperwork.

I might seem a little callous, but after what happened to me tonight, I don't have a lot of sympathy for the guy. As I was saying, it was a high-end sale, not something I would typically attend, but the guy had been a client of the company I worked for, so I had heard about it at the office.

I found a cool-looking old pendant at the estate sale. A layer of dust coated the surface. It took a wipe down with my shirt sleeve to clean off the smudges and reveal its true luster. The metal was tarnished but aged in that wonderful patina that comes from having been handled by people's hands over centuries; the beaded patterns were raised above the surface and polished. The center stone looked like a garnet, but I couldn't be sure.

It looked like a piece of costume jewelry, like something someone would wear with a Viking cosplay: vaguely Celtic with swirls, and not made of gold and fine gemstones... I could have easily sung, "One of these things is not like the others," as I looked at the items displayed on the table. All the other watches and jewelry were high-end pieces, Rolexes or gold and diamonds. Here this thing was, looking like some reject from a historical reenactor's closet.

It looked cool enough for me to ask about it—I mean, really, who doesn't love ancient geeky stuff? When I asked, the agent told me she didn't know anything other than it had been found in an ornate wooden box among the old man's things.

"I supposed it was just something with sentimental value he had picked up in his youth or something. Looks like Art Deco to me, but it's not gold, just bronze, and the gem is only a garnet. If someone cleaned it up, it would be worth a couple of hundred dollars, but I've got to liquidate the estate, so if you are interested, I'll take $30."

Idiot that I was, I jumped at the chance and bought it, thinking it might be valuable since it had been owned by some old rich guy and had been part of a rather pricey collection. I took it to a local jeweler and had it looked at, but no luck. The appraiser told me it was just a costume piece. Bronze and fitted with a garnet. She offered me a hundred bucks because she said it would go well with her Renaissance Faire costume.

She wasn't wrong. Still, rather than Art Deco, it looked like some ancient Viking or Celtic design to me. Except that it didn't look that old. If anything, after the jeweler had taken it out of the ultrasonic cleaner, it seemed almost brand new without the dirt and grime it had previously been coated with. Even so, I couldn't shake the feeling that it was ancient.

Looking back, I should have taken her offer; maybe I'd still be alive.

And that brings me back to what happened tonight. We were just about to get into my old beater of a car: a 1990s Honda CRX that I had gotten as part of the deal I made with Nate for the server build. It had held up surprisingly well on the drive from Dallas despite having over 250,000 miles on it.

That was when we heard a scream from a couple houses over. It didn't sound like someone was just yelling in anger or surprise. It was a sound full of fear and desperation, the 'Oh, shit, I'm about to die!' kind.

Barry hesitated, but I rushed to the end of the driveway to see what was happening. I was just in time to see a couple of guys shoving a big-screen TV into the back of an old van. It took me a second to analyze the scene, but it was obvious. The man screaming must have come home from an evening jog just in time to see his house being robbed and tried to stop them.

Unfortunately for him, besides the two guys manhandling the TV, there was a third robber, and he had a knife. It wasn't just some switchblade or pocket knife either. It was big enough to catch the moonlight and look scary even from where I stood.

Barry had caught up to me and urged, "Just call the cops, man! Don't get involved...."

Barry was smarter than me.

Big-ass-knife-guy had grabbed the homeowner by his shirt, put his blade to the guy's throat, and was hissing something at him, probably threatening him to be quiet. Still, the jogger was too panicked to listen and kept screaming.

I felt ice in my guts. Everything seemed to be happening in slow motion, while at the same time, it was all happening too fast to think.

I instinctively knew Stabby McStabberton was about a second away from slashing the dude's throat. He looked almost as panicked as his victim due to the screams. The guy was going to die if someone didn't do something.

I didn't need to look around again. There wasn't anyone around other than Barry and me, at least, no one who could stop what was about to happen. I wanted to avoid getting involved. I really did. This week in Vegas was supposed to be a vacation to remember for the rest of my life, not because of seeing someone get killed or trying to save them.

My dumb ass couldn't stand still and watch it happen without at least trying to stop it. I'd feel guilty for the rest of my life if I didn't do something.

I wished Barry would do something. He was a black belt in karate. Unfortunately, I knew him too well. It was not in his nature to put himself at risk. He had trained hundreds or thousands of hours in self-defense, not so that he could get into a potentially deadly fight, but because he was afraid of conflict. It was crazy, but it was true. I respected the heck out of his IT skills, but I'd known him long enough to know he wasn't someone I could count on to have my back in a situation like this. I didn't blame him, but still, I couldn't watch someone die.

I yelled as loud as I could, "Hey! Let him go!"

Jack-the-Ripper whirled around, eyes wide, realizing his worst fears had come true. All the man's screaming had drawn attention, and now there were witnesses. He quickly looked around but saw no one other than Barry and me. He hadn't let the man go, however.

One of the two guys at the truck yelled, "Let's go!"

The thug with the knife shook his head, "I can't afford to go back there; we gotta make sure these assholes don't talk. Hold onto this one while I take care of these idiots."

I had been moving toward him while that exchange had occurred. I don't know what I had hoped to accomplish but did succeed in causing Stabby to take the knife from the throat of the guy and shove him roughly toward the accomplices.

"Yay, I succeeded...." That thought was filled with much sarcasm and was about as dry as the desert surrounding the city.

I looked around but found nothing to defend myself with, and now instead of coming to the rescue, I needed saving. I yelled over my shoulder, "Barry, stay where you are and call 911!"

I halted my own advance at the same time, but it was too late. The scruffy thug charged at me with that big knife that looked like a machete now that I was closer. I swear, the damn blade was a foot and a half long, at least. I was about to turn and run when I tripped over a crack in the sidewalk and fell on my ass.

Now I was really panicking and scrambled to my feet, but the guy kicked me from behind, causing me to sprawl out, scraping my hands on the concrete. I tried to roll with the fall, but the best I managed was to stumble back to my feet and turn to face him. I might die, but at least I wouldn't do it with a knife in my back. Besides, he was too close now, and I could not run without getting stabbed.

I'd like to say I faced my death with dignity and put up a hell of a fight, but it didn't go down like that. When I squared off against him, he slashed at my face and cut my cheek from ear to chin.

Despite the adrenaline, it still hurt like hell. Blood was streaming down my chin and neck in seconds. They say head wounds bleed a lot, and this one sure did.

My would-be killer tried to take another couple of swings at me, but I miraculously dodged one, and the next hit my pendant.

I should have been thankful for it deflecting the blow. It would have severed my jugular after all, except the damn pendant chose that moment to make its own attack. In hindsight, it wasn't an attack, but that was how it felt to me then.

The chain, which should have been loose enough to slip easily over my head, suddenly felt tight, like someone was using it to choke me, except the only person behind me was Barry. I could hear him screaming into his phone half a block away for the police to show up, "Because we are being murdered, that's why! Just get them here now!"

I didn't hear whatever else he said because that was when I felt the real pain begin.

There was a stabbing sensation in my throat. It felt like the two points of the crescent moon were digging into my skin, which they were. Then instead of feeling more blood loss where the thing was piercing my neck, it felt like I was being injected with liquid fire.

I don't know if you've ever had an IV or some other shot where they pump something into you, but it was like that, except filled with napalm.

I don't know what happened with the burglar turned murder-hobo, but he was no longer my primary concern. I was literally being choked to death while the pendant injected me with the blood of an ancient vampire.

Actually, THE ancient vampire, the one that started them all.

I didn't know that yet, though. At that moment, all I knew was that my heart was struggling to pump liquid magma through my veins. Every inch of my body hurt more than anything I'd ever experienced. Everywhere, and all at the same time!

Luckily that's when I blacked out and no longer felt like I was burning alive from the inside out.

CHAPTER 2
DREAM A LITTLE DREAM

As my vision began, I found myself standing outside a circular hut of mud-daubed walls and a thatch roof surrounded by ancient trees. A woman in furs crouched over a fire, chanting words that sounded foreign to me, yet I understood their meaning perfectly. Surrounding her was a thick atmosphere of magic and dread as she painted strange symbols around her using her own blood.

I wish I could say it was a fever dream, and I woke up in the hospital, and everything was all better, but there was no denying what I experienced.

I will spare you the details since it wouldn't translate well anyway, and I mean that literally. She was speaking to me in ancient proto-Indo-European or something. It was some pre-bronze-age shit, but I understood her perfectly, thanks to the magic.

I felt like every atom of my being was electrified by her presence as she began telling her story—a story of how, thousands of years ago, a powerful blood sorceress had discovered a way to defy death, becoming the first vampire.

Or perhaps I should say the crazy blood sorceress turned herself into a vampire to keep from dying. Even our ancestors feared death and tried to avoid it.

Queenie, that's what I'm going to call her... was a sorceress who practiced blood magic and was known even before her death as the Blood Queen. She lived in a time when cities were still new, and bronze hadn't been invented yet. She powered her spells with blood because it was the most potent of all forms of magic.

... I'm taking Queenie's word for it. Hell, two minutes ago, I didn't even believe magic existed.

Even in that dark, chaotic time, most considered blood sacrifice an abomination. Still, the Blood Queen had the power, both politically and magically, to do as she wished. She kept her people safe and well-fed through her magic, so they feared and respected her instead of lighting torches and gathering pitchforks. She only ever used the blood of their enemies in her magic, which she primarily spent for the benefit of her city-state.

In time, however, even she could no longer sustain her own life through magic and felt the icy hand of death reaching out for her. So it was that she devised one last terrible spell.

She sacrificed a victim every night for a year. At the culmination of her casting, she put to death over a thousand of her enemies, using their blood and sacrifice to turn herself into the first vampire. She was different from all the others who came later because she did not lose her ability to do magic when she died. She built that into the design of her ritual.

There was no way she would live forever and give up the thing that made her so powerful. There were rules, of course; it might be magic, but everything has limitations. Still, she understood them better than any other. Apparently, mages existed back then, and according to her, the rest of them were crap compared to what she could do with blood magic.

By modern sensibilities, and even by the standards of her own day, she was considered evil. Still, no one ever accused her of being a fool. She made others into vampires over the centuries but never passed on the ability to use magic. Her progeny had great powers and abilities beyond those of mortal man, as the legends suggest... but not magic. That she reserved for herself alone.

It pissed her children off. Instead of being grateful for their immortality and supernatural gifts, they became jealous that she could do something they could not.

Time passed, and more time and my children grew powerful, and vampires were feared across all the earth.

Unfortunately, they could not be satisfied with what they had, but always wanted the secret of my great power. I refused and rebuked them, even sending many to their final deaths.

Later generations grew in numbers and plotted in secret. In time, the old ways were forgotten; even bronze tarnished and gave way to iron. In that ending was sown the seeds of my destruction. After plotting for many years, the eldest and most potent of all my descendants came together and attacked. But they, too, were cunning and knew I could never be defeated so long as I had blood, so their attack did not strike at me but at my people. They raised an army and slaughtered the towns near my home.

Not seeing the threat at first, I was slow to rise. I had known only power and dominance for millennia. I strode onto the battlefield like a titan, ready to punish those who would threaten me, only to discover the mortal invaders themselves lay slain on the field, their bodies drained. Then I was attacked by legions of young vampires. I took some damage but quickly destroyed them all. I sought to pursue the plot's leaders but found the same everywhere. Dead villages and towns, without a drop of blood to drink, and newly made vampires all crazed with thirst. Only then did I realize the true threat I faced. Their strategy was not to do battle but to starve and rob me of what gave me power. Perhaps the leaders thought to weaken me and force me to provide them with the secret of magic, or they simply wanted to eliminate the only one with an ability they did not possess.

Regardless, their plan succeeded. After months of this running battle, with cities and even entire civilizations destroyed, I was ground down, my strength all but drained. At last, as I neared the end, unable to heal any longer or sustain myself. My children drove stakes into my flesh and, with cold iron, removed my head, and with that action, they unknowingly sealed their own doom.

Queenie had the last laugh. She had held two other secrets until the end. First, she used her magic and linked their blood to hers, and with her death, the magic that sustained them lost its source and unraveled, leaving a field full of fanged corpses rather than just one.

So ended the first race of vampires.

The second secret she took to her grave was this amulet. Before the end, she had created an artifact to hold her essence and pass it on when it found someone worthy. Not that I feel all that worthy, but apparently, dying while facing overwhelming odds during a winter solstice with a crescent moon in the sky did the trick. Or maybe it was just that I was facing death, and it was nighttime; I don't know.

Whatever!

I'm undead now, so middle fingers to you, Queenie, for doing this to me. Although I shouldn't be ungrateful, I might be dead if it weren't for you.

Sorry to get a bit flowery there; that was the way Queenie talked. It was all very grandiose and more than a little self-important. In truth, though, I was pretty impressed. She was scary as hell, and her *presence* made me feel like a mouse facing down a lion. That said, I am not sure Queenie killed off all the vampires when she died the way she thought she did. It wasn't a feeling I got in the vision; I'm sure she believed what she said.

It's just the fact that vampires still exist in the public consciousness. There are too many stories and movies for them to have been something that only existed thousands of years ago. I don't know... maybe some of those newly turned thirst-crazed vamps survived the battles, fled into the hills and forests, and laid low until the war was over. Or perhaps someone else figured out the secret to making vampires independently. Either way, I doubted they were all gone.

That event became known as the “Late Bronze Age Collapse” by historians and anthropologists.

Yeah, their fight to kill her literally caused the fall of so many civilizations that scientists are still puzzled to this day on what the hell happened to cause them all to die out at once.

CHAPTER 3
NOW WHAT?

So there I was, lying on a fake grass lawn in some Vegas suburb with Jack the Ripper and his big-ass knife standing over me. His two pals were manhandling the poor guy who started the worst evening of my life with his scream. My friend turned to run away like a little bitch, screaming into his phone for the 911 operator to please send help.

After all, when seconds count, the police are only minutes away!

As I opened my eyes after the vision finished, all of that was frozen in place. I blinked a few times, both overwhelmed by the sudden brightness of the night thanks to my new overly sensitive vampire eyes and in shock at the fact that no one was moving.

It was like someone had a cosmic TV remote and had hit pause. Time was stopped, and that's not just a metaphor. It was like that scene in the movie where that speedster is going so fast that it looks like everyone around him is standing completely still.

Before my untimely death, I was an IT guy, so I kinda understand science. Even so, I had no idea how something like this was possible.

They weren't just going slow; they weren't moving at all. Time was straight-up frozen. The part of my brain that thought it understood the laws of physics was rebelling against this. It shouldn't be possible. If I really was in some kind of Planck time moment between tick and tock on the cosmic clock, then I shouldn't be able to see. The light should not be able to reach my eyes!

Ugh... Queenie was really throwing me for a loop with this one.

After a few minutes of walking around, getting used to my new and improved body, and poking at the thug statues, I decided it was time to stop trying to understand how magic could make physics take a time-out and do something useful instead.

That brought me to a halt. What was I going to do now?

My old life had just ended. I could still see the spot on the ground stained with my blood where I had fallen. As far as the world was concerned, I had just died.

I was a vampire now, according to Queenie. She had told me all about what that entailed and about the magic to which I now had access using the blood of my victims.

Theoretically, if I had enough blood, I could do crazy shit like this time-stop. Except, I had no idea how she had done that. Even with her explanations, which were rudimentary, there is no way I could visualize how this was possible. Based on her explanation, I could make it a reality using blood magic if I could conceptualize something. Only, I couldn't wrap my head around what she had done here or how she had done it. I guess that means stopping time is out for me.

That was a shame. All kinds of crazy ideas were starting to make their way into my brain on what I could do with time stopped. Unfortunately, I only had this one night.

According to Queenie, however long I had until dawn was how many hours I had before I was returned to the normal flow of time. She had done it to give me a head start on my enemies. She had assumed that whatever enemies I faced would be due to them seeking the amulet. She hadn't imagined that the artifact would trigger due to some random punks trying to burgle a TV.

One thing I was sure of. I couldn't go back to my old life. I have seen too many movies and TV shows where something supernatural happens, and the person's family and friends all end up getting dragged into it and dying. At this point, I had to figure wizards and vampires, and who knows what else was real. I didn't want the people I cared about to suffer because of me.

Besides, there were four witnesses who just saw me fall to the ground bleeding out. How was I going to explain that?

I did have the desire to punch a hole right through the head of that asshole with the knife, but again, that would draw attention to the fact that something obviously supernatural had happened here, and that seemed like a bad idea.

First things first, Barry wasn't exactly a close friend, and I didn't even know the jogger, but I couldn't let them get killed either, not when I could easily stop it from happening. Looking at the scene, I gave it some quick thought and settled on the simplest solution.

I walked over, picked Barry up, then carried him closer to the AirBnB and carefully put him down precisely like he had been so he wouldn't trip and fall when time restarted. He would simply be closer to safety. I was amazed at my new strength. Before my untimely demise, I would have struggled to pick my friend up, much less carry him half a block. He had to weigh 200 lbs at least. Now, however, I could have done it one-handed without effort if there had been an easy way to hold him.

Hmm... what to do about the jogger dude?

I couldn't leave him to die, either. Hell, technically, I had just given my life to save his. This was going to be the biggy, though. I couldn't think of any way to save him without it looking supernatural. With Barry, they could have just blinked and missed him taking off at a sprint. That would be easy to explain, but not so much with the jogger.

Maybe...

I suddenly felt a shit-eating grin split my face. There was that movie with the speedster, and when he tapped someone on the forehead while going super speed, they flew backward when time returned to their perspective. What would happen if I kicked knife-boy in the nuts?

I could still manipulate matter. I had just carried Barry half a block and put him back down. If I gave these guys nutshots, I bet they would double over when time started again.

With that plan in place, I first took the big-ass knife away from Choppy McChopperton and stuck it in the ground halfway across the yard next to a small shrub as if it had been thrown there. It had my blood on it, so the asshole would get convicted if he didn't get it back and run the fuck away real fast once time started up again.

Next, I removed the burglars' hands from their victim and gave them each a quick punch to the junk. Not with vampire strength. I was already risking doing severe damage considering the time-stop. I had no idea if I was in some kind of superspeed mode, but I doubted it. If I were, however, their most beloved parts would turn into a fine red mist, and they would probably fly backward about half a mile, or parts of them would anyway. As much as I was pissed at them, I hoped that wouldn't be the case.

After a satisfied smile at that thought, I gently took the jogger dude from them and got his keys into his hand, along with his pepper spray. Sadly, it wouldn't work with physics half-suspended with this time-stop happening, but at least he could hit them with it if they closed on him again. I also moved him down the road to just a little way behind Barry. Hopefully, jogger dude would not be too confused to run.

Last, and definitely the most satisfying, I punched Jack-the-Ripper in the nuts a bit harder than his friends. Fuck him. Fuck him for causing my death!

Fuck it. If I was going to be caught trying to save Barry and the jogger's lives, then I would do this right.

I smirked with satisfaction as I untied his shoes, then unbuttoned and unzipped his pants and gave them a little tug so that if he started running to chase my friend or the jogger, he would not get very far without falling on his face, with his pants around his knees. I wanted to do the same to the others, but that would have been too much of a coincidence to pass off.

There was a lot more I would have liked to have done, but I didn't have any Sharpies, and I didn't want to waste this time on strangers, even though several of my ideas would have been pretty funny.

I wished electronics were working. I would have texted the people I loved. Maybe the authorities would have written that off as a dying man using his last moments to say goodbye.

That made me start thinking about how my family and friends would take the news of my death, but I had to put those thoughts aside. I just couldn't deal with that right now. If I went down that road, I wasn't sure I could function. All this would overwhelm me, and I'd waste the head start that Queenie had sacrificed so much to give me.

Not that anyone was after me, thankfully, but she had been running for her unlife for months fighting a losing battle of attrition, and she wanted to make sure she got away when her blood reawakened in me.

Fortunately, reawakened turned out to be metaphorical rather than metaphysical. Queenie turned me into a vampire– one with some serious mojo, but I don't have a puppet master controlling my body and making me her meat puppet, thankfully.

CHAPTER 4
HITTING THE CASINO

So what did I do with that head start timestop?

What would you do if you were in Vegas and you could get away with robbing a casino?

Oops, spoilers!

Yeah, there were millions of dollars in cash lying all over the place just minutes from where I was and all I had to do was walk in and take it. My biggest problem was how to get the most and get away with it. With time stopped I could literally take an 18-wheeler full of cash, except that I didn't know how to drive one, and even if I did, trucks wouldn't work because time was stopped.

I could manipulate everything around me and there was light from the electric streetlights. Don't even get me started on how the hell that could work with time stopped, but all I can say was that it was halted more than frozen if that makes any damned sense at all. Everything existed, but the laws of physics were half-fucked. If I could physically move it, it would move. I figured this all out in just a few minutes after the necklace let go and the dead Queen in the necklace stopped talking at me. I could open a car door, but the engine wouldn't start. On the bright side, I figured out really quickly that I'm fast. Really fast... faster than a car, fast.

I ran to the strip in less than five minutes. It was so strange dodging between the cars that were stopped in mid-motion. Some douche was flicking a cigarette out of his window, and it hung in the air, its end glowing and smoke frozen, swirling through the air behind it.

Seriously freaky!

I picked the first big major casino I came across, figuring it would have more cash on hand than one of the little boys. Once inside, I looked around to get the lay of the land and figure out where their exchange booth was.

It was tempting to just grab trays of $10,000 dollar chips, but there was no way I'd ever be able to cash them in. From their perspective, the chips would literally disappear in the blink of an eye and they would sure as hell notice something like that when they tallied up their chips. Then they'd be on the lookout for anyone who ever came in using those chips.

Nope, it had to be cash. Cash was king, and that meant getting into that locked exchange booth. I thought about my greater than normal strength which led me down the rabbit hole of thinking about what it would be like to show off to my friends and family. Which, in turn, led me to think again about what would happen to them if they got mixed up with vampires. That would turn tragic real fast...

That thought almost distracted me, I was going to have to deal with some serious angsty introspection, and I knew it. However, this time-stop was a once-in-my-immortal-existence opportunity, so brooding and moping would have to wait until tomorrow. Tonight needed to be about funding my undead life.

It's not like my life insurance policy would pay out after this. That almost distracted me again... *Damn it, that shit needs to wait until tomorrow!*

Looking at the door to the exchange room, I saw that it was magnetically sealed rather than with a physical lock. Access was granted by a combination of a key card and biometric scanner, which would disable the electromagnet that held the door shut. I had run into doors like this in my merely mortal days and knew that no regular human could pull one open, but I figured it was worth a try. Perhaps my vamp strength could do what my mortal muscles couldn't.

I tugged, lightly testing, not knowing how strong I might be and not wanting to rip the door from its hinges in case I turned out to be superhero-strong. I was relieved and disappointed to discover that another aspect of physics was fucked in this weird time-stop realm. The magnetic lock parted without any difficulty, magnetism apparently being malleable or something. It honestly hurt my brain trying to think about how that could be possible.

Fuck it! The door was open so I walked in and looked around. There were three people inside and several carts which held chips and cash: one with chips being brought in, and the others presumably being staged to send back to the counting room. I didn't know how much cash that was, but it made me realize I had made two mistakes.

First, this was of all denominations, so it would not be the most efficient way of making myself rich. The second being that I had no way of carrying the cash. I should have stopped by a sporting goods store and grabbed some duffel bags or something.

Well, shit!

Surely their counting room would have cash bags, but even those wouldn't be large enough to be all that helpful. If time wasn't stopped, I could mojo someone here to tell me where the counting room was, but since that wasn't an option. I'd have to find it myself.

I had seen enough movies about Vegas that I expected it would be downstairs in a secure location. Still, there would need to be a fairly easy route from the exchange booth to the counting room since they wouldn't want piles of cash getting rolled past customers or hotel guests. Sure enough, there was another door at the back of the room with security on the inside. Like the outer door, it swung open without resistance, and I followed the concrete hallway a short distance to an elevator.

That presented another problem, no time = no elevator. I pushed open the doors, and as luck would have it, the elevator was not on this floor. Looking down the dark shaft, I could see it below, but there were metal rungs in the wall for emergency or maintenance, so I simply climbed down and got to the elevator. It had a hatch on its roof which I popped open and dropped inside. The doors were open, and there was a pair of guards and another employee with a cart of cash just exiting.

I squeezed past their creepy mannequin-like forms into another concrete hallway leading to a steel security door that looked like it could resist a grenade. It, too, opened as easily as could be thanks to the absence of certain laws of physics. Not for the first time, I almost wished that wasn't the case, because I knew enough about physics to know this shouldn't be possible. PFM apparently. Pure fucking magic...

Whatever it was, I walked into a large room with all the cash I could ever want. There were tables around the room where counting machines stood in use, with employees feeding stacks of bills into them. Other tables where already processed bundles of banknotes stood stacked and ready to be transported to wherever it was casinos sent their money. A bank, I would guess, although perhaps they had some big vault down here full of millions in cash? It didn't matter as there was more cash in this one room than I could carry, even with vampiric strength.

I walked over and found one table had bundles of $100 notes. They were used, thankfully, and I took a bundle in my hands and marveled at it as I flipped through the bills. Once the wonder wore off, I looked around but just could not find anything useful to carry the cash in. I gave up and decided I should hit a store and grab some duffels.

I could carry three at a time, given how awkward they would be due to their size and the fact that I'd have to get them through the open hatch at the top of the elevator.

It took what felt like half an hour for me to find the closest sporting goods store, and I had to force open their automatic door since it wouldn't move, but they had lots of bags to choose from, so I grabbed three large ones and hurried back to the casino counting room. My inner child was dancing around the aisles of the candy store in bliss. I packed the bags full of bundled cash, mostly $ 100's, but some $ 20's. I wanted to maximize my take, after all. How much cash would fit in three full duffels? It had to be a lot.

It occurred to me at that point that this was going to be something unexplainable to the Casino, a clear supernatural event. If there were mages, vampires, or other things, they would surely be suspected or even called in to try to find me, but hopefully, being out of time, it would not be easy for them. A bomb and a fire would cover my tracks nicely, but I wouldn't want anyone to get hurt.

That got me thinking, though. I couldn't actually create fire, but I could douse piles of money in gasoline and leave something that would ignite it once time started back up for them. That was when I thought of that cigarette the driver had tossed out of his car window... it was already lit. Hmm... maybe I could throw them off the track of it being supernatural altogether? If there was a power outage right as a fire broke out in the counting room, they might think it was a heist and look for regular thieves. That put a smile on my face. A backup generator would kick on very quickly within a minute, I would guess, and that would allow the people to escape the room and get away.

That settled, I ran back to the AirBnB and dropped off the duffels full of my ill-gotten gains, and went door to door until I found a couple of gas cans in people's garages. I also grabbed a lit cigarette from someone outside the casino in the designated smoking area. Back in the counting room, I poured out the gas on piles of cash and placed the cigarette on a pile in the very back of the room.

Once time started again, the lights would fail, a fire would start immediately, and there would be confusion in the room as emergency lights kicked on. The fire suppression system for this room would fail, though. I also made sure the door was open to both the emergency stairs and the counting room. People should be able to get out quickly enough not to get hurt. That was the one thing that worried me. I set everything up to maximize their ability to get out safely, but I really hoped no one would panic and get hurt in the confusion. Even with the fire system for the room broken, everyone should have time to get out.

I spent a good hour making sure everything was in place and would go off as planned before taking three more duffels of cash. I really, and I mean really, wanted to take some chips too, just for the fun of it, but I knew the chips had electronics inside, and even if I never used one in a casino, it would still be a physical object linking me to the place of the crime which was not a great idea.

With an undead sigh, I made my way back and dropped off the other three duffels at the house. With there being no way to tell time, I couldn't be sure how long I had been at this, but it couldn't have taken more than three or four hours so far, leaving me more than half the night to get out of town, or... or what?

What else could I do? I wasn't a native of Vegas, I lived in Dallas. Or rather, I had lived there, but could I go on with my life as it was before? No. I needed to go off-grid. Or was it off the radar? Whatever, I needed to fake my own death somehow and get out of this town. My family would be sad but better that than dead, I reminded myself. I was pretty sure my earlier reasoning was true. If I existed, then it was likely that lots of other things that go bump in the night did too.

Hey, maybe I'm being paranoid, but I was just killed by the amulet of an ancient blood sorceress vampire, so maybe it's not that far-fetched.

Ok, so how do I fake my own death? I already had four witnesses that saw me die, but there wouldn't be a body now...

I needed a body. Fortunately, I was pretty sure that I could make the stand-in look like me with the use of magic. Queenie had explained how to use it, and it didn't sound too complicated. I just needed blood to power the spell. To be sure it would work, I needed the body to be the same height and shape as mine.

I would also need a place that was dark and private and that wouldn't be investigated during the day, like a vacant house. With all this, I wasn't going to have enough time to get out of the city before my time-stop ran out.

One of those things was a lot easier than the other. There were motels all over, and it was easy enough to snag the key to a room from the desk and mark it occupied on the white-erase board they used to keep track of which were empty. Apparently, their computer system was down. I seemed to be awfully lucky tonight—or maybe unlucky; I did die after all.

I stashed the six duffel bags in the bathroom and hung the *Do Not Disturb* sign on the door. I would be back before time started up again and would be in the room to guard the money during the day, so that was no worry.

I won't go into the gruesome details, but let's just say I found a funeral home where the deceased was having a closed-casket funeral followed by cremation. I can't express how icky it was to take the corpse back to my AirBnB, dress him in my blood-drenched clothes, and put him in the spot where I had died.

The last thing I did was something I had been dreading but was eager for at the same time. I cast a spell.

My body was still full of my own blood to power it, but it was scary. The vampire queen had passed on the knowledge of what would happen if I was stupid enough to burn the blood that was sustaining my existence. I should always use fresh blood taken after I was past the point of satiating my hunger. If I was hungry, it meant the magic of the vampirism needed more fuel to keep me alive. I was pretty sure that the fact that I had just died and had a body full of blood—my own fresh blood, plus the blood injected into me by the amulet—meant that I had enough to do magic with. If I was wrong, I might be in seriously bad shape the next day. On the other hand, due to the current crazy circumstances, I might be able to cast several small spells or one or two bigger ones before tapping out.

I had considered drinking blood in order to gain more, as loath as I was to start that before I had to. However, with time stopped, people's blood wasn't pumping through their bodies right now, and I wasn't sure what it would do to them if I tried to suck it out. I figured it would be akin to sticking a suction hose up to their veins. It would probably damage them at the very least, but it might do much worse like stop their heart. Whatever happened under that circumstance couldn't be good.

Well, this was Vegas, so I might as well gamble!

I willed a small amount of the blood in my system to fuel the spell I wanted to cast. It converted into power that I shaped with my will and intention, and the body transformed into me. Or rather, the poor guy who was already dead and had been mourned, took on the appearance of me. The authorities would see my corpse: it looked like me; it was in my clothes and carrying my ID. My friend had seen me die; the jogger had seen me die. They would have no reason at all to suspect the crazy supernatural shit that had happened. If they did an autopsy, I might be in trouble, but at least from the outside, he looked just like me, and he would have my blood smeared all over him.

Once all that was done, I was sure I couldn't have a great deal of time left in my twelve hours of darkness before time would resume so I took the storage card out of my phone, which held the pictures of my family I wanted to keep, and ran back to the motel. I grabbed a couple of extra blankets and used them to ensure no light could get through the windows and fry me during the day.

After that, I looked over the duffels and took the money out, and counted it just for entertainment. The stacks completely covered the two twin beds in the room and totaled a staggering $42 million. I was honestly surprised they had so much cash in their counting room, but there was a major convention in town for the weekend, so perhaps that was why. I was sure of one thing, though, they were going to be pissed.

I was going to need to get the hell out of Vegas quickly, and though I hated to do it, LA was the closest place where I could lose myself and hide while I figured out where to go. I had been there a few times over the years and knew where the airports were. I wasn't about to try and board a plane, not even a private one, in Vegas in the next couple of weeks. The casino would have those watched like a hawk. That meant driving at night, which also meant stealing or "borrowing" a car.

My thoughts were interrupted just then. I could tell the moment the sun rose.

It felt like all the strength was draining out of me, and I wanted very much to sleep. I wasn't helpless, thankfully, just super weak. I quickly stuffed all the money back in the bags and shoved a chair up under the door handle after locking it with both the bolt and flip lock all hotels seemed to have. Then I collapsed onto the bed nearest the bathroom. I didn't like how trapped I felt, but there was nothing I could do about it. Going out into the sun would be death, and with so little time to look for a place, this had been the best I could come up with. With that thought, I was out.

CHAPTER 5
GETTING THE HELL OUT OF DODGE!

THE NEXT NIGHT I woke up dead in a strange hotel room.

On the bright side, I had literal sacks full of cash. On the downside, according to the state, I was officially dead. I needed to stay away from family and friends and pretty much everything I knew because if I didn't, they could end up being hurt. I would need to see them sooner rather than later and tell them the truth. Still, first, I had to get out of Vegas in case the mafia and who knew what supernatural boogeymen might be after me, and I had no way to do that.

Also, I still needed some downtime to process everything that had happened. So far, I was driven by pure adrenaline or something. Did vampires even have adrenaline? Whatever. The point was that I had been pushing ahead so I wouldn't break down and lose it. Tonight had to be more of the same. First order of business: finding a car...

That thought was interrupted by the most intense hunger pang I had ever felt. I wanted food, and I wanted it yesterday! Well, blood, but I knew what I meant; I just didn't want to think of it.

Theoretically, I have lots of advantages: I'm super strong, fast, and tough, I can cast magic spells if I can find blood, and I've got vampiric mojo allowing me to whammy someone into doing whatever I want. I just had to look them in the eyes and command them.

So sayeth Queenie, at least. The problem was that I had never done it before and didn't know how, and I was more than a little afraid my first time would be the most embarrassing thing in my existence.

Let's see, I need someplace without cameras, someplace where many people go. Someplace where I can get people alone long enough for a quick feed.

I looked out the motel window and saw a national chain restaurant across the street, and that answered that. Everyone eats, and everyone goes to the bathroom. Not an ideal spot, but I could get someone alone in a place without cameras or witnesses. I would have to be careful to do it when there was only one person in the room at a time.

I felt like a very lame vampire at the thought of where I was about to hunt and how, but I needed to hurry.

By now, they would know the robbery at the casino had happened and wasn't an accidental fire. They would be watching the airports but couldn't watch every car. Except that the worry in my mind had me picturing police blockades on the roads stopping every vehicle and drug dogs trained to sniff out large quantities of cash. My logical mind didn't think such a thing really existed, but I couldn't help the fear. I was just a regular guy before this.

I made my way into the sports bar, then headed straight for the bathroom. I hid in a stall after checking to see that no one else was in the room. It was early yet for the dinner crowd, so there were few people in the restaurant.

That was good in that the bathroom wasn't crowded with people, but bad because I had to wait a long 10 minutes before someone came in. I was at the sink pretending to wash my hands when my first victim came in. A middle-aged guy with a dad bod walked in and headed toward the urinals. I waited a long minute for him to do his business and walk up to the sink, but the bastard didn't wash his hands!

He was almost out the door before I clued in that he had bad hygiene habits and called out. "Hey Bud, do you mind telling me what time it is?" Not very original, I know, but it was all I could come up with on short notice.

He paused, frowning; no man likes to be talked to in the bathroom by a stranger, after all. He seemed to consider, then pulled a phone out of his pants pocket and looked at it.

I was in front of him when he looked up saying, "7:35..." He trailed off, staring into my eyes and getting lost.

Honestly, I don't know how I was doing it, just that I was staring intently at him, willing him to freeze. "Come with me."

He seemed terribly out of it as he followed me into the handicapped stall. I sat him down on the toilet and took his wrist. I tried very hard not to think about the fact that this guy didn't wash his hands just now after taking a piss, but I did what I had to do. The hunger was driving me. I bit down on his wrist, more or less where I thought the vein would be, and was rewarded with a gush of blood into my mouth.

I would have thought this was absolutely disgusting if I were still mortal. It was blood, after all, and the taste was not something I had ever liked or could imagine ever enjoying. The hunger in me, however, made it seem like a feast. I drank deep, probably taking more than I should have, but I managed to pull away before harming him. I seemed to have some innate sense of his health while I was drinking from him and knew that if I took any more, he would suffer from it. I did as Queenie had instructed and licked the wound before taking my mouth away from his wrist. It closed and stopped bleeding almost instantly, and thanks to the forethought of having some paper towels ready, not a drop fell anywhere.

I would hide the paper in the trash before leaving, but just like that, I had drunk from my first victim. Looking him in the eyes again, I commanded him not to remember this or me and to wash his hands from now on after using the restroom. For goodness sake!

I wanted to get the hell out of there, but I needed more blood. That had been enough to fuel my new existence for a couple of days, but the more I exerted myself, the more blood it burned. Plus, any magic would burn blood, and I did not fancy the idea of finding out the hard way that I had used too much of my own blood supply to keep me going.

Half an hour later, I had enough blood to perform a few minor spells, but it was not inside me. Instead, I had made blood gems, using the most essential spell Queenie had taught me. It condensed and petrified the blood into tiny little gems that looked like little round rubies or garnets about a carat in size. Each one had taken two pints to make, one to cast the spell and the other condensed into the gem. All I had to do to use one was pop it into my mouth or even just be touching it, although it would work better from the inside, or so she had said.

I had five now and popped them all into my mouth and swallowed. They would stay in gem form until I called on their power or reversed the magic, allowing them to turn back into blood. I had to admit, it was very convenient. I could feed several times like I had tonight and not have to hunt again for days if I didn't exert myself much. I would have to come up with a better way to hunt, though; I was disgusted with myself for doing this in a men's room.

Still, I had what I needed, and it had actually been an easy way to hunt.

After my second donor, I had tried to cast a spell, but it failed.

That was super concerning. It was a simple illusion spell to change my appearance, but it had not worked. At first, I was perplexed and a little afraid. I had cast spells the night before, and they worked fine. I wouldn't say it had been easy, but following Queenie's instructions, it had been doable, and I didn't even have extra blood in me then. I had been taking a chance using my own mortal blood that had still been in my veins at the time.

Tonight, however, this simple little spell was beyond my grasp. As I tried again, it was almost as if something were fighting me. Stopping me from casting....

I hadn't had much time to think things through the previous night. Still, I strongly suspected there were supernatural critters in Vegas and most likely associated with the casinos. Otherwise, how could casinos stay in business?

As a vampire, I already knew I could make a killing at poker or any other game that pitted me against a human. My senses were good enough that I'd feel it when even the best poker player drew a good card or had a good hand. I could hear people's heartbeats and see the tiniest change in their pupils. They would be like an open book when gambling.

If werewolves existed, they would have similar advantages, and who knew what mages could do. They could probably manipulate the dice to land on whatever they wanted, or stop the roulette wheel on the number they had picked, etc.

So yeah, casinos had to mean supernatural supervision; otherwise, they'd go broke in a week.

I gave up after my third attempt to cast the illusion. I was spending blood and not getting anywhere. I might be able to overpower whatever suppression field was in place, but it wasn't worth the blood.

Instead, I chose the old-school method of disguise. I whammied a guy and asked him to give me his baseball cap and leather jacket. It was sufficiently different from my typical look that I hoped it would throw off any pursuit. There might be a camera that had seen me enter the building and to the restroom, but sunglasses, a cap, and keeping my head down would keep them from seeing what I looked like when leaving. I had been pretty careful walking in, so I hoped I had avoided any cameras.

My last "victim" was a Long Beach school teacher heading home right after his meal. I took his keys and commanded him to meet me in the parking lot once he was done. In the meantime, I drove the car to the back side of the motel and parked it behind my room. I made sure to check for cameras both in front and behind. In just a few minutes, I had tossed the duffels out the window and stowed them in the trunk of the guy's Prius, displacing his luggage to the back seat. In all, it was only an hour or so after dark when we got on the road. I gave thought to taking back roads but figured that might be the first place they looked for someone sneaking out, and there would be safety and anonymity in numbers on the main highway.

I rode shotgun, and as far as Alfred Smith was concerned, I was just a guy he met at the buffet that needed a ride back to LA who offered to pay for gas. Once we were a good way outside Vegas, I tried my spell again to change my appearance, and this time, it worked. Instead of a slightly out-of-shape 28-year-old with blond hair and brown eyes, I now appeared to be a younger guy in his early twenties with red hair, blue eyes, and a little too skinny. That should help throw off anyone who might be looking for me.

Wow, I realized I was being super paranoid, but under the circumstances, maybe that wasn't a bad thing.

Alfred and I didn't make conversation, although I did direct him to take me someplace upscale near Long Beach. Costa Mesa fit the bill, they had an airport, and Alfred said they had a fancy mall with high-end shopping. Right now, I was pretty much in need of everything. I had nothing but the clothes on my back and six duffel bags full of $42 million in cash. But I didn't have a cell phone; I mean, come on!

The four-hour drive was torture without any games to play or a playlist of tunes. Alfred dropped me at the mall right off the 405 at Anton Blvd. I had a stack of $20s and $100s in my jacket pocket, but the bags stayed in his trunk as he sat in the parking lot waiting for me to do my shopping. I lived in a nice area in Dallas, new and clean, and the mall there was still going strong. Still, this mall was all upscale shops that I never would have gone into back home. For that matter, I doubted many of them would have opened a store back home in Dallas.

The mall was too pretentious for my tastes, but it wasn't the sort of place that would look askance at a customer who pulled out a stack of Benjamins to pay for their purchase. The first thing I did was head straight to the electronics store and find the latest, greatest smartphone and an iPad tablet, and a top-end Microsoft Surface tablet with all the accessories. Between those, I shouldn't be bored on the flight out.

Except, I didn't have an identity, so I couldn't apply for phone service.

In the end, I had to whammy the store manager to set up an account for me under his own name. I gave him enough cash to pay for a year's worth of service and commanded him to make sure the bill was paid each month and to forget he had done this and only remember it when paying his monthly bills. It was a pain in the ass, but it did show me that I would need to create a new identity and get all the paperwork as soon as I settled in somewhere.

For a new wardrobe, I started with shoes. I bought a modest pair of black Johnston and Murphy hiking boots that would dress up or down pretty well and a pair of Ferragamo dress shoes for when I wanted to really dress up. I also bought some ridiculously priced socks to go with the shoes. From there, I moved to buy clothes and picked up a pair of jeans by some new fashion brand I'd never have bought in the past.

I reasoned that I needed to change things up, and they looked great with the J&M hiking boots. I bought a dress shirt and a T-shirt to wear under it. Then I found a leather jacket that was classy and elegant and looked great with jeans and a dress shirt. After making those purchases, I found a dumpster and tossed in my old clothing before hitting the compactor button to make sure no one would dig them out.

And just like that, all ties to my past were severed. I had absolutely nothing from my old life left. I picked up a few more items of clothing, but the fun things were a pen from the Monte Blanc store and a limited edition Breitling watch. I also purchased a nice leather jacket-style wallet and put a small stack of $100s in it so that I looked like some rich guy shopping when I started pulling out cash at the stores. Even in a place like that, the cash raised a few eyebrows, but they were all actual notes, so the workers and managers just smiled and pretty much kissed my ass, thinking I was some rich Hollywood type.

One last thing was a stop at the luggage store. I didn't want to arrive at the airport carrying six generic black duffel bags, so I purchased a full set of luggage of the sort some rich person might have: two large suitcases, a pair of smaller carry-on sized bags, and a nice leather backpack and a leather messenger bag. I decided that was enough spreading cash around in one area and headed back to the car.

My unwitting driver almost didn't recognize me, and when I asked him to drive me to the airport, he obeyed. Still, I discovered when I arrived that I did not have all the information I needed. Planes weren't allowed to take off after 8pm due to the area noise ordinances, and more to the point, I didn't have any idea how to arrange a private charter.

So much for getting out of Califuckya tonight. I sighed and found a dark parking lot to transfer the money from the duffels to the luggage and had Alfred drop me off at the Westin on Anton. It looked like a nice hotel, and with my new look and luggage, I wouldn't seem out of place. I whammied the lady at the front desk not to ask for any ID and paid her in cash for two nights, and she put me up in a room with a good view on the 16th floor.

It was past 11 by that time, and I figured I would repeat my earlier trick to get more blood. Queenie had said in her monologue that I should strive to keep at least 100 blood gems in me at all times, that the reason it took months for her enemies to wear her down was because of how much blood she had stored and kept for emergencies.

I had a grand total of four, thanks to the appearance change earlier. I didn't yet know how much things would cost, but I knew I wanted to follow her advice on this at least. The other shit about making your enemies fear you and squeezing the life out of those who cross you using your bare hands and cursing their families unto the third generation... not so much.

There was a restaurant right next to the hotel, so I repeated my embarrassing 'ambush them in the bathroom' trick from before. I had a few close calls as the restroom was much busier than the place early in the evening. Still, I soon figured out how to pull my blood donors into the handicapped stall and get them to pull their feet up so that no one looking under the stalls would see two sets of feet. I managed another 10 blood gems by 2am when they started to close, bringing me to 14. I might have moved on and found a bar somewhere that was still open. Still, I was starting to become aware that my body was unhappy with its current dead state, so I decided to call it a night and head back to the hotel.

Luckily I made it to the room just in time not to ruin my pants and clothes. I can't imagine what kind of crime scene it would have looked like if I had gone through what came next on the street somewhere.

It all wanted to come out... All the stuff that my undead body no longer needed, the stuff I'd been carrying around inside me for the last couple days that living humans take for granted.

I'll spare the details, but I spent the rest of the night in the shower and on the toilet, flushing away some seriously unpleasant stuff. It's a miracle that the smells didn't wake the people in the neighboring rooms.

When it was all done, I was delighted to see that my new body was not so bad. I had been about 40 lbs overweight before—not obese by any stretch, but definitely not thin or trim. With all that literal and figurative crap out of my system and the fat dissolved, I was rocking a nice body now. Well, by my standards, at least. I had a six-pack because there was almost zero fat left on my body, and that gave me a classic triangle shape, although I was more wiry than muscled. No pects to speak of, no bulging biceps or triceps, but more like a Bruce Lee than a Matt Damon. I could live with that. Ok, poor choice of words, but you know what I mean.

I was happy with the changes. Unfortunately, it meant the clothes I had just bought were now too loose on me. I'd have to buy more, but that could wait until I figured out how to get the hell out of this town and to wherever I was going.

CHAPTER 6
AN EMBARRASSING SNACK

SOMEWHERE ALONG THE WAY, I had decided on Houston. It was close enough to where I was born and raised to feel at home but far enough from Dallas that I wouldn't likely run into anyone I knew. That was not very likely since I could change my appearance, and I had just disgustingly lost over 40 lbs. I also knew Houston well enough from going to IT conferences and working there for a few months on a contract once.

I stayed up and watched the crap that was on TV and browsed the internet looking for info on chartering flights. I found a service and called them the next day around 10am. Unfortunately, they required ID and a credit card, neither of which I had, so I asked if I could present them on arrival at the airport for an additional processing fee. In the meantime, I used the business center downstairs to print fake IDs, Social, and other documents. They wouldn't pass a scan at the airport. Still, with a bit of mojo, the TSA agent would conveniently not scan them and remember that a very nice man passed through security having thoroughly checked out.

The other good thing was that the flight was private, but I would not have to rent the entire plane, I only had to pay for a single seat since they already had a flight scheduled for Houston that had unfilled seats. The upside was that instead of paying over $10K for a flight, I only paid $1700, which fell way below the need for the company to notify the IRS of a large cash purchase, which suited me just fine. The downside was that I had to wait a day as it would not happen until the next evening.

I was thankful to go to bed for the rest of the day and get some rest, although I had discovered that spending a blood gem would allow me to stay awake without the massive strength loss. It became the equivalent of staying awake as a human when you were just exhausted.

I stayed hunkered down in my room until dark but left as soon as I could and headed to a steakhouse I had seen the night before when I was across the street at the mall. Of course, I left the *Do Not Disturb* sign on the door. Wouldn't want some maid stealing my ill-gotten gains.

I wanted to spend the evening learning more about the magic seeing as my life might depend on it, but I needed blood for that. I had thirteen of the little treasures, having spent one to stay awake during the day today. Experimentation meant I needed more to play with. All I knew so far was that a simple illusion or an appearance change cost just a single gem. How quickly did the cost go up? Could I cast a fireball? If so, how much would it cost, and how powerful would it be? I had no idea.

So I settled into the bathroom blood game, snagging a victim as soon as I was alone with them. It went well for a while, and I had managed to make five more blood gems bringing my total to 18 when I got the biggest shock of my unlife so far.

I stared into the eyes of my next victim and said the same thing I always said, "You will not remember me or what I ask you to do, and you will obey my commands."

The guy looked at me like I was a freak and replied, "What the fuck did you say?"

I was so shocked by the guy's complete lack of zombie-like acceptance I almost didn't respond. Thinking about as quickly as I ever had in my life, I stammered out the first thing I could think of.

"Uh..."

Then I managed to get out, "Aren't you part of the game?" I tried my best to look confused, but I was definitely embarrassed as hell, so it probably wasn't a hard sell. I couldn't blush anymore, but I would have been scarlet if I could.

"You are part of the LARP group, right?"

The guy still hadn't said anything else but looked like he was about to call the cops thinking I was some kind of weird pervert creeping on guys in the bathroom.

"Live Action Roleplay...," I continued. "But you are wearing a blue shirt, all the guys on the other team are supposed to be wearing blue like the one you are wearing."

I would say that I acted embarrassed, but it was no act, just not for the reason he believed. "I'm so sorry. I thought you were part of the game. We were meeting here at the Gold Claim tonight, and I thought you were in the game because of the color of your shirt."

The guy was still looking at me like a freak, but now he at least had a context for why I was acting a freak and wouldn't likely call the cops. He looked to be a beach-boy jock type, so he had probably beat up guys like me in high school, and now I was firmly categorized as a NERD in his mind, but at least I wasn't someone he would take action about. He kept a wary eye on me and left as soon as he finished washing his hands.

I, on the other hand, had learned something I did not know was possible. Some mortals are just plain immune to our mojo. It was rare, but it did happen, and from now on, I'd be ready for it. My quick thinking got me out of it this time, but I'd need to have this practiced for when it happened again. Luckily my surprise and embarrassment were genuine and helped sell the ruse.

It was time for me to get the hell out of there and move to another restaurant and try again. That guy would very likely be watching for me to come out of the restroom, and if I stayed in, he'd report me to the manager, at the very least, if not the cops.

As I headed to the Mexican place next door, it occurred to me that vampires must still exist. We had all these myths about them, and they were in the public consciousness to the point there were roleplaying games about them and movies. So that meant either Queenie hadn't killed them all like she thought, or someone else had managed the same feat she had by turning themselves into the undead. I would need to be careful.

For that matter, the guy might not have been human. He might have been something else, something that my powers didn't work on. That was a sobering thought, and I was much more careful the rest of the night.

I stalked the Hacienda's bathroom for almost four hours, then hit a sports bar that was open till 2 am. With my improved technique and experience, I managed to get twenty-three more blood gems made, bringing my total to forty-one.

After that, I headed back to my hotel room for some experimentation. Magic experimentation, that is. I opened my bags and cast an illusion on them to make their contents look like mundane clothes instead of piles of cash. I didn't think that would hold up for the security screening at the airport. Still, I was hoping a little mojo on a guard would ensure that the luggage was manually checked rather than x-rayed. I was going to a private flight, after all, not one of the major airlines, so I would have to go through security, but not through the main lines—I hoped.

That done, I pulled out a quarter from my pocket. I knew I could make illusions and change the simple appearance of a human, but that was not really changing the substance of a thing, just how it was shaped. I wondered how much it would cost to turn the quarter into gold?

As usual, I burned a blood gem and pushed my will at the thing, trying to force it to BE gold instead of the thing it was. It felt like I was trying to push a boulder up a hill. I burned another gem, and the boulder got significantly easier to push but it still resisted the change. It took two more blood before it took on a gold sheen and changed into what I wanted it to be. If I could sweat, I'd be doing it right then. I took a deep breath and sagged back on the couch, just staring at the gold quarter. Had I done it or just made it look gold?

I reached out and picked it up and immediately felt the weight difference. It was heavy like gold. I flipped it in the air with my thumb, and it made a pretty ringing sound, but I had never held a gold coin before, so I had no idea if that was what gold sounded like. Then, because I had seen it in countless movies and TV shows, I bit the coin, not hard, but enough that I could feel the metal deform slightly under pressure from my bite. It sure as hell seemed like real gold. I grinned and put it in my pocket for good luck. That had taken four gems, bringing me back down to 36. I was damned sure going to keep track of that shit and not get caught with my pants down! I didn't know if I could really make a fireball or not, but I'd napalm a bitch before I let myself be killed if I could.

I still had a pile of coins on the desk, but I wasn't going to waste four blood on turning them into gold. I'd do a brick or something more significant, but that would be a dumb thing to do before traveling on an airplane. I already had $42 million in cash, which weighed quite enough already. Also, I was curious to know if the coin would stay gold or if it would revert back to whatever a quarter is made of these days. I'd have to remember to look at it tomorrow.

The pile gave me another idea, so I spent another blood and willed them to float into the air and then started moving them around in interlocking circles like they were being juggled. Ok, so telekinesis, check. One gem. But what about something more massive?

I spent another blood and lifted the couch, that wasn't too bad either, but I could feel a slight difference. The coins were still weaving around in their rhythm, but the sofa seemed harder to manipulate, and I had the feeling it would fall to the floor long before the coins did.

Ok, so lighter is more manageable and takes less power. Judging by the difference in feeling between the coins that weighed a few ounces at most vs. a couch that weighed 75 or 100 pounds, I thought I might have been able to pick up something much heavier like a truck with a couple more blood. Still, more mass seemed to translate into more energy needed. Ok, so magic obeyed some kind of laws, even if I didn't know what they were yet. Interesting.

I continued to test, burning through more gems until I was down to 30. What I knew so far was that the more complex a task, the more fundamental a change, or the harder the task, the more magic it took to make it happen. On the other hand, magic was able to wave the middle finger at the laws of physics and would let me do just about anything so long as I could pay the price. Or so it seemed. Another thing I learned was that changes made seemed to be permanent. However, telekinesis ran out faster or slower depending on complexity or mass, meaning the harder something was to do, the more magic it took and the faster the magic ran out.

I'd check again tomorrow to make sure, but I felt pretty sure the quarter would stay gold. A fundamental change once made seemed to be permanent, but the price was steep due to overcoming some barriers. I didn't know what to call it, cosmic inertia. Or was it just hard to manipulate the foundational aspects of matter? I wished I had understood Einstein's theory of relativity better just now. $E=mc^2$ I knew energy and mass were somehow connected, but that was all I could recall.

After that, I settled in for another day of sleeping like the dead. I would need to be up and moving as soon as night fell. I had scheduled an Uber for fifteen minutes after sundown to take me to the airport.

CHAPTER 7

FLYING THE SINFUL SKIES

I WAS PLEASANTLY surprised to find out that I didn't have to go through the regular security checkpoint. I was dropped off at a private hangar, and although there was an agent there to check everyone in, he didn't scan bags or anything. He just asked us to open them and then sent us on our way. I was sharing the plane with four other people who had chartered it. They had let the company include me in order to drop their cost some. It was a pastor, his wife, son, and his secretary. They were far too chatty, but thankfully I claimed to be tired, and they let me take a nap, which I faked, but it was better than dealing with them. I did get a kick out of watching them, though. They had an interesting dynamic. The pastor and his son both eyed the secretary; she, on the other hand, played innocent, but I could see subtle signs that she was encouraging them both. Meanwhile, the wife was so self-absorbed that she seemed oblivious to the tension between the father and son or the sexual tension between the three. They were a biblical scandal waiting to happen.

I was very grateful when we touched down at a small airport about 90 miles from Houston, and the driver I had arranged was there to meet me. I bade my group of fellow passengers a quick farewell and got the hell out of there before their deity dropped a lightning bolt on the whole lot of them for their sins. I really dislike evangelist types, who preach hellfire and damnation and demand their congregations pay for their private jets, all while porking their secretaries in private. If god is real, I'm sure he has a special place for them.

That brought up more questions for me. What was I in store for once I finally died? Did god have a special place for the undead, assuming he exists at all? Or do we get the same judgment chances as everyone else? I was raised religious, but since becoming an adult, I kinda liked Penn Jillette's philosophy about religion. People aren't good because of religion. I rape and kill as much as I want, which is zero. The threat of eternal damnation doesn't make me love god, nor does it make me avoid doing bad things for fear of it. I don't do those things because I know they are wrong. After all, I wouldn't want someone else to do them to me. It was that simple.

Also, now that I am a vampire, I don't know if I believe or not anymore. That's something that will have to wait until I have time for some more serious introspection. I do know that holy symbols have no effect on me.

Of course, I didn't think I'd want someone to Shanghai me in a bathroom and jack my blood either, so maybe I wasn't the best person anymore. On the other hand, I didn't hurt them, and they left never knowing anything had even happened. Now that I thought of it, the scales seemed a bit tipped toward me being the baddie. I would have to keep that in mind and try to balance the scales from now on.

Maybe I could do something good for my blood donors in exchange for their involuntary gift to me. I could give them each a hundred bucks. That's more than twice what people get for donating blood at a blood bank. I could provide them with a command that would be beneficial, like a post-hypnotic suggestion to quit smoking or something. Or to study hard and get good grades in school? I'd have to think about it...

Another thing I thought about and ended up dismissing was the idea of either working with a blood bank to take whatever blood they had that expired or setting up my own blood drive.

The first problem with that was that I figured any kind of blood drive or blood bank would be closely watched and monitored by the existing vampire population of a city. After all, if they didn't already have some kind of agreement with the blood bank, I'd be astonished. As for a blood drive, that would be like announcing an all-you-can-eat buffet. Some vampire was sure to show up and want a little taste, which would have led to them discovering me.

As much as I liked the ideas, they were just full of too much risk.

Even so, I wasn't entirely opposed to the blood-drive idea. I wouldn't be consuming it all myself or using it all since that would be noticeable even by the mortal authorities. Still, if I could skim a little off the top during the day, then if some vampire came around that night and took more, it would be on them, and they'd be the ones to get caught for stealing. The rest would actually go to the blood bank, as it was always needed.

However, I did an experiment, and the results were disappointing. It was no wonder vamps in the TV shows always turned their noses up at bagged blood. After about a 48-hour period, it lost about half its potency before stabilizing somewhat. It was like the mana was evaporating from the blood or something.

As I did more testing, it seemed to me that when it was fresh, the blood was charged with mana, but that excess power dispersed pretty quickly after it was drawn. It still had mana in it after that and would sustain a vampire for a night, but it took nearly twice as much to provide the usual effect.

I could live off blood like that, but for storing magic, it was a wasteful proposition. I would feel terrible using up so much blood that could be saving mortal lives.

Still, if I ever got into a position where I didn't have to hide from the other vampires of the city, then a blood drive would be a great way to gain a lot of power fast. Maybe I could work with some big company to do a blood drive every few months and be able to create a hundred blood gems in a day or two.

Get half a dozen companies doing the same thing, and I'd be set!

I sighed in disappointment as reality set in. For now, I'd have to keep doing it the way I had been. It was about as unglamorous as you could get, but it worked, and I was able to secure a lot of blood without too much fuss. No hunting people on the streets or trying to pick up women in clubs.

CHAPTER 8

SETTLING IN

THE DRIVE to Houston was boring but allowed me to do more research on the area. I had spent some time there going to IT conferences and even lived there for six months while working on a security implementation contract once. That is to say, I knew my way around, but that had been some time ago when I had first gotten out of college. For now, I needed a hotel until I could find a place to buy or rent. I picked the Westin Oaks, having had a good experience with the Westin in California. It was right by the Galleria, and that area was nice back in the day. Hopefully, it still was, or I'd have to find someplace else.

Why Houston, though? Sure, it was in my home state, but so were Austin and San Antonio. My reasoning was that it was on the coast and a major city, big enough that I could be lost in the crowds if I wanted to be. It had an international airport if I ever needed to get out of the country fast. It was a major port of call for shipping, so I could also get away by boat. It wasn't too far from Mexico if I needed to flee by land. Last but not least, plenty of businesses would deal with international trade and offshore banking.

In short, it seemed like the perfect place where I could settle in and live a quiet, peaceful unlife, not bothering anyone and being left alone. That was my hope, anyway. I had no other plans for this new life yet; I just wanted to survive.

You might get the impression I was as nervous as a cat in a room full of rocking chairs, and you'd be right. I was a newb, and I didn't want to get pwned by the sharks swimming beneath the waters of this new life. I knew vamps must be real, but what about wizards, werewolves, or fairies? I did not want to cross fairies if their reputation from folklore was accurate! A werewolf would be a nasty fighter, but a fairy will fuck you up.

Until I know more, I'm going to be as quiet as a church mouse and figure my shit out. Then and only then will I relax a little bit.

It was only 10:30 by the time I got to the hotel, so I stowed the luggage and cast a spell so that only I could get back into the room through the door. It was thoroughly locked from the inside. I headed to a local steakhouse a few blocks away and repeated my feeding trick. This time I did not run into any surprises and added another ten blood gems to my total.

After that, I headed to the Guy's House on Westheimer; it was an all-night diner that was popular with the bar crowd as a place to go after they closed. From that, I managed a full twenty-five more before heading back to the hotel for the day. That brought my total to seventy-five. It wasn't quite the minimum 100 that my maker suggested as an emergency supply, but it was getting close. One more night and I should be there. I was tired, but I stayed up long enough to make a couple of phone calls to arrange appointments for the following evening.

I called two different financial advisor agencies and asked about someone with solid experience in offshore banking. I wanted them to meet me at the steakhouse for a consulting meeting. I needed to discuss some liquid assets I had recently inherited that I wanted to move offshore legally. I offered to buy their dinner and pay a $1000 consultant fee if they could help me or connect me with the person who gained my business. Both companies assured me that someone would meet me to discuss my issues.

One was scheduled for 7 pm and the other for 8 pm. The first guy arrived fifteen minutes late and seemed reasonably knowledgeable on the subject, but he didn't give me the impression that he was an expert. In other words, not someone I would trust with my money. The irony of "my money" was not lost on me.

The second guy was early and sat down with the other guy. We all chatted for a few minutes before I thanked Mr. Ryan of the losing agency. He left a thousand dollars richer but without my business. The second guy thanked me for the meal and asked me a lot of questions about what I wanted to accomplish, and rather than bragging about himself and how awesome he was, he simply told me he had established offshore accounts for over a dozen clients who were looking to shelter a portion of their wealth outside the United States for safety reasons. He didn't hesitate to describe the process he typically went through and even discussed the "customary fees" aka bribes that would need to be paid to avoid customs and suggested that if I was planning to travel with a large sum of money, that I hire at least one bodyguard, but preferably two.

He wasn't judgmental, nor did he try to talk me out of taking my money offshore, but he did warn me about all the legal ramifications and risks. I had an excellent feeling about Mr. Pope, but I wasn't about to take chances and whammied him to tell me the truth and make sure he wouldn't embezzle or set me up. Under strict instructions not to betray me in any way, I asked that he put me in touch with a pair of bodyguards and asked that he arrange a private flight, with the understanding that I would pay him back once my new Cayman Islands untraceable bank account was set up. As an incentive, I gave him $5000 up front and promised $100K once it was done. I also offered him a job managing my money for me and investing a portion of it. The trip would be scheduled a week from that night, and I ensured that all flights and travel would occur at night. The thing I was not looking forward to was being out in the sunlight.

One of the secrets Queenie had imparted to me was that I could make myself temporarily immune to the sun, but the cost was high. It would burn five blood per hour that I was in the sun, plus the blood gem to stay active during the day. I had a week to build up as large of a surplus of gems as I could. I wanted to have at least double what Queenie had called the emergency cache of gems. Also, I wanted to experiment with the sun thing since I didn't want to rely on an untested spell when my life depended on it.

You know, it occurred to me then, that no other vampire besides Queenie would have been able to use that trick to go out into the sun. They could burn blood to stay awake during the day by feeding extra, but the sunlight trick was only possible due to the magic. No wonder the other vamps had hated her so much and wanted to destroy her.

Hell, if I were a regular vampire and knew she had that ability and didn't give it to me, I'd hate her too!

On the other hand, I wasn't going to go around and gift every vampire with the ability to do magic. That seemed like a recipe for disaster. In other words, I couldn't blame Queenie for keeping the ability to herself.

So it was that after the meal, I again haunted the steakhouse's bathroom until they closed, followed by the rest of the night at the Guy's House diner.

Despite the fact that I got more efficient and practiced at the art of the feed, I had gotten a late start that night, so I only ended up with thirty-two before I was tired of the game and wanted to get back to the hotel and relax. That meant that after the test the following day, I ended up with the 100 gems that were supposedly the minimal safety net of magic. Perhaps that made my maker happy, but I still didn't have a good gauge of my capabilities, so I was still nervous.

Besides, I wanted to make sure I had at least double since I did not know how much I would have to burn while on the island. That meant I would need to average fourteen gems a night plus a few to spare. I decided I would want to get at least thirty per night so that I could spend more on staying awake some during the day over the next week so I could start looking at houses and take care of other business.

To that end, I popped a gem that morning to stay awake and active and called around looking for a good real estate agent, and called my new finance guy to ask for a recommendation on an executive assistant. I would need someone fairly high-end to handle my affairs. Since I was so rich, it would be silly to spend all my time on mundane things like paying the water bill and calling the city to dispute a property tax increase or one of the myriad annoying things I used to have to deal with as an adult who couldn't afford to have someone else do it for me. I spent that day talking with people downstairs in the hotel's bar area. It was nice and internal to the building, so no sun streaming in through the windows turned me into the human torch.

Of course, before I took even that small risk, I cast the spell to protect myself from sunlight and stuck my hand behind the curtains into the direct sunlight. It was warm but not hot, and I didn't burst into flame, so I threw open the curtains and looked at the sun for the first time in days. I needed sunglasses. Even with the protection spell, my eyes felt sensitive to the light. Still, I'd had that problem even as a normal human if I went from being in the dark to the bright sun suddenly. This was a bit worse than that, but not too bad.

Feeling bolstered by the knowledge that I had enough blood inside me to render myself immune to the sun for several days if necessary, I headed down to the bar for my first meeting.

CHAPTER 9
EXECUTIVE ASSISTANT

Mr. Pope sent a friend to see me, someone he had worked with over the years, someone who had strong business sense and good soft skills. Katherine Clearwater was her name, and she was quite a good-looking woman for being in her 50s. I'm a guy. Sorry, it was the first thing I noticed, but only for a split second before I seriously evaluated what I was seeing. She dressed professionally like she was going to an interview, which this was. Still, she looked comfortable in the attire, rather than like someone who only dressed this way when she had to. She had good poise, posture, and a confident air, and she looked me directly in the eyes with the self-assurance of someone who knew their own worth. I was impressed, entirely apart from her rather good looks. That smile was the kind that drew people to a person.

After we sat and got comfortable, the first thing she said was, "If this were a corporation, I would stick with Katherine, but it looks like you want someone to directly oversee your business interests and keep you on task. That speaks to a somewhat less formal setting, so please call me Kat."

We sat and had a good conversation. Kat told me about her background, credentials, and what she had accomplished business-wise over the years. Like Mr. Pope, she asked questions, too, ones that showed she was thinking two or three steps ahead about my needs.

I did it. I whammied her, just to make sure she would be loyal and not reveal my secrets or do me any harm at all.

Once that was out of the way, I told her what I wanted from her, which was basically to keep my life and my business running smoothly. I asked her if that was something she felt comfortable doing, seeing as she had the chops to be a director or VP for a Fortune 500 company.

"With the size of the capital you have to invest, and your net worth, I think working for you will not seem boring."

I smiled at that but needed to make sure she was going into this with open eyes.

"I have to be honest with you. Working for me, you could find yourself in danger. I do not have any enemies at the moment, but that could change at any time, and the sort of people that I might cross are the sort that might target those around me to hurt me. What I am saying is that working for me puts your life at risk, but the rewards will be high as well."

She shrugged, "I can't say I like the idea of being killed over who I work for, but as long as you aren't a criminal or getting me into danger due to you being a bad person, then I can accept that. For appropriate compensation, that is." She grinned at that last statement.

I could tell she was serious, but I didn't blame her in the least. I'd want danger pay, too, if my job had the potential for it.

"You're hired." I grinned right back at her.

Kat had really impressed me. "Ok, the first order of business, I need a place to live. I won't be able to buy until Mr. Pope and I get my accounts settled, but I'd like you to start coming up with some options. I want two places, a high-rise penthouse with a great view, like an upper floor in that 90-story tower just outside the loop, what's it called, the Williamsburg Tower? Anyway, it can double as both an office space and my personal home. But I also need a workshop, someplace fully equipped for woodworking, metalworking, and jewelry-making tools. Basically, Adam Savage's workshop; check out Youtube to see what I mean, and I'd like that to be fairly close to my home/office."

She looked shocked by the request for an entire floor of the Tower.

"I will have to check on buildings with vacancies of an entire floor, but you would be talking in the neighborhood of a million a year, I think, in the current Houston market. At least."

Almost as an afterthought, "That wouldn't include the cost to renovate and decorate the space. As for the other, Houston doesn't have zoning laws like most other cities, so finding a place to rent for a workspace should be easy by comparison."

I could see the frustration on her face as she thought of another problem.

"Although zoning isn't an issue, I doubt an office building that is meant for businesses would welcome someone living out of one of their suites. That might be the biggest challenge to what you want. You would need special permission from the building's owners or management."

I chuckled. "Trust me, I can be very persuasive. You find me the vacancy and then get me a meeting with the person in charge, and I'll not only secure their agreement, but I'll also get them to throw in parking as well."

It was time to see if I would break her or if she was flexible enough for the job. "One other thing you need to know if you are going to work for me. Magic is real, and I'm like a wizard or something."

Kat frowned, "What do you mean magic is real?"

She was suddenly questioning my sanity or whether she was being punked. I could see it in her eyes. Only the fact that her longtime associate Pope had sent her on this interview and talked about how rich this guy was made her hesitate.

I burned a blood point and lifted her in the air with my mind while theatrically waggling my fingers in her direction. "Exactly what I said."

She waved her arms about, at first flailing in instinctive reaction, then as if feeling for wires that might be holding her up. I hadn't been obvious about it since we were in a public place. Still, there was no one where they could see her and no cameras, so I let her hang there a couple of feet off the ground for a minute until she was satisfied that nothing was touching her.

"Ok, I can't explain that, but *magic*? Really?" Her eyes narrowed, then she asked, "Is that how you earned your money? Do you have some new technology that defies gravity?"

I put her down and flipped her my gold quarter, which she caught without dropping it. She looked it over and then looked back at me questioningly. "It's a gold quarter...."

Smiling, I responded, "I turned a regular quarter into that. Changed it at the atomic level, and no, this is not technological; this goes back many thousands of years. It's something our ancestors knew that we lost along the way. I just recently found a piece of that lost heritage, and it granted me the ability to do things that defy the laws of physics."

My smile turned to an evil grin. "Still want to come to work for me? Now is your chance to back out before you know too much. Red pill or blue pill Mrs. Clearwater? You decided."

She rolled her eyes at my movie reference but then asked, "Which one is which? I never can remember which color did what."

I laughed, "Me either."

Her slightly shell-shocked expression dissolved into amusement, then outright laughter as she joined me in the ridiculousness of the situation. "Well, now I really can't walk away. I have to know which pill does what."

Grinning, I said, "I think we'll get along just fine, but be careful. No one can know any of this outside of you and me. Even Mr. Pope has no idea. This is *need to know* and right now, no one besides you needs to know."

She grew serious for a second, "Just to be clear, if I find out this was all some big setup and I'm on Candid Camera or something, you and Pope will both die a prolonged and painful death."

Then she smiled and added, "But if it is, it is one hell of a setup. It's real enough to fool me."

My grin turned into a rueful smile, "Believe me, I understand. If it hadn't happened to me, I'd never accept someone else telling me it was real."

I couldn't help but think back to Nate. He had tried to tell me my pendant was magic, and I had utterly dismissed him without a second thought. Until I'd experienced it, nothing could convince me.

CHAPTER 10

CHAPMAN HURLEY, MEET DANIEL FOX

We wrapped up after that, and she left to begin working on my requests. A little while later, my new tax guy showed up with Mr. Pope, another recommendation. Since nothing was official yet, nor did I know how things would work out, we kept things simple and just had a meet-and-greet session. I did the mojo thing on him as well to ensure loyalty, and after talking for an hour, I was satisfied he would be able to handle it all. They both knew without too much being stated that the offshore account was really to legitimize the money, a way to have it and keep the government from looking into me too closely. We'd bring at least some of that money back into onshore banks in order to do business, but we would pay taxes on it and appease the IRS that there was nothing to see here.

This led me to my last appointment of the day, yet another recommendation from Mr. Pope. This was a guy who could build me a new identity and provide me with all the documentation to back it up.

Who was this Pope guy that he had so many interesting connections? Something I wanted to know more about but could dig into later.

Mr. Green, that's what we'll call him, was not an above-board businessman. He was a criminal mastermind when it came to building new identities. We talked for a good three hours about what all it would take, the pros and cons of US vs. other citizenships. His specialty was fabricating a background for the person with a credit history going back several years, so when someone did a credit check, which happens way too often in modern life, they would see an actual history of paying bills and making purchases. It was all a genius idea he had almost 20 years before. He established dozens of identities and maintained them over the years, selling them off one at a time and establishing new ones.

I would become Daniel Fox, a Texas-born native who lives off dividend stocks from investments his parents made before they died. Or at least that is what the US government would think. It was a legit name. The actual social number belonged to a child who died at birth, so Green used that name and social to build from when he made the identity. Since there was no living person, there were no pictures, no driver's license, or anything like that. Still, there was a paper trail and credit history that looked absolutely legit.

The Daniel Fox identity was 22, so it wasn't too big of a stretch that I could go down to the DMV and get a license.

From that point, I'd be in databases with a picture ID. The one thing was fingerprints, and there Green had done his job well. He had the original birth cert. The one in the county had "accidentally been destroyed" thanks to Green's bribe to the County Clerk. His method was to digitally alter the prints on his copy of the cert and then give a legit-looking copy back to the county, and they would then be filed. However, since I could change my own prints to match the baby prints, that was unnecessary.

It would take a few days and would cost me an incredible 3 million since this was a service so long in the making it could pass even direct government scrutiny. Still, I figured it would be well worth it to have the ability to buy and own property in my own name, or rather in my new name. Of course, given my abilities, I could always not bother with owning anything and just occupy properties by using the mojo to manipulate people into owning them for me.

The rest of the week went by in a blur. I tested more spells to better understand what could be done and what it cost, but primarily I built up my blood supply. By the evening of the flight to the Caymans, I had 223 blood gems. A solid amount to work with. I was also starting to understand that when it came to spells, anything was pretty much possible, it was really only a matter of cost.

Of course, I didn't know what human mages could do, but from my testing, small-scale things tended to be in the one to three-point range, such as a candle flame up to a bonfire. More significant effects ranged from four to seven points, burning down a house with a fireball, depending on the size of the house. Eight to ten would be something like a meteor shower spell that took out several city blocks. Not that I cast any actual fireballs or burned any houses down.

Theoretically, it could continue to scale up so long as someone could pay the cost, up to and including nuking an entire city or causing the eruption of a supervolcano. Not something I'd ever want to do, but the fact that it could be done was scary as hell. Another thought occurred to me: if the blood held magic and human mages existed, I had to assume they could only hold up to around ten magic points at a time. If that were the case, then a mage would only be able to cast spells big enough to destroy several city blocks. There were many assumptions in that line of reasoning, however, and I would not bet my life on it.

At this point, you might think everything was coming up roses and I was happy with my new life. I hadn't thought about my family or friends even once since abandoning Barry to his fate at the hands of the thugs.

You'd be wrong, but I can't blame you for that.

I've avoided mentioning any of the angst I was feeling over my choice to leave my old life behind. Why? Because it was depressing, and I don't really want to dwell on it. I could go on and on about the hours I spent alone and lonely in my expensive hotel room, living my new unlife each night, brooding and getting weepy over my situation. I could tell you how I wallowed in self-pity for hours at a time, bemoaning my loneliness and how badly I missed my parents, nephews and nieces, and friends.

Or I could tell you how I was surprised I didn't spend even more time feeling depressed than I did. I chalk it up to a couple things.

First, I was starting to believe that even though Queenie wasn't pulling my strings like a puppet master, she might just have placed some kind of whammy on me to force me to survive. No matter how I felt, I couldn't just lie around being miserable. I felt compelled to be active and get things done. If I wasn't hunting to build up my blood supply, I was watching movies or researching vampires and other supernatural things on the internet. Mostly, I was trying to figure more out about the magic and how I could use it to improve my odds of survival. Last but not least, I was actively working with my new employees to set up a comfortable and safe existence. Doing things like opening bank accounts so I could buy a secure home.

CHAPTER 11

WELCOME TO FANTASY ISLAND, NOT!

THE FLIGHT to the Caymans was uneventful other than a bit of turbulence due to the small size of the jet. On arrival, we were greeted by a Customs agent that looked through our luggage and went away happily with a $1000 bribe, er, I mean gift. My bodyguards, Ralph and Jasper, flanked Mr. Pope and me as we headed to the bank.

As we left the airport, we didn't get far before we were also stopped by a patrol of policemen who also needed to be bribed, this time only $300. I don't want to make the place sound like some third world dictatorship where everyone you meet is some corrupt official. We could have gotten away without paying any bribes. Doing so just made sure we weren't hassled and didn't have to go through the scrutiny that otherwise might have arisen. I also think the Customs guy we bribed had a cousin that was part of that patrol and tipped him off that I was doing something shady.

Even so, I would have been super happy if that had been all.

Unfortunately, we didn't make it to the bank without incident. I am 90% certain they didn't track me or the money. If I had to guess, I'd say they had someone waiting on the island to catch whoever had robbed the casino. Maybe it was a mage; perhaps they had a werewolf that was trained to sniff out large piles of cash; I don't know. Hell, maybe that Customs agent tipped them off.

I'm getting ahead of myself.

We arrived at the airport right in the middle of Georgetown, and the bank we were heading to was on the west side of the island, just past Hero's Square, where the government buildings were. I had never been to the island before. I had only seen videos and movies set on the Caribbean islands, so I was shocked to see that this was nothing like I had expected. I was picturing a small island with barely paved roads and lots of airy beach bungalows. What I wasn't expecting was a well-developed modern town.

That area of the city where we were heading had quite a few decent-sized buildings, five to seven stories tall. On the other hand, the government buildings were smaller than I would have expected and almost bunker-like with tiny windows. Overall, it didn't seem all that different from Galveston, which I was familiar with from a few trips I had taken during my mortal life. The humidity was a bit lower than in Houston, though, which was a nice change. I hated the humidity.

Hang on, I have to say one word about that. One of the big downsides to Houston, Texas, where I had decided to make my new home, was the damned humidity. If you've ever heard someone talk about it, you'll know it is a common complaint. Inevitably, one of the people in the conversation will say, "It's not the heat that gets you; it's the humidity!" And everyone around will nod along sagely in agreement.

It might be a cliché, but it's so fucking true! I lived most of my mortal life in Dallas, where it was actually a little hotter on average but where the humidity was somewhat less, being farther from the coast. I had spent some time in Houston for IT conferences and even lived there for a very short time while I worked a contract job implementing a new information security system for a company in the Oil and Gas sector. The biggest thing I remember from my time there was how absolutely oppressive the humidity was. It had been summer and 97 degrees with 100% humidity, and you felt like you would die. Five minutes outside, and you would be absolutely drenched in sweat.

The noticeably lower humidity here on the island made me realize how much of a relief it was no longer having to care about it. If she were there, I'd hug Queenie for the fact that I no longer produced sweat! As a vampire, that was a thing of the past.

Don't get me wrong, it still felt like you were swimming through the air. It was so humid in Houston, but I would never again have to peel a shirt off that was soaked in sweat and then stand in front of a fan for several minutes to cool off and get dry!

Sorry, back to the matter at hand. We were being driven toward the bank in a nice limo but weren't out of the woods yet, although we didn't know it. Pope and I were in the backseat, and Ralph and Jasper were in front of us.

I didn't really need bodyguards since I had better reflexes and strength. Still, they were a good deterrent to casual mortal criminals who might try something. They were also experienced professionals with skills that I lacked. One of those was observation and the instinct to know something was up.

My first clue that something was wrong was when Ralph looked at Jasper and raised an eyebrow, and the other mercenary-turned-bodyguard gave a slight nod. Their body language had just gone from relaxed to tense. They were reaching into their jackets and loosening weapons in their holsters.

Pope noticed, too, and asked, "What's wrong?"

Ralph shrugged and nodded behind Pope and me, "We should have taken a left at Harbor Dr and headed south; instead, we're heading north toward N. Church St."

I had made a wise choice when I took Pope's advice to hire them. They had done their homework and knew the routes we were supposed to take to the bank.

Without that, we might have driven into an ambush completely unaware and unprepared. As it was, we only had a little warning. The car only traveled a few blocks before pulling off the main road and into a sketchy-looking property that was surrounded by a tall metal privacy fence and tropical vegetation. The gate closed behind the limo as soon as it had passed, leaving us trapped in what looked like a cross between a jungle, a junkyard, and a storage facility populated by shipping containers.

We were driven into the middle of a large group of stacked shipping containers that made a large open square. From what I could tell, the property was perhaps three or four acres in size, big enough that with the vegetation and junk around us it would be a good place for an ambush that wouldn't draw attention from nosey neighbors.

The driver hit the intercom and said casually in his island accent, "Not to worry, this is just a formality. I was notified by Customs a couple minutes ago to bring you to this facility to inspect your baggage for possible quarantined produce. It happens from time to time. There was a big problem with a disease that killed off a lot of the coconut trees a couple years ago, so they just need to make sure you aren't carrying any coconuts in from the States. You should be in and out in no more than five minutes."

I gave my bodyguards a look and said quietly, "Yeah, right. Custom's facility, my ass."

Jasper nodded in agreement, "Yeah, a few years back, there was a lot of drug trafficking going through the island. The US put a lot of pressure on the government here, and they cracked down on it pretty hard, but I'd bet a year's salary this was one of the places the cartels were using to stage shipments back in the day."

We had the duffels full of cash in the back of the limo with us, and my bodyguards each had a small bag that was filled with “essentials”. They contained a couple of flashbang grenades, tasers, and half a dozen magazines each for their 9mm pistols.

Depending on what was about to go down, that would either be overkill, or we'd desperately wish we had more. This car wasn't bulletproof, and we were now surrounded by metal shipping containers. They could have gunmen atop the stacks and fill us so full of lead that they wouldn't need cement blocks to make our bodies sink to the bottom of the ocean.

I felt responsible for my bodyguards and Mr. Pope. Unless there were supernaturals among our attackers, I could survive, but my team couldn't.

That's not to say I wasn't scared. I'd been paranoid since stealing the money that they'd catch up to me and send some kind of supernatural team of badasses after me. I wasn't ready for my potentially immortal life to end only a few weeks after it started. Worse, I was the bad guy if these were people trying to recover the money from the robbery. If I killed people being paid by the people I robbed, then that made me a bad person. That's not who I wanted to be.

The heist was supposed to be a victimless crime in my mind. It was a casino, after all, and they had insurance against getting robbed. They wouldn't even be out any money in the long run. If people died today, then it would be my fault for stealing that money, and more than the fear of the situation, that idea was making my stomach do flips.

My mind raced with ideas on how to get out of this. If it was just humans, I could whammy them into letting us go. The contents of the bags already had an illusion to make it look like our clothes and toiletries instead of bundles of Benjamins. Maybe we could just get away with it.

As much as I wished that was true, I wasn't hopeful. If they were any good, they were sure to have at least a couple people with rifles posted atop those stacked containers doing overwatch duty. A simple call or something going down that looked sketchy and they might open fire.

And then we were parked and guys came walking out from around the containers. Maybe five of them had some kind of uniform on, but they looked sloppy. Another six guys wore shorts or other casual clothes. A couple were even shirtless, and those guys didn't look anything like official customs agents. Giving them the benefit of the doubt; maybe they were just yard workers at this location.

Yeah, and I'm the governor of Grand Cayman! In other words, not bloody likely.

On the upside, only the guys in uniform had guns. The rest had sledgehammers, pry bars, big-ass metal wrenches, baseball bats, and other improvised weapons. The supposed yard workers were just standing around near the containers looking intimidating. Still, the guys with the guns were surrounding our car.

Pope, who I was already impressed with, spoke. "Let me try to talk to them. Maybe we can get out of this with a good-sized bribe."

I opened the duffel closest to me and showed him the clothes inside. "It will have to be. I've got

$500k on me, the rest was sent to the bank via an alternative method. I was afraid something like this would happen."

My financial advisor looked confused, sure those bags had been filled with cash back on the plane. He muttered under his breath, "How the hell did..." then trailed off before chuckling.

"Okay, that should make things easier. They might be mad, but if we give them what we've got, that should do the trick. There's no way they could know how much we came here with in the first place since only you and I knew that."

I tried to smile reassuringly, but my guts were in knots. The only way I would get out of this situation a winner was if no one got hurt. Giving them half a million was nothing to me if it would buy us a way out.

One of the men in uniform, who was dressed slightly better than the others, approached the car and knocked on the driver's window.

They had a quick conversation that I could hear, thanks to my vampiric senses.

"Good to see you, Paul. Are they in the back? Do they have the cash with them?" The leader asked.

My traitorous driver readily answered, "Yes. I picked them up directly from the plane, right on the runway. They unloaded their bags and got right in."

"Good, good! Tell Mary I'll come to dinner sometime next week, and we can celebrate your new baby."

"Of course! We'll see you then." He paused for a second then added, "Let me just tell them to get out for the inspection."

The intercom crackled to life, and Paul spoke, "The Customs Inspector asks that you step out of the vehicle and present your bags for inspection."

I noted that he did not get out and open our doors for us or put himself in the line of fire. A second later, the doors unlocked.

Looking at my team, I gestured to Mr. Pope. "He'll do the talking. You guys look menacing and give them a reason to hesitate to use force. I planned for this. We'll give them the money I have on me without a fight, then we'll head to the bank afterward. No fuss, no mess. Got it?"

They nodded. All their goodies were on them now, and their bags were empty. I earnestly hoped they were cool under pressure. I wasn't, but I was faking it for their sake. I didn't want to look like a loser in front of professionals like this.

We stepped out and withdrew all our bags. Ralph and Jasper went first and stood flanking the car door, guarding us as Mr. Pope and I dropped the duffels in the dirt.

The leader stepped up to Pope, who looked like the guy in charge of our group. He was mature and experienced and looked calm, despite the circumstances.

However, the guys with the guns looked a bit twitchy over Ralph and Jasper's presence. My guys were wearing shoulder holsters, so their pistols were concealed. Even so, they stood like professional mercenaries and were intimidating, even surrounded and outnumbered.

I knew it was only my vampiric condition that kept me from shaking in my boots. There was a serious amount of tension in the air, and I felt terribly afraid this would all break down into violence, and then my people and many of these guys would die. I was scared for my own life but figured I had a decent chance of surviving.

Unless my spell protecting me from the sun failed....

That thought did not bring me peace! I had cast it, but it wasn't a cast-and-forget type of magic. It would protect me for a while, but if

I got hit with bullets, that could disrupt what little concentration the spell required, and I could go up in flames.

Now there's a pleasant thought!

This day just keeps getting better. Thank goodness for that illusion that I had put on the cash in case customs at the airport decided to get nosey.

The “Customs” guy spoke first, "I am Nigel Bennet, Customs inspector for the Department of Agriculture." He then went into a spiel, spouting off some bullshit about coconuts and quarantines and needing to look in our bags.

Mr. Pope shrugged. "That's fine. We have no produce, which we already attested to during the inspection at the airport."

"Understood, but we had a report about produce, so we must inspect the bags and confiscate any contraband we find." The man was pretty cool with his lies. When he was done, he kneeled down and began to unzip the first bag.

I could hear his heartbeat and knew he was lying from his body's reactions, even if this whole scenario wasn't so blatantly false. I think I actually heard his heart skip a beat when he opened

the bag and saw clothes instead of money.

His face fell before he rooted in the bag looking through what appeared to be Mr. Pope's wardrobe. He frowned, looking toward where the driver sat in the front of the limo.

Not to be deterred, he moved on to another duffel and repeated the process. His face grew darker with each bag and I could hear his heart racing. He was getting angry.

I began to get angry as well. It occurred to me that these guys wouldn't be doing this unless they had been tipped off. Only my guys and I knew about the cash, and even Ralph and Jasper had no idea how much I was bringing; only Pope and I did. Not even the pilot on our plane knew we were carrying bags of cash.

Who could have tipped them off, then? Could it be the casino somehow? That couldn't be right, though. If the casino knew who I was and knew enough to have someone intercept me before the bank, then they could and probably would do a lot worse to me than this.

So who could have done it? I was stumped but couldn't get an answer at the moment.

Finally, the inspector got down to the last bag. He looked like a blood vessel was about ready to pop on his temple. To say he was feeling anger and disappointment would be a massive understatement. I was a little afraid he might tell his men to open fire just to take out his frustrations on us.

I had left a small plastic-wrapped bundle of Hundreds visible in that bag, not covered by the illusion.

There was an almost palpable relief on the man's face when he saw it. "Ah, ha! This is undeclared contraband! I will have to seize this on behalf of the government."

Mr. Pope, bless his heart, looked angry and demanded, "But that's not coconuts; we came to the island to do banking. This did not need to be declared."

The man turned to Pope, squared off against him, cash in hand, and waved it about. "Coming into the country with undeclared cash like this means you are most likely a criminal. You are lucky my men do not take you straight to jail. If you can prove this money is legal, then file a complaint and I am sure they will give it back to you. In the meantime, you should go and do not let me see you again, or I will arrest you!"

Pope groused but got back into the car, myself and then the bodyguards following. I hit the intercom button for the driver. "Take us to the bank now. We need to withdraw some cash in order to get home."

Before he drove off, I heard the driver explain to the fake inspector. "I don't know. Blevins said they had a lot of money!"

"Bah, this isn't more than a few hundred thousand American dollars. I'll wring that man's neck next time I see him! I risked my position to do this, and I'll have to share most of this with the men, there will be little left for you and Mary and the baby!"

"We'll talk about this later, uncle! I must deliver them to Blevins now."

And then we were driving out of that death trap.

I was incredibly relieved there had been no bloodshed, and the whole situation had made me realize that this new life of mine was serious. It wasn't all just some victimless game. I did not want to become someone I couldn't stand. Being immortal and hating yourself would not be good. Once I got settled, I needed to find a way to turn my ill-gotten fortune into a legitimate one.

I mean, I had died at the outset of all of this, and that was serious. But with that crazy time-stop, and the ability to rob the casino of all those millions, I hadn't really been taking things seriously, starting out that way had skewed my perspective. I needed to balance out the craziness of the situation with the need to keep my humanity.

I sighed and refocused.

Turning to Mr. Pope. "Do you know someone named Blevins? I think I heard them mention that name as I was getting into the car."

Pope's eyes got big. "That asshole! He's the banker we're here to meet. I'll ruin him!"

He thought momentarily, then added, "I did not tell him how much money we were bringing, just that we would need to set up some large accounts."

I put a comforting hand on my finance guy's shoulder.

"Don't worry about it. I'll take care of him while we are meeting. He just cost us $500k and tried to turn us over to people who might have killed us if things hadn't gone well. We'll see how much he is worth and make him wish he'd never heard of us."

I had to hide my smile from my team because I knew my fangs would be showing with the desire to rip that guy a new one.

The experience at the bank was more pleasant. Mr. Pope used his connections to speak directly to the bank manager, Michael Blevins. I mojo'd him to keep our meeting off the record. He personally handled the deposit while Ralph and Jasper lounged outside the room, keeping watch.

The man was an older fellow, balding and getting a bit obese. He had a loosened look to him as if there were not enough muscle under the fat of his face. It bothered me and made a bad impression. Of course, he'd already gotten in my bad graces by selling us out to the fake customs agent and his crew of thugs. He was going to have a bad day, starting as soon as he completed setting up my shiny new bank accounts.

Incidentally, I usually felt guilty when I whammied people, but not this guy. Even aside from what he'd already done to me, I had the distinct impression he would sell his own mother for a dime. Luckily, I no longer had to worry about that. He and Pope were under oath, so to speak, not to reveal anything about this, so even if they heard about the Casino heist, they wouldn't feel any urge to spill the beans.

After we were done, Blevins would not remember seeing me, all he would remember was that he had betrayed me and I had turned out to be a little fish that wasn't worth the effort. He would not, however, have any memory of setting up my accounts.

Once I was done ensuring his trustworthiness, it took some time to count out the whole pile of money and then do all the paperwork necessary to set up the accounts and make the deposits. In the end, I had an untraceable bank account that only I could access. I also had several secondary accounts with lesser amounts in them so that I wouldn't always have to hit the big account for small things and potentially expose my net worth to people or organizations like the US government. Two of the accounts we did specifically make legit by filing US taxes on them in order to keep them off the IRS's radar. Once I started doing little things like leasing million-dollar office spaces and renovating them, that would be pretty important. The last thing anyone wants, especially a vampire, is for the US Government to suddenly take notice of your finances.

All of the details made my eyes glaze over, and I kept having to burn blood as the day dragged on since Mr. Slackface's office was in the direct sun, thanks to a wall of windows. The upside was that he had a good view, and I did get everything I needed done. I was now the proud owner of several anonymous bank accounts and two very legitimate ones.

Of course, any money put into those accounts would have to be justified to the US Government by filing statements on where it came from. This time it was an inheritance from a relative who passed away. In the future, it would have to result from "foreign investments" with at least enough of a paper trail that it wouldn't raise eyebrows, but that was what I was paying Mr. Pope to handle so that I didn't have to worry about it.

Finally, a bit after 2 pm, it was all done, and we were able to get back to the plane and head back to the States. I thanked Ralph and Jasper, each with a $500 bonus, and Mr. Pope with an offer to go to work for me full time; he'd get a $500K a year salary.

I did not force him to accept but let him decide entirely on his own. He accepted but negotiated a bonus for each major action that was required of him, such as traveling outside of the country to open foreign bank accounts or sudden inflows of cash that had to be legitimized. It was smart of him. He clearly saw that I had come by the money in some nefarious way and was okay with that. Still, he ensured he would profit from what he saw as my future endeavors.

He did ask me point blank before accepting if my money came from or would in the future come from harming innocent people. I was able to look him in the eye and say no, and he took me at my word. He seemed to be a shrewd judge of character, so he probably would not have worked for me if he thought I was some kind of mafia boss.

CHAPTER 12
BUYING A BUNKER

THAT SETTLED, I checked back in with Miss Clearwater. She had found that the 61st floor could be leased. It required taking over the remainder of the lease for an office that was currently occupied. Still, they wanted to move to a cheaper location anyway. I could move into the unoccupied portion immediately, and the company would vacate the other space by the end of next month. At that point, we could begin the reno of the entire floor. She had arranged for an architect to meet with me over dinner to discuss what I wanted for the space. That was a relief; I wanted someplace to start calling home already.

As for the Maker Space I wanted to set up, she had already made the arrangements; it just needed a signature now that I had access to the funds via a legit bank account. We took a short drive in her Lexus over to the building. It was just off Richmond Ave, on the inner side of the 610 Loop, less than a mile and a half away in a rather nice neighborhood. The businesses there were mostly high-end shopping and dining, but my building was a block off the main street and would not disturb the neighbors.

From the outside, It looked like a Spanish-style building with a stucco exterior, but that was only a façade. It had originally been a small communications bunker for the phone company, built during the cold war, with concrete walls several feet thick. On the inside, however, it had been gutted and was all open with no interior walls other than a small office on one side and some storage over that office. It was 5,000 sq.ft. of space completely empty, but with good electric already run due to its history. Since then, it had been used as an automotive shop. It even had a basement where the mechanics had done oil changes to get under the cars, but the openings had been concreted over, leaving the lower floor accessible only through a single stairwell by one wall. It had one 16' shop door that could be raised to bring in large equipment or cars. I would want to do something about that to make it far more secure, but I wasn't sure yet what could be done.

"Kat, please have the architect come by here as well to look the place over. I'll want to make some changes. I like being able to get cars or large equipment in and out, but I want something a lot more secure than that thin metal rollup door."

She made the note. "So, I take it you approve and want to purchase?"

"I do; please arrange it. The funds are available, so let's move quickly."

I was ready to get stuff done and not feel like I was on the run and hiding anymore. Well, I would always be hiding from now on, but at least I would have a home.

Despite my eagerness to leave the hotel, it still took another week to get all the legal stuff done with the lease and another two weeks to close on the workspace building. In the meantime, I met with the architect to explain what I wanted to accomplish and made a lot of decisions about décor and furnishings. I really wanted to move into the Tower space ASAP. Still, Kat convinced me to move into the shop building instead for the time being since contractors would be doing a lot of work, and having me living in the space would become very annoying, very fast, both for me and the workers. I saw the logic and agreed, but that meant I was stuck in the hotel for another three weeks.

To make matters easier to bear, Kat ensured the building would get hit like a tornado the second we signed the papers. She had staged the contractors like it was the invasion of Normandy on D-day. The day we closed, multiple cleaning crews hit the place and made sure there wasn't a cobweb or speck of dirt anywhere to be found. Then before the day was half over, furniture started to arrive and was moved in. She even had a decorator on hand directing the crew on where to put everything. Expensive rugs were placed down on the bare concrete floors, and the furniture was arranged on those. When it was all done, it was a lot like a loft apartment with a large empty space sparsely furnished. Still, I had all the comforts of home now, including a massive 85" TV, and state-of-the-art sound system, and an impressive gaming rig PC with a top-end VR setup. It was all the things that would make this new life enjoyable as a bachelor. There were even tapestries and art on the walls. Most of this stuff would be moved to the Tower once that was complete, but it was my home for now.

In the basement I put my bed and a jewelry workshop, and contractors were brought in to secure both the big rollup door and the stairs to the basement. For the rollup, they installed an industrial steel outer door on rollers that slid to the side with the press of a button but would lock in place with some very sturdy hardware that even vampires or werewolves might have a hard time busting through. We did the same to all the other doors as well. Still, we kept those looking fashionable on the exterior so that it didn't look like I was turning the building into a bunker, although that was exactly what it was. This would be my safe space that I could retreat to if necessary and where I would do my work. I had already thought of something that I was ready to try. If magic worked, then why not magic items? I was crafty, having been a bench jeweler for a couple of years during college, and dabbled in both smithing and leatherwork as hobbies, so it seemed only natural to want to put magic into things. I knew exactly what I wanted most in the world to make. Something that would protect me from the sun without having to constantly pay such a high price in blood to prevent damage.

But the blood queen was thousands of years old and had never made such a thing, you ask? Well, she didn't know modern science. It had taken Her Evilness a year of human sacrifices and then 1000 more the night of her transformation, and the downside was she could never again see the sun, or at least not without using magic at a ridiculous cost to do so, but she was countering a magical effect of our very condition. I figured if I could just nullify the effects of certain frequencies of light the way a polarized pane of glass did, then badda-boom badda-bing, Bob's your uncle, and I'd be good to go. That shouldn't cost nearly as much as trying to overcome a multi-thousand-year-old spell's side effect. The cost to make something like the sun ring permanent would be astronomical, but I hoped it would be doable.

This maker space would allow me to experiment and try such things out. After three weeks of nights, all spent moving from restaurant to bar to club, I had just over a thousand gems, aka about the equivalent 1000 carats of diamonds, but in 1-carat gems. Altogether, they would have been about twelve teaspoons. Still, because spheres don't stack well, it was about ten times that volume, or big enough that I could feel them uncomfortably in my stomach, or whatever passed for a stomach in a vampire. If I put all that into a single spell, I could wreak some serious devastation or make something really impressive.

I made a pendant shaped like a shield with the Fox clan crest and motto engraved on it. That took me several days of work, but using magic to assist the mundane art of creation, it went fast and was very well made. I made it out of titanium to be light and very strong, which in turn made it super annoying to engrave. After the 11th broken graver tip, I finally resorted to magic to strengthen my tools, which helped considerably. When done, I tested the spell before trying to find a way to enchant the piece. It actually took me another three days to figure out exactly how to cast around myself to block the light without it being noticeable. Then it took another day of experimenting to temporarily place the spell in an item so that it would still work on me when held or worn.

Finally, I was ready.

I slept well the day before and meditated for the entire night, preparing myself. On top of that, I used a spell to keep myself focused. Then in the morning, when the sun and moon were in the sky together, I went up on the roof of my building and placed the amulet on a silver plate which in turn was on a gold plate, eclipsing its surface.

I had found that symbolism mattered in spell casting; it gave a boost to what you wanted to accomplish. Words and circumstances, burning candles, sacrificing things of value, these could all affect the ability to cast, the cost to cast, and the effectiveness of your spell.

Don't ask me why that was true, but it definitely was. Queenie had given me the quick magic 101 class during my death vision. Her lecture had been big on practical advice but could have done better on answering the why of things, and it was at times like this that I wished I could talk with her more and ask questions.

Regardless of why it worked, I maximized everything I could on this cast and still burned a full 250 blood gems, the equivalent of 25 human sacrifices if this had been done by the Blood Queen. Thankfully, my way didn't require such gruesome acts.

One thing that surprised me a bit about this was the actual casting of the spell and how I perceived it. I hadn't thought about it with the small spells I had been casting, but it became noticeable when casting such a big spell using so much mana.

I figured blood magic would be dark and creepy, with a gruesome aura, something that others would shriek in horror to see. To my great surprise, it was far from that. There was a certain earthy dark undertone as I converted the blood gems into mana. Still, externally, as the mana entered the pendant, it was pure, untarnished light. Just as I was trying to create an artifact to protect me from the sun, it seemed to be a mixture of golden and silvery beams twisting around one another as they mixed and sank into the pendant.

I was fascinated by what I was seeing, but I had to maintain concentration and focus my will on what I wanted the magic to do. When my mind tried to wander for that second, the thick strands of mana seemed to shake and go out of control, but they tamed quickly as my mind returned to the task.

Even so, it was a long process and with a fraction of my mind I couldn't help but revel in the beauty of what I was seeing. The pendant lay there, and it was as if it were greedily drinking in the mana. As time passed, I noticed that it was beginning to glow stronger and stronger, as if it was straining to hold all of the mana being forced into it. It seemed that I had gone beyond its natural capacity to hold magic energy and was compressing it into the metal. Near the end, it had floated off the surface and hung suspended in the air, surrounded by the bright glow of magic.

That tiny fraction of my mind, not focused on the enchanting, couldn't help but worry that such a powerful casting was creating a beacon that could be seen from across the city.

As the power sank into the amulet, I could feel that I had used more magic than necessary, so I focused my will to channel the extra energy into making it indestructible and inconspicuous. It wouldn't be invisible, but it would deflect the notice of others so that they would simply overlook it as if it wasn't there.

Interestingly, the look and feel of the magic changed as my purpose changed. When I shifted my will to making the pendant indestructible, the mana took on a metallic hue, more like steel. When I shifted to making it inconspicuous, the mana turned shadowy.

Apparently, my mind was affecting how the mana looked and felt. I guess it was all subconscious on my part, and I imagined that another mage might enchant something with the same functions, but their spell effects might look totally different. That was just a guess, however. Unfortunately, since I had no mage friends, I was not likely to satisfy my curiosity about this anytime soon.

As the pendant finally lowered back down and rested on the surface, I felt absolutely exhausted. Still, I mustered the energy to hang it on a titanium chain and put it around my neck. I couldn't feel anything, but I let my spell of protection drop, ready to dive through the hatch in the roof and back into the protective darkness of my bunker.

I waited.

I was poised to jump at the first hint of pain or damage, my muscles on a hair trigger. I almost couldn't believe it when nothing happened.

I stood there in the full light of the morning sun, its rays shining down upon my undead body and doing no harm. The UV was channeled around me without hitting me as if I wasn't there.

The pain of being fried wasn't the only worry in my mind that morning, however. I also hoped it wasn't possible to sense when someone was casting big spells because if it was, I had just lit the beacon fires of Gondor on my workshop roof.

Putting the instruments of my work aside and locking the building, I casually walked around the corner to a coffee shop and ordered a latte like nothing was happening. I sat on the rooftop balcony they had, from which I could see my own building, and waited to see if anyone would show up. I tried to sip the coffee but had to spit it back into the cup. I couldn't eat or drink normal things any longer, it seemed. No digestive system, I supposed? I'd have to figure that out someday.

CHAPTER 13
OOPSIE, THAT WAS A MAGE...

EITHER NO ONE could sense my use of magic, or anyone who did decided that discretion was the better part of valor and left me alone. My security system didn't detect anything, and the people I had stationed around the area to watch for those who might be watching my workshop didn't notice anyone either.

Hooray, for cheap private detectives that don't ask questions and just do what they are paid to do!

That put my mind at ease, and though I had to spend an extra blood gem still to stay awake that day, I could now go out in the sun anytime I felt like it.

It was weird. Here I was, just a couple months into my undead life, and I was profoundly glad that I had overcome this curse that kept me from enjoying the daytime. The irony wasn't lost on me that there had to be vampires out there who had gone centuries without seeing a sunrise or sunset. Yet, here I was, feeling relieved because I had missed going outside during the day.

I couldn't imagine how they must feel. No, I take that back; they'd be jealous. Enough that they would kill and risk their immortal lives for the chance to get it back. They had killed Queenie, after all, and they had destroyed civilization at the time in order to do it.

That was something I needed to remember!

Still, the sunlight pendant would only be the first of my creations. So, if they would kill me over that one item, what would they do over all the other things I would make now that I had proven my ability to enchant?

That drew my mind back to my plans. I hadn't decided what to do next. I was sure there were tons of great items that could help me survive better and make me harder to kill, but I still needed perspective. I also was distracted by the Tower situation.

The work was going well, but not fast enough for my liking. It would take two months before I could move in. Still, I went there daily to view the progress and make notes on things I wanted done or changed.

I saw Kat daily, Mr. Pope weekly, and my other guys as needed, but I was starting to feel isolated. There was only so much planning and work one could do. For that matter, there were only so many vampire dramas on TV that could be watched before becoming bored and feeling lonely. Although I had to admit sitting in my fancy recliner watching the shows on my 85" TV was a great way to do it. First-world vampire problems, am I right?

Did I mention that I had been binge-watching every vamp show I could to see if there was anything I could learn that I didn't already know? So far, I wasn't too impressed. It was all either a bunch of old horror crap where the vamp was a monster or a modern teen angst fest that was even more crap than the old stuff. Mixed in were a few classics and good ones like the Lost Boys. Still, mostly it boiled down to what I knew from personal experience: the mojo, being stronger and faster than mortals, healing incredibly fast from wounds, not getting staked or beheaded or set on fire, and sunlight being bad.

Interestingly, a couple of different series had vamps able to go out during the day due to magic rings. I guess I wasn't the only one to think of that, but the fact that multiple shows had the concept meant it was probably based on fact. Despite how angsty the shows were, they made me want some companionship. I was missing having friends and family. I had never been alone this long in my life.

In my old life, I had my family and a strong circle of friends, Marcy, Jake, Megan, Taylor, Katy and myself. We used to do everything together; we'd hang out two or three times a week and even take trips together, like going camping.

I blinked in surprise at that thought and froze in place.

How the hell hadn't, I thought about that over the last couple of months since becoming a vamp? Why hadn't I contacted any of them? I mean, I know I decided right away that it would put them in danger, but who just abandons their lifelong friends without a word? Even if I weren't going to talk to them, why hadn't I checked up on them or gone to see them privately in a way that couldn't be detected?

Sure, I had been super busy trying to establish this new life, but that wasn't an excuse...

"Queenie! That fucking bitch!"

I suddenly realized the depth of what she had done to me. I mean, I had thought it before, but I never really grokked just how much she had whammied me. Just like I used my vampire mojo to give my blood donors post-hypnotic suggestions to forget me or wash their damned hands when they go to the bathroom in the future, she had done the same to me. I don't know exactly what she had implanted in my brain, but it was obviously to do with surviving at all costs.

I was decently diligent at studying in school and getting good grades, but I had never had this level of focus in my life. Spending weeks of days and nights figuring out how to do enchantments with almost no break other than to feed and build up more blood as a safety net. Sure, I was watching some TV, but even that was in order to find out about vampires and other things that go bump in the night. In other words, it was research that might help me to survive better!

That bitch... was my life even my own anymore?

Don't get me wrong, I'm glad Queenie wasn't able to turn me into a meat puppet and literally possess me. Still, she was controlling my life now through this *drive to survive* compulsion.

I took some deep breaths and tried to calm down and think it through. On the one hand, I wasn't unhappy with the results. I now had protection from the sun, one of the most significant factors that could kill me, and it made my life way more manageable since I could go out during the day like a regular person. On the other hand, it had kept me from some of the things that made life worth living, like friendship and family.

Was there anything I could do about it?

Did I want to do anything about it?

Was the fact that I just thought that last question part of the compulsion, or was it me thinking it through with a clear head? I felt clear-headed and in control of myself. At the same time, I knew I would continue driving toward eliminating any other source of danger that I could. I had ideas for shield enchantments to prevent me from being staked, and that seemed like a really good idea to pursue, compulsion or not.

I sighed and gave up.

There probably wasn't any way to remove the compulsion, only to satisfy it. But at least I was fully aware of it now, and maybe that would let me mitigate its influence to a degree?

I guess it wasn't all bad. I wasn't completely alone, I just didn't have real friends at the moment, but I could change that.

Kat was the only person alive that knew I wasn't normal, but she was an employee rather than a friend. There was something to be said for simply having people around you. I wasn't physically alone; after all, I was still going out nightly all over the city, feeding and stocking up on blood gems.

I had gotten quite good at it by now, having done it hundreds of times in only a few weeks, but I felt like I was being reckless to feed so often and so many times from the same place at once. Still, thanks to the compulsion, I wouldn't rest until I had a significant supply of magic, and I wasn't sure how else to accomplish the task. I could do one or two per night, but that would take years, and the thought of taking that long gave me a very uncomfortable feeling that I knew was the compulsion talking.

One last thought struck me. How much of my desire to just live quietly and peacefully was part of Queenie's doing? I hadn't really thought much about what I wanted to do with my unlife beyond making myself safe. Theoretically, I was immortal unless killed; surely I ought to have more ambition in life than just survive....

CHAPTER 14
TIME PASSED

AND YET, thoughts of a greater purpose didn't stick with me for long. The day-to-day grind to build myself a safe, secure life was more immediate.

Two months later, by the time my new home was ready in the Tower, I had topped 2,000 blood gems, but I still didn't have any way of knowing how that compared to other mages or how dangerous other vampires were compared to me. For all I knew, these modern vamps might be vastly stronger and tougher than me. They might be from a different bloodline, after all.

That question ended up being answered in the scariest way possible, and I was very lucky it didn't happen sooner before I was settled into my new life and used to my powers and abilities.

I was in a restroom at an Indian restaurant one evening when it happened for the second time. I went to mojo a guy, but unlike the first time in Vegas, this guy knew what I was and raised his hands in a defensive stance, and flames sprang up around them. It was scary as fuck! I could feel the heat trying to burn even as we both got some distance from one another.

"Oh shit!" I stepped back and held up my hands in the universal gesture for "Please don't kick my ass; I've just made a terrible mistake and suddenly regret my life choices."

He didn't pay attention to my pleading gestures and began to send the fire toward me like a spell or something. As they got closer, the heat felt like it was going to singe my eyebrows off; it was so intense.

I backed as far away from the fire-crazed mage as possible until my back bumped against the wall. If he took one more step I was going to be an undead torch. Well, perhaps not. I didn't know if vampires were actually flammable, but I desperately did not want to find out!

Luckily, he stopped advancing and lowered his hands just enough that I could see his face. The guy looked a bit scared and very wary.

"Give me one good reason I shouldn't fry you right now, bloodsucker?"

"Easy, I wasn't going to harm you. I was just looking to have a quick bite and let you go on your way in peace. I didn't know you were a...."

I cocked my head, puzzled, "What are you, by the way?"

He lowered his hands a bit more, looking puzzled, "What do you mean what am I?" He waved the flaming hands around, "I'm a mage, isn't that why you...." It was his turn to trail off, sensing things weren't quite what they seemed.

Just then, we heard someone else coming into the restroom and the mage let the fire disappear and pretended to be washing his hands as an older gent walked in and headed toward the urinal.

I tossed a paper towel in the trash and nodded toward the doorway. If he wasn't going to kill me with other people present, then maybe I would survive this unfortunate encounter.

"Would you care to chat over dinner? I've never met a mage before and I've got a million questions. I'm a bit new at all this." I had said it very quietly, but he must have heard because he nodded slightly.

I quickly made my exit from the restroom and considered sprinting for the door. I didn't think he could catch me if I used my vamp speed. Still, he seemed almost as nervous as I was, and he'd been unwilling to show his power when a single guy had walked into the bathroom, so I was willing to bet he wouldn't try and nuke the whole restaurant just to kill me.

Looking around, I sat at a booth near the back where I would have a good view of the doors so as not to be surprised.

The mage joined me after only a few seconds, but not before going to tell his friends that he needed to talk to me and would return shortly. With my hearing, I had no problem catching his conversation. Which reassured me a bit.

Now that I had a chance to get a better look at him, he seemed young, college-aged, maybe. He was definitely not a jock type either. He was pretty nerdy but seemed to be trying to look tough as he slid into the booth across from me.

He quietly announced, "My friends over there are all mages, and they will fireball this table if you make a move." It was all bluster.

I smiled and tapped my ear. "They don't know what either of us are, do they?"

He sighed and looked startled by me calling his bluff. "Fine, but I can still burn you if you try anything," he warned.

That much I believed and surreptitiously checked to make sure I still had eyebrows. I did, thankfully.

My smile turned rueful then. "Look, I seriously didn't mean you any harm. I just needed a little blood and didn't know you were a mage.

How was I supposed to know that anyway? I've never even seen a mage before."

"Really? Huh. I figured it must be a deliberate attack since you were here." He sat back in his seat, relaxing a bit. "By the way, I've got a truth spell going, so I *will* know if you lie."

My jaw dropped open. "I didn't even think about that. That would be a handy power to have."

He smirked, "It is. But why are you not hunting the clubs, one of the vamp-owned venues in town, or one of the blood banks? You guys are supposed to stick to those places unless you feed in private in your lairs, that was the agreement."

I frowned; that was going to suck. "Like I said, I'm new at this. You could say that I was created and orphaned on the same night. No one told me any rules; I've been figuring this out as I go. For the record, I have not killed anyone or done anyone serious harm. I only take as much as will not hurt my donors. I would have taken about the same from you as if you had donated blood, then let you go unharmed. I also try to leave them better off - I usually ask my donors what something they would like to change about themselves and give them a little help via a vampiric post-hypnotic suggestion. A student having trouble in school might get a suggestion to relax and have better recall, etc."

The mage's eyebrows shot up. "Wow, you are not the evil scum I expected. Not that what you are doing is right, but I see you are telling the truth and not hurting people." He visibly relaxed some. "So you really don't know anything about vamp society or mages or any of the rules?"

Shrugging, I answered simply, "Nope. Just what I've seen on TV. Do you know any vampires I could talk to? Or can you tell me any places where they frequent so I can meet them? I don't want to be killed for breaking rules I don't know."

He nodded, "No idea about any specific vamps, just what I've been told by my teachers. Stay away from clubs because vamps tend to hunt in them. Some bars around the city too. As far as the rules go, we all follow the golden rule: don't let normal people know about our existence. Anything that breaks that rule will pretty much get you killed or have other bad consequences, depending on what group you are part of. Vamps kill. Mages, well, not so much with the killing, but breaking the rules can result in worse punishments than death."

"Worse than death?" I wondered if that meant mages were psychopaths, or what?

"Yeah, it doesn't often happen with mages, but when one goes rogue and does something terrible, the punishments aren't quick, and they aren't pleasant. When you can bend the laws of physics and reality, punishments can get very creative. If a group of mages has to hunt another down, they make the punishment permanent, such that it can't be undone by any single wizard or small group of them."

That made sense. "Can your abilities be taken away or something?" If a mage could be blocked from using magic, it might be possible for them to do it to me?

"Yes, but that is a very extreme punishment, and it takes a conclave of powerful mages to do it."

This guy was being very informative, and I wanted to keep him talking. I wanted to know his name and get his contact info, but I didn't want to risk spooking him by asking.

"Powerful mages? That implies that some aren't powerful; how does that work?"

My information source shrugged. "Why are some people born good at sports, and others good at piano? Genetics I would guess, but yeah, some of us are born more capable of casting powerful and complex spells than others. I'm pretty strong, but definitely not considered among the more powerful."

I nodded, eager to hear more. "This is fascinating. I'm learning more from talking to you than I have in the weeks since I was made into this. I wish I had had someone to tell me the rules. Tell me, though, how do you judge how powerful you are compared to others?"

My new acquaintance smiled, "We call it the 10-point scale, and it's a typical bell curve. A tiny few who can do magic are very weak and can only do extremely minor spells, and a few at the other end of the scale can do really powerful magics. Most of us fall in the middle somewhere along the curve. I am between a six and a seven, meaning I can do some decently powerful magics like teleportation. You've got to be at least a five minimum to teleport, but at that rating, you can only go short distances. I can move across the continent anywhere in North America, or if I was on the East Coast, I could move to England or Spain. Or I could move to Hawaii from the West Coast, that sort of thing. If I were a full seven, I'd be able to jump from here directly to England. An eight could go anywhere in the world."

"Man, that is so cool. I never even thought a mage could do something like that. But put it in perspective for me, if you used fire as a metaphor, or rather as a scale, how would the various ranks be measured? I assume a one could light a candle? What could a ten do?"

Now to see if my theory held up...

Chuckling, he said, "That's easy; everyone always uses fire. Yeah, a one could basically light small fires like candles. Someone like me, between a six and a seven, could fill a space of about 350 square meters. A ten could do around 500 square meters. That's square meters, not cubic meters, mind you."

That left me very thoughtful. I wasn't totally accurate in my theory, but very close. That meant a human really was limited by their bodies on how much mana they could burn at one time. I didn't have that limitation. I could burn as much as I could hold gemstones inside me. Instead of burning a maximum of 10 blood like a mage, I could burn 100, or even 1000, and actually nuke an entire city. That was a sobering thought. No wonder those ancient vamps had been jealous of the Blood Queen. In her vision, she mentioned her enemies had allies, and that must have been the mages. If the vamps were pouty over what she could do, the mages of the time must have been apoplectic knowing someone was running around able to do entire orders of magnitude more powerful spells than them. This guy seemed nice and mild-mannered, but I sure as hell wasn't going to let him know I could do magic now that I understood this.

I asked a different question, changing the topic. "Since my change, I've been watching a bunch of shows and movies on vampires figuring some of what they are based on must be true. In more than one show, I've seen the concept of vampires having magic items that let them walk around in the daytime. Is that a thing?"

My new “friend” became suddenly wary. "Don't even ask. That's one of those forbidden things that will get a mage Punished with a capital P."

I held up my hands in a placating gesture. "Ok, so you confirmed that it is a thing, but it's forbidden, so I will not ask. I wouldn't want to get you in trouble."

Changing the topic again, "What about magic to see other supernatural people so that you would know what you were looking at when you meet someone, that way, I would never again accidentally mess with someone I should avoid?"

He looked thoughtful. "Well, certainly, there are spells for that. I know one myself, and it's only a two on the scale, but magic item?

That's way too expensive to make. Enchanting takes a group of mages weeks, months, or even years to complete due to how much power it takes to make a spell permanent. Even the most powerful of us rarely ever enchant items alone. The cost is too much to deal with when we can spend a little power and cast the spell when we need it instead, especially low-power things like Aura Sight."

If I could sell the things I could make, they'd be worth an absolute fortune, but it looked like I'd have to keep my enchanting very much on the down low. "Um... if it wouldn't be considered rude or offensive, are there any books or teaching materials on mages and what you guys can learn to do? I'd love to know more about you guys."

Egbert, I was thinking of him as Egbert because he looked like an Egbert, looked wary again. "I probably shouldn't have even had this conversation with you, so no. I'd say you are not likely to find anything like that."

"Got it. Sorry. I really don't want to get you in trouble. It's just that you're the first person I've been able to talk openly to about this stuff since it happened to me. Do you mind giving me your contact info and what I can call you? I'd love to be able to talk again sometime, although I promise to avoid any subjects you tell me are sensitive." I hoped he would, as he would be a valuable resource, and it would be really nice to be able to talk to someone.

He looked sympathetic but still wary. "Names are powerful, so definitely no on that. But you can call me George, and I don't mind giving you my email if you will give me yours. I think that's as close as I'm comfortable being for now. Mages and Vamps don't typically hang out and chat. My people would worry if it became known and might wonder if I were being courted to do magic for you, which is forbidden." He got out a business card and passed it over. It was Magnificent George's Wizardry: for parties and events, contact me at this address. $300/hr.

I nodded, impressed. "That's clever. Hide the truth behind the misdirection of a plausible alternative; very magicianly of you." I chuckled and rattled off my own email for him to write down.

He laughed at that. "That's a great address, and I can tell from the spell you aren't lying. How did you get such a good one?"

I smiled, "I had to buy it off the guy who originally grabbed it. Cost me $2,000, but it's worth it for all the looks I get when I give people my addy." He was glancing over at his friends at the other table like he was ready to leave, so I added one more quick question. "I don't want to keep you, and I really appreciate you trusting me enough to chat, but can you tell me anything about the other vampires?"

He frowned, "I don't know much, just what I've heard. They are dangerous. Most of them kill people callously, although they are careful not to raise any alert. They make it look like criminal activity or regular murder, things like that. Many are part of organized crime, or so I hear. Some are parts of gangs, and some are lone wolves, so to speak. Some old ones are super rich from centuries of manipulation and investments. The older they are, the more powerful, or so I hear."

George paused for a second to think, "Basically, all I know is second or third-hand, you are the first one I've ever had a conversation with, and you seem as regular of a guy as I could imagine, but then you are brand new and don't even know what your kind is like. I honestly hope you stay that way and don't become a killer. I'm pretty young myself, although I've been training in magic since I was a teen, and if I had to I could take you out. Don't let me find out you've started harming people, if you do then don't ever cross my path again, or I will end you. And don't reveal yourself to the mortals; the Cabal will come for you if you do that."

He had grown earnest at the end there. He actually believed he could and that it was his duty to do it if he had to.

I nodded solemnly. "I'll remember that, and I have no desire to become a killer. Hopefully, I can stay out of vampire business and society and keep to myself."

What he had said right at the end caught my attention, so I asked, "Cabal, what's that?"

In the vision, Queenie had mentioned something about a group of mages and other supernatural critters that worshiped a dragon or something crazy like that. Some secret society of supers that went all the way back to the beginning.

"The Cabal is a shadowy organization that polices the rules. No one knows who is a member and who isn't. Still, suppose a mage starts openly tossing spells around in public, or a vamp goes on a spree, kills a dozen victims, and leaves their bodies drained for the human authorities to find. In that case, the Cabal will send a team to catch and punish the rule breaker. It keeps us all safe from the humans, but they have a dark reputation for being excessive in their punishments."

George shuddered thinking of it, then fell silent, obviously not willing to say more.

I doubted I'd be able to, or even want to stay away from vampire society forever, but I really didn't want to become some kind of monster, or mass murderer the way Queenie had been. I was also still very apprehensive about how powerful I might be compared to the modern vamp species. There was absolutely no way to compare until I met some. Now that I knew I wasn't supposed to be feeding in places like this or stick to clubs and bars and things, I would be limited on how much blood I could collect if I followed their rules.

We didn't shake hands but did nod to each other as a show of mutual respect as we stood and parted company. Without another word, we went our separate ways, possibly to never see each other again. On the other hand, this restaurant was right down the street from the

Tower, so it was possible we might run across each other someday. I made a mental note not to feed and hunt near my home again and to be much more random in the future. I'd only been undead for a few weeks, and I had run into both a mortal immune to vampiric mojo, and an actual freakin' wizard.

Granted, I had fed a couple thousand times, but that was still pretty high odds to hit the 'jackpot' twice in such a short time.

CHAPTER 15
AURA DETECTION

AFTER THAT FRIGHTENING EPISODE, I made a point of learning to cast an aura detection spell. It only took a couple days, and once I had it mastered, I tested it out by going to crowded places like sporting events. There were tons of people, so I was sure to see different types of folks.

I still didn't know what each aura meant, just that they were different from normal. I tweaked the spell to highlight only the abnormal ones and only show me something in particular about mortals if I concentrated on them. That way, mages, werewolves, fae, and whatever else existed would stand out like a beacon. I'd know to avoid them instead of accidentally hunting someone that might be able to squish me like a bug.

When I had it mastered and tweaked, I bought a lovely lab-created sapphire and then enchanted it with the aura-seeing spell so that I would always have it on me and active. Then I mounted it in an earring and stuck it in my left ear. Not that many men wore earrings these days, but enough did that it wasn't considered outside social norms. That enchantment only cost me 150 blood gems. When it was done, I was able to appreciate it all the more for knowing how rare magic items were and how unusual my ability to make them was.

After that, I was more careful where I hunted and more confident, knowing that I wouldn't accidentally stumble across someone dangerous.

Time passed, and my penthouse office was completed, much to my delight. It was just about the best view you could get in Houston. I could see downtown to the east and outward many miles on every side overlooking the city. At night the lights were beautiful, seeing the city spread out to the horizon in every direction.

The business part of the floor was on the south side of the building and took up about a quarter of the space. To get to my suite, you had to go through the business. There were private window offices for Kat, Mr. Pope, and my CPA and a greeting area for guests and visitors, where an executive assistant to my senior employees sat. There was also a large conference room for me to hold business meetings with the team. Finally, there was a small server room with all our computers and networking gear.

On the east side of the building was my private bedroom/living room, as it had the best view, in my opinion. There was no bed exactly. Instead, I had a sunken couch area for lounging and sleeping. The floor would slide over it, concealing it when I slept and making it seem like a ballroom when it wasn't visible. In that room was also a baby grand piano. Not that I played, but I loved listening, and I thought that if I ever had a big party, it would be great to have someone playing. Besides, now that I was immortal, why not learn to play?

On the walls were replicas of some of my favorite pieces of art. There were also alcoves with pedestals with sculptures on them. It was all exquisite and classic. It wasn't just Greek and Renaissance pieces, however, there were optical glass sculptures from Jack Storms.

I had found those fantastic even before I was turned into a vamp, but with my improved vision, the prismatic effects of the light were downright mesmerizing.

To the north, I had more casual living spaces, such as the dining room, kitchen, and a couple of guest bedrooms. Between the east and north, I had my private bathroom, with its Roman style bath for soaking and relaxing. The views from the tub were spectacular. On the west was the library and conference room. Between the south and west sides was a computer gaming room with state-of-the-art gaming systems and VR equipment for solo or team fun.

Between the west and north was a Gaming room of a different sort, where I planned to hold D&D-type tabletop games. Each area was decorated to the 9s, as I had spent almost 5 million dollars on the renovation and décor. I didn't have any real Van Goghs or anything crazy like that, just replica pieces. Still, everything was high quality, and it was all me. Well, I had professional help, but the ideas and choices were all mine.

The entire suite also had the best security I could buy, although I figured if something other than mortals came at me here, they would not be deterred or stopped by mundane security. Someday I would have to prepare magical defenses, but I settled for normal ones in the meantime.

The windows were coated to block the spectrums of light that would harm a vampire. I had installed an escape tunnel from my bed to the inner core of the building where the piping and utilities ran. From there, I could make my way down to the ground undetected if the need arose. I also had a window pane on each side of the building rigged to blow outward in an emergency so that I could dive out and fly away.

Flight was within my ability now, although I hadn't done it yet. I knew I could and even how much it would cost. I'm not afraid of heights, obviously. Otherwise, I wouldn't have made my home dozens of floors off the ground. Even so, I wasn't too eager to jump off a building, even if my vampiric nature or magic would allow me to survive.

Before it was done, however, while the floor was gutted, I had made sure the ceiling and floors were all completely secure from those above and below. In all, I had made this place as safe as I could without using magic yet.

On the other hand, my workspace building underwent another renovation once I moved to the Tower. It still had the basement bedroom, but that bedroom was now secret, with a concealed entrance that even the builders no longer remembered.

I had reinforced the main floor knowing that it would have to support the weight and operation of heavy power tools, which made my hidden bedroom even safer. It, too, had a secret tunnel exit now. I also put the jewelry workshop upstairs in what used to be the office space, and the basement bedroom now doubled as an armory that would make Burt Gummer green with jealousy.

Speaking of tools, I had a full woodworking shop, full metal working setup, full blacksmithing including two power hammers, and both a coal and gas forges. There were also CNC and plasma cutters, as well as 3d printers. I had a crafting room for leatherwork or other non-specialized crafts in one corner. Basically, it was heaven for a creative person. Every tool I could want to make things with and supplies to make them were in that shop.

If it could be made, I could do it in my shop!

5000 sqft might sound like a lot of space, but with all that stuff in there, it was cozy but very well organized. I had pros come in and help design the place.

I guess I should mention one other thing. Down below the Tower in the garage levels, I had a private space created to park several vehicles, a sports car, a luxury sedan, two motorcycles, and a truck capable of going off-road. One bike was a cruiser style, suitable for looking like a biker, and the other was a sport bike, street legal but it would practically fly down the roads and was capable of going off-road if needed.

All the vehicles were registered in different names to different people that were all whammied to be loyal and handle the taxes and registration for me. That way, I could drive out of there like Batman from the Batcave, and no one would have any idea who I was. With my magic, I could look like a redneck in that truck, a middle-aged grizzled biker on the motorcycle, or the CEO of some company in the luxury sedan.

They were all hidden behind the garage doors so that no one would be able to see what was in there. Better still, there was a hidden emergency tunnel from the utility shaft to the garage, so if I ever had to escape in secret, I could do it without ever going through a public space in the building that any normal person would have access to or even know existed.

Call me paranoid, but I was one of the undead now, so I figured I was entitled to a little paranoia. Besides, I could blame Queenie's compulsion for the extremes to which I was going to ensure my safety and survival.

'Queenie made me do it!' I couldn't help but laugh. It made for a good excuse, and it was even true. On the other hand, I was the architect who masterminded the whole thing, so I couldn't entirely blame her. It was my life that might be saved after all.

CHAPTER 16

MOAR ENCHANTING!

So where did that leave me?

I had the ultimate bachelor pad, and it had cost me a literal fortune. I also had the ultimate shop. I wanted companionship but still felt vulnerable and anxious about my survival. I wanted to make more magic items that would help me, so what did I do? I pulled out every gaming book I could think of and combed through them for ideas.

Many were ridiculous and would never be worth creating, even if they could be done. But some... some were good ideas. Just perhaps not as described in the books.

Bracers of Defense, or the equivalent? Great idea, but lousy execution. I could get away with wearing rings and earrings, but big ol' metal bracers covering my whole forearms?

Sorry, not fashionable this season in Paris.

Not that I really cared about fashion, and I thought the idea of bracers would look cool. Still, they would be obvious as hell, and everyone I met would give me the side-eye and call the fashion police on me.

A Rolex of Defense, on the other hand.... Well, maybe not that brand, but a Tag Heuer or Breitling, now that I could get behind. I would want something that offered armor-like protection for my whole body but also to specifically deflect shots aimed at my heart or head, anything else I could heal from. Time to make a list of everything I would want to create, at least for now.

After a good deal of consideration, here is the list I came up with:

> Magic Items:
>
> General armor protection when struck - Watch Band Link
>
> Deflect blows to heart or head when attacked - Ring
>
> Spidey-sense - Detects harmful aggressive intent - Ring
>
> Truth-sense - Ring
>
> Invisibility?
>
> Silence?
>
> Storage ring!!! - Not sure if this one is even possible, but I absolutely WANT!
>
> Light?
>
> Regeneration / preservation - bring me back from the brink of death and keep me from dying if massively wounded. - Ring
>
> Hiding Aura to disguise as human - Watch Band Link?

So many other items sounded handy but were not essential in the real world. These could be pretty great, especially combined with my vampiric abilities, they would make me much harder to kill, and some would help me to avoid fights altogether. I wasn't about to wear that many rings, though, so how to avoid that?

The items I most wanted, the storage rings, would take some deep thought. If I was making extra-dimensional spaces, I had to figure out how that could work in the real world, or rather outside it. Invisibility would be the easiest of everything as it worked on the same principle as the sunlight protection amulet I had already made, but it was also the least needed item.

So much to do.

One thing that helped is that I realized I could actually combine at least two or more items into one. Each storage ring could also hold another artifact in its structure. For example, I could make a signet ring, and the ring itself would be the storage item, but then inlaid on the top would be the secondary item. That would allow me to knock 4 items down to 2.

> Storage ring 1 - Spidey-sense & Truth Sense (those two things are related in that they sort the intent of people)
>
> Storage ring 2 - Aura Hiding & Invisibility (Those also are related since they both hide from the sight of others)
>
> Watch Band - Armored Defense, Silence, and the ability to add many more spell effects later.
>
> Toe ring - Deflection
>
> Toe ring - Regeneration, Preservation (related)

I could make multiple items using each link of the watch band. However, I didn't want to rely too much on any one item in case it were to be lost, so I kept it to two for the moment.

I started with the Toe Ring of Deflection first. It was both an easy item to make physically and magically. I just needed to enchant it to turn any blows aimed at my head and neck or my heart to be deflected, which meant they had to trigger on those specific actions. I toyed with spells for a couple days before I felt I had it both correct and powerful enough to deflect the blow of a supernatural creature or the round from a .50 cal Barrett. Not stop the round; just deflect it away from the vital spots. The armored defense spell would hopefully do that or at least reduce the power enough to be survivable. One thing was for sure, no wooden bullet or hand-wielded stake was going to make it to my heart through that magic.

Since it wasn't expending power at all times, only when triggered on intent, the ring wasn't as costly as I feared. I only spent 150 gems on it, but I was also improving at using non-blood aspects of magic to lower the cost. Rhyming couplets in ancient languages, a hand-engraved altar, burning wood, metal, and ammunition, a target where the bullet missed the bullseye... and more. It all helped. Maybe not significantly, but even reducing the cost by 10% would make all the mumbo-jumbo worth doing. Still, it actually saved me an entire night's worth of blood gathering. That was worth feeling a bit silly.

But why a toe ring? Simple. Who the hell is going to expect you to be wearing a magic ring on your foot? If someone even suspected I was wearing magic items, they'd be looking for pendants and rings, they wouldn't look at my feet!

Next came the Toe Ring of Regeneration and Preservation - it was intended to speed my recovery up by at least half again over its normal rapid pace. But the preservation was the sneaky thing. If someone didn't destroy my body, even if they staked me or put a bullet through my brain, the ring would restore me to the point where the regeneration effect would kick in. It wouldn't be fast, but it meant tossing me into the sunlight or leaving me for dead with my brains splattered all over a wall would not actually kill me. Even sneakier, it would trigger my people to come look for me, thanks to a companion set of rings that linked to the ring that I would give out to people I could trust to try to mount a rescue.

Each new item made me feel more confident and less like a sword was hanging over my head.

I tackled the watch next. It was actually two items, the bezel contained the Armored Defense spell, and one of the links held the silence. The whole watch band was engraved with scrollwork, even though it was just decoration. These took less time as they were both straightforward. Like the deflection, the armor only activated when damage was incoming. The silence, however, had to be activated by command and then ended with a touch. The silence cost a mere 100 gems, but the defense cost a massive 500 due to the needed strength required to stop such strong attacks.

Not to suggest I was a good person for only using these blood gems that I had collected in a relatively benign way. Still, if Queenie had made those items, it would have meant the death of at least sixty people to power the magic. I had no illusions that I was some upstanding moral guy; on the other hand, I did feel good that I hadn't killed anyone and that I was trying to give my "donors" some kind of payment for what they had involuntarily given me.

Now I was breathing easier, but a few months had passed between the engraving and all the spell research necessary to make these items. It was months well spent, however, as I was not only feeling far safer with the added protection, I was getting quite good with the spell work after all the casting and experimentation. I didn't know how I compared to a fully trained mage, I'm sure they could cast better, faster, and more efficiently, but I could cast vastly more powerful spells.

I also doubted that mages who had spent their entire lives enchanting could top what I had accomplished in mere months. At least, that was probably true if what George had told me was accurate. I couldn't know for sure at this point, but I hoped to find a mage enchanter someday and learn more.

That wasn't all, however.

In addition to the months spent on those first items, there were also another six months spent on the storage rings. I took my time making those rings since they were the things I cared about most as well as being the most complex.

One was a signet in platinum, with gold inlay on the top. I made it the Clan Fox crest and motto like the pendant since that was my assumed identity. The inlay held the spidey sense and truth sense, and that was the easy part. The storage ring portion was the tricky bit.

I used so much symbolism, it was ridiculous. I cast in the darkness of a new moon to signify something unseen but still available, I sacrificed amber that held plants and insects in it, I performed the ritual on the roof of a storage unit, and the list went on and on. I did everything I could to reduce the amount of blood gems needed to power the enchantment, and still, the cost was astronomical. I spent a staggering 1000 blood gems to create a small pocket dimension that I connected to the ring.

That was just the cost. I also needed to do many weeks' worth of internet research and actual study of scientific papers related to cosmology and quantum mechanics. The one downside to the magic was that if I couldn't picture how a thing could exist, I couldn't make the spell do it.

I didn't have to fully understand everything about quantum mechanics or string theory. Still, I did need to *believe* it would work and be able to imagine how it was possible. That had been the most challenging part.

On the bright side, it worked, and I didn't blow myself up during the enchanting process. Something I was actually afraid might happen, considering how much power was required.

With a thought, I could send an item I could carry into another dimension. It would stay there unaffected by time or temperature until recalled. The space was large enough to hold a great number of items, entire semi-trucks full.

Aside from the cost to enchant them, I probably spent another thousand gems on experimentation during the research process. I keenly felt the loss of that many blood gems. Queenie's compulsion to stockpile a significant quantity of magic made me regret the expenditure. Besides blood gems, it also came with a cost in time, both to hunt for more blood and to research.

And let me tell you, six months of research and enchanting had felt like an eternity. I still wanted to be out there checking up on my family and friends, but the compulsion was pushing me to complete the things that would make me safe first.

Luckily the second ring only took a month. Most of that was time spent making the Aura Hiding and Invisibility spells and enchanting them separately. The second ring held an Onyx carved with a fox head. It, too, cost a full thousand gems, but thankfully there were no research costs with the second one.

And with that, I felt my gear was now complete.

I had spent uncounted hours in my workshop during the year or so that I'd been enchanting. That meant I was no closer to having any friends. Still, my employees were great. They kept my wealth managed, and despite the initial spending I had done in my first year, they were investing my remaining money in stocks and bonds, or at least the portion I had allowed to come into the US.

I still had 25 million just sitting in those bank accounts, hidden from the world until I needed to use it. The rest was growing, if not quite at my spending rate. I had a plan for that, however.

Kat had been working on setting up a mining operation in Alaska and had acquired several virgin claims, but they were mountainous and required real mines.

I hired a crew to do some digging and make it look like a real mining operation. They were getting some gold to be sure. Still, I was using my magic to transmute regular sand into gold and then had my crew melt it together along with what they were actually getting, making it look like we were a legitimate successful company. As far as the world was concerned, we were acquiring our wealth from the gold claims.

It looked like we had made a super lucky strike to everyone else. The operation cost two million the first year getting it going, but "made" four million. It would cost only half a million in the next year to run, but it would pull in five. In the long run, it would provide a seemingly legit reason for me to be a rich bastard living in a penthouse and driving expensive vehicles.

Despite the ridiculous amount of blood I had burned to create the items, I had been hunting along the way. By the end of that first year in Houston, I was still at over 2000 blood. I could hold more than that in my body, but beyond 1000 it started to become uncomfortable. From this point, I intended to store at least 1000 in each ring and 1000 inside my body.

If anyone ever came at me the way they had at Queenie, they would have a damned long chase to bleed me dry. Especially since I now knew teleportation was possible and that I could go anywhere in the world for a mere 8 blood.

Of course, I could only go places I had been, so it was time to start traveling and committing places to memory. It would begin with some day trips to cities within a short driving distance: Austin, Beaumont, Lake Charles, Galveston, Corpus Christie, and San Antonio. I would be systematic about it and knock out the close places in a week, giving me some close escape options.

I wish I could just do it from pictures or even old memories from when I was mortal. Sadly, I needed to "get a feel" for the place using my new senses to make it a valid target for teleporting. The upside was that I didn't have to really memorize the area in any detail, there was just a certain sense of each place that was different from any other, and once I had felt it, I could travel to it.

There was one other way I could think of to travel, but it seemed dangerous, and there was no reason to risk my immortal life trying it out. I suspected that I could travel to something or someone I had a connection with. In other words, I could take a pair of my boots, have them shipped to Norway, and then use them as an anchor to open a gateway to that destination.

The more I thought about that, the more convinced I was that I could do it. There were downsides, however. It would mean letting things I was connected to be out of my sight and control, and I couldn't really be sure what I'd be venturing into. Also, a gateway would use two or three times as much power as a simple teleport.

I'm calling it a gateway but really, what I'm talking about is a wormhole punched through the fabric of space to somewhere else. It would be stable, though, and there wouldn't be any spaghettification that you might get with a black hole, which was pretty important if you wanted to survive the trip.

Still, that was theoretical and dangerous, so I was committed to enjoying the safe approach. At least, I hoped it would be safe.

CHAPTER 17

STOP, KAMI-TIME!

I PUT Kat on setting up a trip to Japan, with a stop in Hawaii for next week, and had her pay for a return flight even though I wouldn't use the return ticket.

I would teleport back. No way was I going to deal with the hassle of flying even if I could afford first class, not when I could jump back home instantly. It might be a risk to not have that seat filled on the flight back. However, if someone ever tracked me down, I could simply claim I had flown back on a private jet at the invitation of a wealthy friend.

The next trip would be to the UK for a month, and I would return by way of New York. I detested the idea of New York, but it would be an essential place to set up a teleport location, or perhaps several. However, there were some things there that I would love to spend time on, such as the museums. I would return home for a month and then take a trip to New Zealand.

From each of those locations, I would venture out to neighboring cities the way I planned to do in Texas this week. By having those few locations, I would be able to have dozens of places to teleport in just a few months. It seemed fun, but even with the excitement of an adventure, I couldn't help but feel a little sad that I had no one to share them with.

I really needed to make some damned friends. Well, preferably ones that weren't damned, but you know what I mean.

I took the cruiser-style bike out for the trip to San Antonio and Austin and had Ralph, one of my bodyguards, meet me there so he could ride the bike back. I wasn't about to make round trips for no good reason and drive the roads twice. Besides, I wanted teleportation practice. I had done it between the Tower and maker space a few times now, but that was as far as I'd gone.

The ride to Austin was nice. I made it during the day on a weekday so the roads weren't too crowded. Even so, once I got into the city, I was glad of the vampiric reflexes, as the traffic in Austin was just as bad as in Houston. I hit a few sites in the city and committed them to memory, such as the Capitol, Threadgills, a city park with lots of gardens, and the UT campus. After that, I headed to San Antonio, memorized some spots around that city, and ended the day at the River Walk. That was where I met Ralph and gave him five hundred bucks to enjoy himself for the evening and told him to have the bike back the next day. He gave me a big grin and tipped his hat to me.

"You're the best, boss!"

I did some hunting on the River Walk but was careful to watch for auras in case there might be non-humans around; it was a very popular destination, after all. I did spot a few, but I wasn't too worried with my own aura hidden. I didn't get close to them, however, as I still didn't know what aura types signified which type of critter. The teleport back was easy enough as to not be remarkable. It honestly didn't feel any more challenging than jumping from the Tower to the maker space despite it being more than a hundred miles.

The next day I went in the opposite direction and hit Beaumont and Lake Charles. In Beaumont, I stopped by the Spindletop Museum, downtown, and a rather lovely comic shop off Phelan Blvd. In Lake Charles, I only bothered to memorize the casino. Still, I noticed that there were people with non-human auras in there that seemed to be working for the casino. Probably making sure no supernaturals gambled and bankrupted them with magic or something.

The next day I hit The Strand, Galveston's downtown area, and then the beach. Afterward, I made my way down to Corpus and picked up several locations there. I was making a point of doing it during the day in order to see the places and get a better idea of what it all looked like. Although I can see in the dark almost as well as a human can see in the day, it's not quite the same. You don't get the color and depth of field from it that you get in sunlight.

Kat made sure my passport was up to date, and my itinerary was all laid out for the Japan trip. I did a direct flight from Bush Intergalactic Airport to Honolulu and had a layover of a day there. *Intergalactic*... I joke about that, but that airport is freakin' massive!

Anyway, I stayed long enough in Hawaii to get out and see the beach and Pearl Harbor. That night I slept back in my bed at the Tower and teleported back early the next morning to catch my connecting flight to Tokyo.

I had hunted in Hawaii to cover the cost of the teleporting. This one was noticeably more costly than just jumping around Texas and took me 7 blood gems each way. That was about 3 hours worth of hunting, so not cheap in terms of my effort.

Tokyo was bustling and was the most populous city I'd ever been in, and it was also a new challenge to me as I did not speak the language. I figured that magic could solve that, but it would need some experimentation.

I purchased a rail pass and spent the next three weeks traveling all over Japan. I loved the country, from its busy cities to its serene shrines, to its rural farmlands and mountains. I memorized dozens of locations there, including the top of Mt Fuji.

By the end of the first week, I had created a spell that allowed me to understand what people talking in other languages were saying. Still, it took another two weeks to complete the opposite spell and enable them to understand me. That one was tricky because it had to make my words come out in the language of my listener and make it seem completely natural so that they didn't realize something unusual was happening. It wouldn't be good for them to see my lips moving out of sync with the sounds they were hearing. It would be like a bad version of one of those old Chinese Kung Fu movies.

Thankfully, those spells were only two blood each to power. Still, I decided that before my Europe trip, I would want to make a magic item that did the translation for me. Oh, and another spell to understand written languages as well.

Kat was able to reschedule the flight to the UK, so I spent a month turning another link in my watch band into a Universal Translator, or Babel Fish spell. With that addition, I was set to enjoy my European trip.

Like in Japan, I bought a rail pass and spent a month sightseeing in the UK, from the Orkneys in the north to Canterbury in the south, to Galway in the west over in Ireland, with stops in every major city and tourist attraction.

I tried to see Newgrange in Ireland but was disappointed. It was still closed since that terrorist attack that had happened the previous year that had damaged the passageway into the tomb. I couldn't believe some asshole would damage a historical monument like that!

On the bright side, I particularly liked seeing the oldest pub in England, Ye Olde Trip to

Jerusalem, which was carved into the base of the mount where Nottingham Castle once sat. I was surprised to discover it was owned by a vampire. He was the first I had seen, and apparently, he had been around since the days when the pub was first opened. I didn't approach him but kept my distance and pretended to be a mortal tourist, but I was close enough that with my enhanced senses, I could tell he was undead.

Ok, so red spiky aura = vampire, Check! Not a big shock there, but good to have it confirmed.

If I had to guess, I would say the ethereal blue auras meant Mage and the Green wispy ones were Fae, but those are just my guesses. I had also seen brown auras, grey, and black ones, but I had no idea what those meant and didn't want to speculate until I knew more.

Actually, scratch that, the grey ones I have only seen in Japan so far. Now that I think of it, those were probably kami or oni of some kind.

I hunted all over the UK during my trip, but never with the frequency and efficiency I had back in Texas. This was a vacation, and although I still wanted to increase my supply of magic to draw from, I didn't need to rush. I was steadily working my way toward the 3000 I intended to keep as my base amount.

One nice thing about the storage rings was that I only needed to carry a small backpack with me on my trips for appearance's sake. I could keep all the comforts of home stashed away in my rings, ready to pull out in an instant. My iPad, my Windows tablet pc, my mp3 player, anything and everything. I even had an arsenal consisting of dozens of guns in various calibers and thousands of rounds of ammo.

My trip to England also made me realize I wanted an enchanted weapon. I could grow my claws and use those if needed, but seeing all the ancient swords on display in the museums... I had caught the enchanting bug again, and I wanted swords and daggers. Not that I ever wanted to get into a fight, but how cool would it be to reach into your coat and whip out a katana and chop a bastard's head off? *Talk about style points!*

However, I still had one stop to make on the route home, and that was New York.

I hit the Statue of Liberty, Brooklyn Bridge, Wall Street, the Met, Central Park, Times Square, the Empire State Building, and more. I had to admit, there was a lot about the city to like, but damn, that shit was waaay too crowded for my taste.

Houston was a big-ass city, but it was spread out decently. Houston has a radius of about 25 miles from the center to the point to where you are no longer really in the metroplex. Whereas NYC is almost half that but has about four times the population. I shuddered at the thought of living in the Big Apple. No thanks. I would appreciate it in short visits and retreat to my nice, comparatively uncrowded Houston.

Arriving back home, I checked in with my team and ensured the business was on track, and everything was going smoothly.

I had another trip coming up to head to New Zealand, but I had time before that to jump back to Japan for a few days. I did some research and discovered that Yoshimbo Musihara was the foremost sword maker in Japan, so I determined that I wanted him to make my sword. His works started at $30K for a common blade and $50K for a masterpiece. Still, I wanted custom, so I was prepared to pay $100k or even $150k to get mine made specifically for me.

With my being a foreigner, I expected Musihara to be reluctant to just jump me to the head of the line. So I came prepared with a gift; a

50-year-old Balvenie Single Malt Scotch, which had cost me $40K. It was a lavish gift worthy of what I wanted him to create.

I called ahead, asked to see the smith, and was given a time to arrive the next day. I came prepared to talk the smith into taking my commission but figured I would have to use my mojo. I wasn't prepared to walk into the forge and see a man with a grey and red rayed aura looking at me with piercing eyes. I bowed respectfully and received a bow in return.

The smith was short but broad-shouldered, his long black hair pulled back into a topknot. His eyes were dark and intense, and his calloused hands looked strong and powerful, able to crush anything they could reach. He carried himself with a regal air like this forge was his place of power, and he was the lord of his domain.

Greetings were exchanged, but then the master smith ordered his apprentices to leave us. He was holding a hammer which I could see was no ordinary tool. Like its wielder, it also had the aura of a kami. I hoped the smith wasn't getting ready to use it on me from the wary look I was receiving.

Even so, I couldn't help being struck by the hammer's beauty. The Japanese-style forging hammer looked like a perfectly balanced piece of artwork. Its leather-wrapped handle was sturdy and made of aged oak, while the head of the hammer was dark steel that glinted red in the light of the forge fires. It had an air of power to it, like that of a divine force emanating power and strength.

To put it bluntly, both the smith and the hammer were impressive, but the hammer seemed more ancient and powerful, although it didn't seem to be sentient.

I knew that kami could be most anything, but I hadn't realized they could be living people. Traditionally, according to what I had read, some important people like the Emperors or heads of major families were said to become kami after passing away, but this guy was very much alive. I assumed that was because he embodied the spirit or tradition of katana making, which was culturally significant to the people. I wasn't about to ask, however. Things seemed dicey enough without potentially being rude by asking questions he might find inappropriate.

I was relieved when he spoke first.

"So what does a Western devil want with me?" I could tell from the way he said devil; he didn't mean American, or White Man; he meant vampire.

It seemed that he could tell what I was despite the magic concealing my aura.

I held the Scotch forward with both hands, in the traditional offering gesture I had learned on my first trip to the country.

"You are the best smith in Japan. I would like to commission weapons from you."

Seeing that I was not being threatening, he stepped closer, reached out with one hand, and took the decorative wooden box holding the Scotch. He moved to a bench and sat the hammer down before opening the box. Seeing the contents, he looked back at me and raised an eyebrow.

"This is an expensive gift. I would not normally take a commission from a Westerner, much less from one of your kind. But tell me, why do you want a katana? Do you not already have weapons that would be more deadly than one of my swords?"

I nodded, "I do, but I've always admired the katana as being a very elegant weapon, and I am willing to pay triple your usual fee for a custom blade made specifically for me."

The kami—because what else could he be?—tilted his head in thought.

"I still doubt that this would be a wise action. Besides, even a blade of my making would not survive the strength with which you would wield it. I have heard your kind are very strong."

I shrugged, "True, we are strong, but the best warriors are not those who overpower their opponents with brute strength, but rather those who strike with precise attacks."

The other man nodded acceptance of that but still looked doubtful.

There was a feeling I was getting from the man that he could see deeper than others, and he was waiting for something from me, so I took a chance. "If you make the blade for me, it will be enchanted to withstand my strength and never corrode or be marred. Your work will remain pristine for centuries, or perhaps thousands of years, a testament to your skill as a maker."

A small smile formed on the other man's lips. "This is closer to the truth. Good."

I sighed and gave him the rest of it, "Mostly just because I want it. I've never been in a fight in my life and honestly hope I never have to, but it would be treasured for as long as I exist." Well, that wasn't exactly true, I had died during a knife fight, but that didn't really count. I hadn't intended to fight at all, and I had done more falling down and dying than anything else.

The man's smile grew. "That sounds like truth. Very well, I will make the blades for you, but it will also come with a promise from you to never do me or mine harm."

I grinned but countered, "Unless in self-defense. I could not keep such a promise if I were attacked."

The smile grew more expansive on the older man's face. "Done."

"By the way, are you a kami?" I asked, hoping not to offend.

He laughed, "As is this hammer. Many things are kami, but yes, we are."

"May I watch you work as you make the blade?"

The kami shrugged, "During some processes yes; during others, no. Return in a month. That is the earliest I can begin your sword."

Let's be clear. Did I need a katana? No, of course not. Was it because I had seen Highlander while growing up? Guilty. I could justify it to myself in all kinds of ways, but the reality of it was that I just plain wanted one, and my vampiric state and my fortune presented the opportunity for me to have one, so I was going to get one.

CHAPTER 18
BLADES UP!

Returning home, I prepared for my next trip to New Zealand. I was looking forward to the sword creation, but I wasn't going to put everything else on hold for it, and I had always wanted to see where they had filmed the Lord of the Rings. The flight sucked; even in 1st class, it was brutally long. First-world undead problems, I know. I was thankful when the plane touched down, and we got to get out and stretch our legs.

What can I say? It was a beautiful land and friendly people. I toured both islands and decided I would set up an emergency home there to fall back on should something ever happen to my home in Houston. It was remote enough that no one was likely to chase me there while still being a modern Western nation mixed with ancient Maori tradition. I memorized dozens of sites in New Zealand and was very glad I had made the flight out. On the bright side, Australia was just a short hop by plane from there, so I wouldn't have to fly back across the globe.

The trip there was a good distraction to keep me from focusing on the days until I could go see the sword being made.

When it was finally time, I jumped to Japan and booked a hotel for the time I would be there. I would have liked to see the process from start to finish, including the creation of the tamahagane, as I would have loved to cast spells into it. Still, I didn't want to throw off the creation process by altering the characteristics of the material.

For days I went to the forge and watched. The skill and tradition that went into every step was fascinating. Yoshimbo was a true master, but then he was a kami, as was his hammer. As I became more familiar with the forge, I noticed that many aspects of the place had subtle auras, but that was the thing about kami, they weren't all grand spirits taking the form of forging masters. Some were just the minor spirits of a place like that, which had seen generations of smiths lovingly and painstakingly create works of art.

The blades were a set: katana, wakashi, and tanto. They took many months, and I did not stay in Japan the whole time, only popping in occasionally to witness the progress and particularly vital stages of its creation. I spent the downtime hunting and experimenting with the spells I wanted to embed into the blades.

Indestructibility, the ability to cleave through nearly anything, and the ability to cleave and deflect magic. That last one was the hardest because it took creating several magic items and then learning how to cleave through their effects. I destroyed those items, and it cost me a lot of time and hunting, but I felt it would be worth it in the end. I had nothing against mages, but they had sided with the ancient vamps against Queenie, so I figured that if they ever learned of my existence, they might well come at me, and I wanted to be ready for that.

I provided input on the design and materials of the fittings in which the blades would be housed, ensuring the tsuba, menuki, and kashira all had a fox motif, but allowed the artists to make them as they saw fit. I wanted the master's work, after all, rather than my own. If I had wanted, I could have simply made a sword myself and transmuted it into steel, then cast the spells into it. I could even have made them beautiful, but they wouldn't have been authentic, and I would not have treasured them the way I would these.

Before presenting them to me, Yoshimbo and a group of Shinto priests held a ceremony to bless the blades, which I attended. Once it was complete, he offered them to me in all their glory, and I could only bow deeply in respect for their perfect imperfection.

The hamon line was stunning and genuinely artistic in its execution. I showed as much respect and appreciation for his creation as I sensed the master was comfortable with and then departed. I wished him well, and he did the same, but neither of us had forgotten the promise.

Rather than return home, I jumped to Fujisan, that is Mt. Fuji, one of the most sacred places in Japan, and performed my enchantments there. It seemed more appropriate than doing it at my studio, and during the casting, I felt the magic flow and settle into the blades easier than my tests had gone. Perhaps that was due to the quality of the blades, or the fact that they were made by supernatural beings, or maybe it was the kami of the most sacred place on the island aiding the magic.

Whatever the case, when it was done, I felt that the blades were a part of me and added two more bits of magic which also seemed appropriate. They would return to my hands when called. That way, if I were ever to be disarmed or they were stolen somehow, I could retrieve them.

Lastly, they would not harm me, which turned out to be the easiest of all the magics to cast on them. They had literally been custom-made for me, so by their metaphysical nature, they did not want to harm me.

And with that, I felt my collection was complete.

Funny how I keep having that feeling and then discovering something new that I need to add...

Still, it *was* a good feeling, and I was happy with what I had acquired and accomplished.

I stood that night under the full moon on the summit, moving through katas with the sword, feeling like it was now part of me.

I suppose I should mention that during the months of waiting for the blades to be made, I worked with a Kendo master who trained me in their use. If this were a movie, I'd play a montage training sequence showing how I had gone from a stupid useless newb to a master through hard work and dedication, all in the thirty seconds it takes to watch in fast motion.

Bullshit to that.

I had trained hard, and thanks to my vampiric speed, strength, stamina, and dexterity, I was picking it up super fast, but I was no master. Reaching that stage would take years of dedicated practice even with my advantages. However, I didn't believe I'd chop my own hand off or embarrass myself in a fight if I ever had to draw the blade.

I watched dawn appear over the horizon with the blade in hand and let the rising sun baptize the katana with its rays. That felt right.

Back home, I placed the blades in my storage ring and slept for a couple hours before the setting sun forced me awake. That was some severe jet lag, but thankfully my vampiric constitution didn't leave me suffering much. It just threw my time off a bit. Seemed like it should be mid-morning when it was instead sundown.

I went out to hunt, but just a normal one. Despite the insane amount of blood gems I had burned enchanting the blades, I was still over

3000, which was where I wanted to be. I had been hunting during those months of waiting. However, I took fewer "donations" per night than I used to. I had slowed down, no longer needing to reach a goal.

Hell, now that my enchanting was done, I only needed to feed once per night to maintain my levels. Perhaps two donors in case I needed to stay awake during the day.

CHAPTER 19
A MESSY RESCUE

AFTER A HUNT, I was on the customized Triumph Rocket, a cruiser-style motorcycle, on my way to meet someone about gaming. I had met him in the comic shop on Hwy 59 a couple of weeks previously, and we'd started talking about D&D. I mentioned I wanted to get into a game and that it had been years since I had played. We agreed to meet so he could introduce me to the others he usually gamed with. It was a test run to see if I would fit in with them and vice versa.

However, I heard a scream as I was getting close to the bar, also off 59, not too far from the comic shop. It was night, and this wasn't that bad of an area, but still, it was a cry for help, and it was cut off abruptly.

Worse, it had been a woman's voice. How do I know that over the sound of the motorcycle, you ask? Vampire hearing, duh. I pulled into a parking lot, turned off the engine, removed the key, and listened using all my special hearing mojo. I could hear the muffled sounds of a woman crying while someone had their hand over her mouth. Several men were laughing and making crude comments about the fun they were about to have.

Shit.

I was no superhero, but I wasn't about to stand by and let a woman get raped. I zeroed in on where the noise came from, just down an alley about half a block behind me. I took the keys from the bike and ran toward the noise.

The woman screeched, "You aren't supposed to be here! This area is supposed to be safe!"

I heard one of them saying, "We'll go wherever we want. By the way, Theriot sends her regards to your great aunt. Be sure and let her know we took *good* care of you."

I thought that was a bit odd, but I guess the attack was personal and not a simple crime of opportunity. It didn't matter; I wouldn't let someone get hurt if I could stop it.

I mean, I had already proven I was dumb that way when I died, right? The irony was not lost on me.

When I rounded the corner, it was clearly some young gang members. The woman had her skirt ripped up the front, almost falling off, and she stood there struggling against the ones holding her.

They didn't hear me coming, and I had the initiative...

I charged at one of the closest two with their backs to me. I rammed him with my shoulder as hard as possible using my vampire speed. The hit made a sickening crunch of bones in the guy's spine before he flew into the brick wall of one of the nearby buildings.

We were in a small parking area behind the old brick buildings that made up this block. There were a few cars, but mostly it was just an asphalt and gravel-covered courtyard where the business owners parked their cars during the daytime.

I took that all in as I hit the first guy. I had just enough time to stop after the hit and swing my left elbow at the other guy that had been standing next to him. I vaguely noted this guy was bald, having shaved his tattooed head. In the heat of the situation, I wasn't thinking about the fact that I could be killing humans right now. They were rapists caught in the act.

That was when I noticed that they had red spiky auras, which relieved my conscience. The woman was human, and they were vampire predators. That put my mind at ease, and I committed to doing what needed to be done.

The guy I had just elbowed also made a disturbing cracking sound before he went flying. I had used all my strength in that hit. He made an even more gruesome sound when he hit a nearby car.

That was all the time I had. If this were DnD, then I got off two attacks during the surprise round, and now they had the initiative.

Fortunately, this wasn't a roleplaying game, so when they charged, I didn't have to stand around and let them have their turn uncontested. Two of them charged at me so fast that a human would not have been able to follow them. Being a vampire myself, they weren't quite fast enough. I wasn't necessarily quicker than them, but I could perceive what they were doing and react.

I stepped out of the way of one and dodged the knife the second thug tried to stab at my throat.

I really wasn't keen on being stabbed, so I punched him in the face with all the strength I could muster.

He went crunch, and blood splattered everywhere before what was left of him hit another car parked behind the building. Like the other guy, his body wrecked the poor vehicle he hit, the side of it crumbing like it had been T-boned.

I had no idea my strength could do that... With the part of my mind that was marveling at this and not freaking out, I thought maybe it would be a good idea after this to test myself out and get to know my physical abilities better.

Which was why I missed his friend's attack that came at me from behind.

Thanks entirely to my magic items, what should have been an absolute killing blow to my heart, instead sent me flying. Like the ones I had sent flying, I pancaked against a car, caving in the rear passenger door.

I heard and felt bones cracking in my back and ribs, sending tremendous pain throughout my body. I knew that if I was going to survive this then I couldn't let the injuries stop me. I had to keep attacking and not let them have a chance to regroup. Luckily for me, I didn't have any shattered ribs sticking out through my skin or piercing any organs, unlike the guy I had hit.

On instinct, I burned five blood gems to accelerate healing. It wasn't something I had ever done before, but it had seemed like something that ought to be possible. Don't get me wrong, I knew I would regenerate damage naturally and that it would only take minutes rather than the days and weeks that a human would under these circumstances. This was even faster, however. Burning the blood seemed to take the automatic function that my body did and pump it full of steroids.

By the time I was jumping back into the fight, my ribs had already started to mend, and my spine was straight.

I gave the guy who hit me an evil grin, launching myself back toward him in a rush of vampiric speed that surprised him.

I had no desire to leave this guy alive two seconds after he had just tried to kill me, so I drew the wakizashi from my storage ring as I drove toward him. I played Highlander, sending his head flying.

I can't even describe how that felt. The magically strong and unnaturally sharp blade went right through the vampire's spine with barely any resistance.

It kinda freaked me out a little. It shouldn't be that easy!

Still, in the middle of a fight was not the time to have an existential crisis of conscience, so I steeled myself and refocused.

I quickly looked around to see what the other three were doing. The one holding the girl was staring at me with an open mouth, looking at me as if I had just done something impossible.

He stammered out, "Don't you know who we are?!? You... you'll pay for that! Even if you kill us, Theriot will kill you, but not before she makes you watch everyone you care about die!"

I would have loved to know who the heck they were talking about, but I was a little too busy at that moment to stop and ask.

The two that I had flung against the wall were only now starting to recover, shaking their heads and trying to get up. Still, I could see that they were broken up pretty severely by the impacts. One had a rib sticking out of his shirt, and the other seemed unable to make one of his legs work.

I started with the one holding the girl.

I charged at him the same as I had the last one, and he tried to dodge, but he just couldn't move fast enough. He seemed like he was almost in slow motion. I also removed his head, then turned to the final two who were trying to recover.

I felt sick.

I had never killed anyone before, and although these guys were rapists and probably a lot worse, these last two were clearly incapable of fighting back. That made what came next an execution rather than a fight.

If I were human, I would have lost my lunch over it. I took each of their heads just to be safe, then turned back to the girl.

She had fainted, thankfully, but she lay there half-dressed, and there was blood on her from cuts they had made on her body.

I cleaned my blade on the shirt of one of the dead vamps. Then, not wanting to, I dragged their bodies into a pile, including their heads, and burned five blood gems to burn them into ash.

They clearly worked for someone pretty nasty. From what I had heard, this had been aimed at someone. This Theriot person had told her minions to attack this woman to send a message.

That was not something I wanted to get involved with, but I had anyway, unable to stand by and let something like that happen. Thankfully, that one serious hit I had taken hadn't been worse. If I had landed differently, it could have broken my neck, and then I'd be dead right now.

Well, more dead. I chuckled at the thought.

Apparently, Queenie's parting spell forcing me to survive at all costs didn't prevent me from following my conscience in a situation like this. This time luck got me out of it.

I looked around but didn't see any cameras, thankfully. I spent another three gems to eliminate any traces of the fight so that no blood or ash remained. If these guys had friends, I wanted what had happened to them to be a mystery rather than have the city's vampires hunting me.

Sadly, there was nothing I could do for the two cars. Their owners would just have to claim the damage on their insurance. At least I had been able to use my magic to remove any blood and DNA evidence that the vamps had left smeared on the wall and cars. Their owners wouldn't have to deal with that.

I returned to the girl and checked her over. Except for the torn skirt, she looked like she'd been in a car accident. No doubt they had been feeding from her before what they had planned next, but they used knives rather than their fangs to draw blood.

That was interesting, but I supposed it was one way not to advertise that they were supernatural. I'm sure whoever this woman's great aunt was, she would know, but the authorities at the hospital wouldn't have. I wouldn't let that happen, though.

I bit my wrist and fed her a few drops of my blood the way I had seen vamps do in the TV shows and the movies. Sure enough, she healed almost instantly and regained consciousness. I helped her up and used my mojo to make her forget her ordeal. I told her she had tripped and had a nasty fall that tore her skirt and that she would hurry home and get cleaned up, being none the worse for the experience.

Seeing the trauma drain out of her expression was eerie, but I felt good that I could help her that way. I ensured that she returned to the street and headed toward her car, which was parked about half a block further back. I watched for cameras as I moved back to my bike but didn't see any that could have captured what had happened. It made sense, though; the gangbanging vamps wouldn't have attacked someone where they would have been caught.

After the incident, I went ahead and met up with the roleplaying group at the bar. The two guys and two girls were friendly, and I thought I might like hanging out with them in the future. Even so, my mind was too scattered with what had just happened for me to concentrate, and I felt terrible for being distracted.

After a bit, I excused myself, saying I had had a long stressful day at work and had to get home but would love to meet again.

Out of an excess of paranoia, I rode the bike out of town and teleported us back to the garage so that no one would be able to track me back to my home in the improbable event that I had been captured on video along the way. That was the first time I had teleported, taking something as big as a motorcycle. It cost an extra two points of magic but it was good to know it was possible.

I spent the rest of the evening reviewing the fight in my mind. Had it just been a matter of surprise, or had I been more powerful than those vamps?

Maybe they were overconfident and not used to dealing with other vampires, and so had not taken it seriously until it was too late? I couldn't be sure one way or another.

I had caught them completely by surprise, taking two of them out of the fight in seconds. The next two attacked me, and I dodged, but they might not have given it their all since they didn't know what they were up against.

They seemed a little weak, but I wanted to err on the side of caution and assume it was that rather than me being some super vampire. The one holding the girl may have been weak, or he may have just been caught entirely flat-footed by seeing his friends die. And if he could see auras somehow, he would have thought I was a human confusing him even more.

That could be it...

I would tell myself that until I met other vamps and had a chance to measure myself against them somehow. In the meantime, I was going to lie low for a bit just in case their disappearance stirred things up.

CHAPTER 20

TESTING AND TRAVEL

I GOT Ralph to introduce me to the owner of the gym he trained at, and I mojo'd the guy into letting me in after hours one night. I wanted to see what I could do.

As a human, I had been pretty average. I wasn't weak, but I wasn't terribly strong either. I could bench press around 150 lbs and squat about 225-ish lbs. That was my baseline when I hit the gym, and I wanted to see what I could do now.

The gym had only free weights, no machines, so I found a bar and added weights; one fifty-pound disk on each side, plus the bar weighed fifty-five pounds by itself. That was my max as a human when I was in college, the last time I had lifted weights or been remotely in decent shape before becoming a vampire, at least.

I lay on the bench and looked up at the bar. I knew I'd be able to lift it, but I also knew I would have been a little intimidated to try this without a spotter once.

Taking a deep breath, I lifted the bar off the stand.

It felt like nothing.

I did a couple of reps, then put the bar back and got up to gather more weights. I loaded it down with 1000 pounds of weight. I was afraid to put any more than that for fear it would bend the bar.

I lay down on the bench again; I was a little worried this time. I knew I was super strong now, but this was a lot of weight. A quick internet search on my phone told me the world record bench press was around 900 lbs, and there were some claims of 1000 or more; however, those were outside the Guinness Book.

I stopped hesitating and lifted. It was a strain. I'm not denying that, but I could bench it and do fifteen reps before I decided to stop. I didn't really get tired as a vampire, but overuse of my abilities would burn blood.

With a sigh, I returned the weights and cleaned up after myself. I could have gone higher with the weights, maybe a lot higher, if I had burned some blood. I was definitely outside the human realm in terms of strength.

I could have tried deadlifting, but there wouldn't have been a point to it. I was definitely beyond human standards, and the bar couldn't hold enough weight to challenge me. It would have bent or broken long before I hit my limit.

I decided to test myself during my travels. I would see if I could find heavy things to lift to get a feel for my capabilities.

With that in mind, I teleported back to New Zealand and arranged a private flight to Australia. I would spend a week or three seeing the land down under, and when I got back, I would see about meeting a vampire and seeing what I could learn. While there, I hit all the major towns and Coober Pedy and Uluru because they were cool. I was tempted to toss some boulders around at Uluru, but it was considered sacred, so I restrained myself.

Since I was close, I took a plane to Papua New Guinea, memorized a spot there, and then hopped planes across Indonesia, Malaysia, and the Philippines. It was a long few weeks, and I ended up gone longer than I had intended. Still, it was productive, both in terms of memorizing new teleportation spots and testing my limits.

I found some excellent strength-testing options while I was gone. There were granite boulders at some not-sacred locations I visited, and I had tested ever larger ones until I hit a limit. I don't know how much the biggest stone weighed, but it was big enough and heavy enough that I had no doubt it would crush a car if I dropped it on one.

Next trip, I'd hit the small South Pacific islands or maybe southeast Asia. I would only rest once I had seen every major area of the world. Aside from memorizing teleportation spots in the event things ever got dicey, I was seriously starting to enjoy seeing new places and learning about different cultures around the world.

One of the surprising enjoyments of the travel was the universal translator that my magic provided. It allowed me to speak to people directly, and I found that in most places, I received a far warmer welcome as the people thought I had learned their language. I felt a little guilty about that, but it seemed to make people happy to meet a foreigner who spoke their language. I have to admit, I was not using my own face. I changed appearances in each country so that I would not leave a trail of security camera footage all over the world of my face. With big data and face recognition technology, it would be possible to track my movements if I hadn't taken that precaution.

I also had a series of fake passports from multiple countries that I used as I border-hopped around the world, crossing from one country to another. Eventually, if I lived long enough, I would get around to buying property in many places around the world and building safe houses, but that would be a much lengthier endeavor than just memorizing teleportation locations.

When I returned to Houston to spend time at home, I checked in with the gaming group and set up a new meeting time. I did still want to play some good RPGs, after all. We met and played D&D. The guy named Todd DM'd and started a new campaign for us. In addition to me and Todd, there were three other players in total, another guy and two women. I played a rogue and had fun backstabbing goblins in the first session. All in all, they were fun to hang around with. It was a nice change from the paranoia and empire-building I had been engaged in.

Most of all, it felt good to interact with people on a purely social level for the first time since I'd been turned.

I promised to game with them again the following month. The plan was to do a monthly session to start and see how we all felt about the game in a couple months.

It was weird for me. Back in Dallas, I had a very tight friend circle that I had grown up with. Except for Marcy, who had joined the group when she was a senior in high school, we had all known each other since Elementary school.

There was Jake, he was a bit of a horndog and kind of annoying, to be honest, but he always had your back. Taylor was a jock and had played pretty much all the sports in school, and we'd always been there to cheer him on. Megan was his on-again/off-again cheerleader girlfriend, but she was pretty damned smart and had gotten a law degree after high school. She had only just passed the Bar exam a year or so ago and was doing corporate law now. Marcy had moved up to Dallas after her sister died in a car crash. Her parents had died some years before, and she was officially under her sister's care. Poor Marcy had to take care of her nephew and niece after that, which was a bummer, but she was really cool, even if she had a thing for Jake.

Last but not least was Katy. She and I were the ones who never really dated within the group. We were good friends, but she had felt like a sister to me, and there hadn't ever been any attraction.

We were all tight friends, though, we hung out practically daily when we were in school, and even after graduation, we still managed to get together at least a couple times a week.

I almost choked up thinking about it. We had been so tight; we were chosen family to each other.

Since becoming a vampire, I had pretty much been alone with nothing but employees around me, and meeting these new gaming folks was a bit of a kick in the nuts. It reminded me of what it was like to have friends again, but at the same time, the bonds just weren't there with these gamers the way they had been with my friends back home. It reminded me of what I was missing.

CHAPTER 21
HONKY-TONK BIKER FANGBOIS

SPEAKING OF EMPIRE-BUILDING; I had kept Kat busy.

Over the last year, we had established the mining operation in Alaska but had also formed a company that specialized in mineral surveying. The idea was to identify untouched natural deposits of gold, gems, and valuable resources. We would sell some of that data to big corporations like BP, Exxon, etc., but for things like gold, we would stake our claims for later mining.

I hired experts and, using my mojo, ensured they had the qualifications to excel at their mission. We would then expand the mining to some of those new locations, where we would legitimately extract the resources, but that would give us an even better cover as I used my magic to augment what we found in the ground. Where a starting business might struggle for years to make a profit, we were profitable from day one, but not so much that it would raise suspicion.

Over time those operations would increase and give legitimacy to my cover. Someday I'd have to change my appearance and "inherit" the business and property, but that would be many years away since my persona of Daniel was only in his twenties. Of course, I could simply age my appearance to look like I was living an average human lifetime, then when I was old, I could have a new persona take over as my heir.

Note to self: in a decade or two, have a fictional child so that documents will exist when I need them....

About a week later, I went to a honky-tonk bar in North Houston off I-45. I hadn't specifically intended to find a vampire bar, but I had just been looking for a place to hunt. You can imagine my surprise when I see three spiky red auras among the people inside. Instead of heading to the restroom to feed, I wandered over to the bar and took a seat.

The bartender was one of the vamps. He eyed me but left me sitting there for a bit. I was casual about it, but I was keeping an eye on the other two auras. Sure enough, one walks over to me.

I kid you not, he plays the classic, "You're in my seat."

This guy looked more like a middle-aged banker than a biker, but he had a leather jacket and a cigar in his mouth. Don't get me wrong, he was slim and well built, but he had that certain clean look that weekend bikers have, the ones who are trying to seem tough and remind everyone they weren't always middle managers at some corporate job.

I just looked at him as if he must be kidding. "This your bar?"

"You could say that. You going to move out of my seat?" He was trying to loom, but I was not having it.

"Sorry, find another seat; this one is taken."

I smiled. There was a challenge in it, but not outright hostility. I still didn't know what my power levels were compared to other vamps, so I wasn't going to take shit for no reason. Still, I wasn't going to go out of my way to make this guy a mortal enemy either.

He leaned in and tried to mojo me. He got an intense look on his face and his eyes suddenly seemed immense, as if they were the center of the universe. I felt a little tickle in my head.

"You really want to get out of my seat right now." He was pushing his intimidation as hard as he could, trying to will me to give in. I could feel the pressure, and if I had been a mortal, I am sure I'd be quaking in my boots and pissing myself with terror.

I wasn't a mortal, however. Despite the tickle in my brain and the pressure I felt, I was otherwise entirely unaffected.

I sighed and mojo'd him right back, "Why don't you have a seat right there and play nice."

Knowing he was a vamp and that it wouldn't be easy, I mustered my will and pushed hard to reinforce the words I spoke.

He got a confused look on his face and sat down. After a moment, the dull, blank stare that mojo victims always get wore off, and he shook himself and looked a little nervous.

All the fight had gone out of him, and now he seemed to be like a little dog that was all bark and had just gotten faced down by a much bigger, badder dog.

"Uh, sorry, man, I was just testing, ya know?" He did seem to be sorry, but I wasn't sure if it was my mojo or if he had accepted that I wouldn't be pushed around.

I stole a glance at the bartender, who was looking at me with surprise and slight worry on his face. The other vamp had stayed put, but he was observing what had happened also.

I looked back at the man. "You test everyone like that who comes in?"

"No, I know most people and where they fit in. You, I don't know, so I had to find out if you were some snot-nosed punk wandering into my territory or what. I expected you might be some new-turn that had yet to be claimed by one of the elders, but I didn't expect that you were an elder yourself. If I had known, I would have shown respect."

He hastened to add, "I'm claimed by Thaddeus, by the way."

He had said that last as if it was a shield that would prevent me from killing him.

I asked, "What about the others here, they with Thaddeus too?"

He nodded, "Yeah, we all answer to him. He's over four hundred, came over from the old country on one of the first boats after the Mayflower or some shit. He's strict but lets us do what we want as long as we serve when he calls and pay tribute."

He looked worried, "You aren't here to make trouble are you?"

I shook my head and said, "No, I'm not here to challenge anyone, just stopped in to get a bite to eat so to speak, and didn't know this was your place. I'm new to the city and don't know what spots have been claimed or haven't. I didn't aim to make any claims; I just needed to feed."

I saw both of the other guys relax at my words.

"I'm Tom, by the way. Glad to hear there won't be any trouble; I try to stay out of elder business."

He added, "I can tell you the places I know, but you'd need to meet with another elder to learn more. We keep to where they assign us so we don't violate another's territory. That tends to start conflicts."

I didn't offer him my name in return. Any information would be something they could potentially use to track me back to my home, and I wasn't ready for that.

"I can imagine it would. Tell me, Tom, how difficult would it be to meet with Thaddeus or one of the other elders to introduce myself?" I cocked my head in question and added, "Is there a neutral spot where they typically meet?"

Tom shrugged but looked nervous. "I can pass the word to him that you have arrived in town and would like to meet. Do you have a number or a place you are staying that I could give him?"

The place I am staying? Like hell!

Instead, I replied, "Hmm... tell you what. Give me your number, and I'll check with you in a couple of days."

He frowned but grabbed a napkin, took a pen out of his pocket, wrote his number, and then passed it over.

"Nice meeting you, Tom." I turned to each of the others and nodded to them as well before walking out of the bar.

I wanted nothing more than to wring every bit of information I could out of him, but every question I asked would also reveal more about me. Tom didn't seem too bright, but he wasn't stupid either. If I started asking questions every newb should know, he'd know something was up, especially since he mistakenly thought I was an elder.

I needed to find another vamp, one that I didn't have to worry about. Someone like one of those bikers I had killed. If I hadn't been all keyed up by the situation that night, I should have questioned one of them before killing them. Of course, then, I might not have been able to do it.

Killing in the heat of the moment was one thing, but after talking with someone who couldn't defend themselves... I wasn't sure if I was cold enough to do that.

Besides, I doubted little fish like those gangers would know the elders or who the other players in town were anyway.

CHAPTER 22

I SCRY WITH MY LITTLE EYE

It was time to develop a new spell. I needed to be able to locate these guys so I didn't stumble into them accidentally like this. If I could sense when I was coming within a quarter of a mile of one, I could take steps to avoid them before they could know I was there. That gave me another idea. If I could do a detection spell over the entire city or even just a five-mile radius, I could track their movements. I'd have to key the magic to the spiky red auras, though, so that I didn't trip any alarms among the city's mages. I would not want them to come looking for me. I still worried my enchanting would draw their attention, but it didn't seem to have been noticed so far.

At least, I didn't think so.

Just to be safe, I headed to the Rice University area to a little rooftop café I knew was closed at this hour. I made sure no one was looking and leaped up, grabbing the edge of the roof and vaulting over. Sure enough, it was empty, and there were no cameras or anything to tie me to this place. I settled into a chair and focused my mind, picturing the round table as a five-mile radius around where I was and willing red dots to appear on the surface, showing me the location of any spiky red auras in that area.

I burned one blood gem after another until I reached five, and red dots flickered to life, glowing like tiny balls of light on the surface. One, then two, then three, and on it went until nine showed on the surface. Some of the balls were moving, but others were stationary. I let it go, and the lights flickered out.

I sat there in the dark for a good two hours just to see if anyone would come to investigate.

While I did, I planned for how I could better use this new spell. The first thing I would need was a good map of the city, a big one, big enough that I could see at least down to the scale of city blocks. I would also need someone to record the movements of the dots for me, so I could figure out where they went to ground each morning. Give that a few days or weeks, and I'd know where every vampire lair in the city was. At least those who my spell could find.

It was always possible some powerful elder might be able to conceal their aura the way I could. It occurred to me that knowing such information could give me an incredible amount of power. I imagined most vampires who were not very powerful concealed their resting places to not be staked during the day. This was the modern world, after all, and it wouldn't be much trouble to hire mercenaries to take out an enemy while they slept.

Since no one came to investigate my magic scrying spell, I would have to assume it was safe to use. I headed back to the Tower and cleared the floor in the library, moving the tables, chairs, and rugs to the sides, leaving an extensive section of the floor open. I called Kat, something I rarely ever did off hours.

"Hey, Kat. I'm sorry to bother you in the middle of the night, but I've got an urgent request. I need maps of the Houston metroplex, and I want them scaled to fit the floor of my library. I need them to be detailed enough to show city blocks, and even better if they can show buildings the way you can when you are zoomed in on google maps. I'd like to have them before the end of the day tomorrow if possible. I also need someone to work an all-nighter tomorrow and for perhaps the next two weeks to record and track the movements of some people that I will mark on the map for them."

There was silence on the other line for a moment before Kat let out a long sigh. "Ok, boss, I'll get on it right now. Will likely be tomorrow afternoon before I can have them delivered and in place."

"Thanks, Kat. I wouldn't bother you if it weren't important. Don't worry about it being pretty. It just needs to be accurate and as detailed as possible for now. If this works out, I'd like to see about maybe doing some kind of digital wall map where we can electronically record what I want. We could use the computer gaming room for it, but we can discuss that tomorrow. Don't stay up all night working on this. Get some sleep, ok?"

"Will do. Talk to you when you get up tomorrow." She hung up, and I knew it would get done. Kat was the kind of person that made things happen.

Once that was settled, I headed to bed. I would need to wake up before the sun went down the following evening to cast my spell, and it would need to be a lot more powerful than the one tonight. I planned to record the dots while they were still stationary before they had woken up for the evening. I would start with their lairs and then follow where they went for the evening.

When I met with Thaddeus, I wanted to know as much about the city's vamps as possible. That also meant I would have a better idea of the 'territories' that they each claimed. Of course, it would take weeks to put names to the dots, but I was pretty sure I could do it using my magic and the fact that I could hide my aura. Once I had names, I could begin to trace the connections between them and figure out who each elder claimed, whatever that meant. If I knew the city's power structure before my meeting, it would go a long way toward showing the elders that I was not someone to take lightly.

The next afternoon I woke around 3 pm and spent the blood gem necessary to remain awake without penalty. I quickly showered and dressed, feeling a bit more human, so to speak, and surprisingly well-rested.

When I was done, I walked over to the library to find Kat and a younger woman arranging map sections on the floor and taping them down. Looking it over, I was impressed.

"Wow, Kat, nice job on these maps."

She smiled tiredly. "I have a friend that owns a print shop, the old school kind, where they print blueprints, large diagrams, and maps. He already had the maps we needed on file, so I twisted his arm and got him to rush a print job for us." She chuckled, "I owe him a bottle of bourbon by the way. You're paying."

I laughed but felt terrible for putting her on the spot as well. "Thank you again for jumping on this and making it happen. I'm sorry to have woken you up in the middle of the night, but it is important to me as you are about to see. Also, give your friend something nice, whatever the best bottle Specs has under $500. That should buy just about the nicest bottle of Bourbon they've got."

Gesturing at the younger woman, I asked, "I see you brought some help?"

I suspected some relation to Kat. They both had the same shade of dark hair and similar features. I would have guessed her daughter, except that I knew Kat didn't have any children from the many conversations we'd had over the last year or so.

"This is my niece Heidi. She's been helping me out a bit in the office, and I've been giving her a little internship-style training."

The young woman smiled and waved to me. "Nice to meet you, Mr. Fox. Aunt Kat asked me to help out and said you needed someone to do data entry overnight?" She walked over and confidently extended her hand to shake.

I took it and was impressed with her steady grip. She wouldn't be a pushover. I couldn't help but notice how incredibly vibrant her green eyes were. It was almost the only thing I saw for a moment.

"Nice to meet you too, Heidi."

As I spoke, I surreptitiously checked her out and was impressed. She was quite pretty, with brown hair cut short, almost boyishly, but it suited her well. She had fair skin with freckles and was a touch on the short side. She had nice curves. Overall, I'd say she had some Irish or Scottish in her ancestry.

As I realized how thoroughly I was checking her out, I was suddenly reminded that I hadn't had any female companionship since my death well over a year ago. I noticed all of this without being obvious, doing my best to maintain a professional demeanor. I wasn't sure how Kat would feel about me hitting on her niece, and I valued her talents too much to jeopardize losing her over messing with someone she cared about.

Forcing myself to focus on the task at hand, I began, "Yeah, I know Kat hasn't said anything about me, but before we get started, you need to know what you are getting into."

I smiled and gestured for her to take a seat at the desk, and I sat on the chair next to her. I looked into her eyes and kicked in the mojo. "You will not betray my trust in any way, and you will keep secret anything you see or hear while with me."

She glazed over and nodded. "I will not betray you and keep your secrets." Then her eyes unglazed.

I smiled, "I know you won't. Anyone Kat trusts enough to bring here would not be the sort to do that."

"But what did you want to tell me?" She asked.

I was impressed. Even after just being whammied, she was sharp enough to keep her wits. That spoke volumes about how strong her mind must be.

"I am not a normal person. I can do magic, and that's a super big secret. You will believe me in a few minutes once we get started."

I grinned at her disbelieving expression and stood up to get ready. "I'm going to cast a scrying spell to locate some people. When I do, glowing red dots will appear on the map, and I want you to mark the location of those dots with a marker. The “people” are all vampires, which are real by the way. The dots should be showing us where they are sleeping during the day. I want to circle that dot to designate it as a lair. Once night falls, many of them will start moving, and I want to draw dashed lines showing their movements. We'll make another mark wherever they stop for longer than a few minutes. Most of those will return to the original point by sunrise. Some may not, and we'll want to note those especially. Some vamps might have multiple homes or safe spots, others may just crash anywhere, but my guess is the majority will have someplace they have fortified that they consider safe to go to ground when the sun comes up."

Kat cleared her throat; disbelief was evident on her face. "That's crazy. I know you are not normal, but vampires? What else is real?"

I shrugged, "I don't know; I've only been at this since shortly before we met. So far, I've met a mage, a few vampires, and a kami or two when I went to Japan. I have to assume most things are real, though; it's the only safe assumption."

She thought momentarily, then said, "We've got one problem through, or may have. What if there are more dots on the map than the three of us can mark and trace?"

I hadn't thought of that, but it was a good possibility based on my test last night. "Hmm... we'd better call in some help. Who else do you have available?"

Kat considered, then said, "I'd suggest calling in Ralph and Jasper; they already know you and are under NDA over your business and activities. Hopefully, five of us will be enough."

"Sounds good. We can get started, as it will be a couple of hours before the dots start moving anyway."

CHAPTER 23
I LOVE IT WHEN A PLAN COMES TOGETHER

I STOOD on the Tower where it was depicted on the map. I waved my hands around over the pages while chanting, "Ostend nobis lamia," over and over while focusing my will to show dots to represent every red spiky aura in the range of the metroplex represented by the map, and to keep it active until one hour past dawn the next day. It burned a surprising 15 blood, whether because of holding it active so long or because of how difficult it might be to locate them, I wasn't sure. Like the night before, however, the glowing red dots appeared, but there were far more of them than I expected. Instead of a couple of dozen, there were around 200. Some with large areas around them with no other vampires, and some where clusters of them gathered together in groups as large as six or seven.

"Well damn. I didn't expect that." I looked over to Kat, who was shocked at seeing so many vampires in the city. "We'd better call in more help. Let's get the guys in the office over here. They are still at work anyway, so we'll ask them if they can stay for a special project."

Kat nodded distractedly and then shook herself and headed for the door.

On the other hand, Heidi looked shocked but in a different way. She had just seen magic for the first time. Honest-to-goodness magic, and she was having to readjust her worldview.

Of course, she didn't accept it without testing. She looked at the ceiling for laser pointers, then waved her hand over several of the dots trying to shade the map and figure out where the light source was, but when it became clear that there was no external source of the dots, she began to accept.

I gave her a few minutes of silence to come to terms with her new reality.

Meanwhile, I moved to grab a marker and started circling the dots. For the nests, I circled individual dots even though they were practically on top of one another so that we would be better able to follow them and have exact numbers. I was thankful that my aura was different enough that it didn't appear on the map. That would have been awkward to explain to my team. As the new team members came in, I gave them a fresh mojo to make sure they could not speak of what they were seeing and learning in this room and that they wouldn't even think about it when they weren't present here.

Soon we had all the dots circled and had ordered pizza for everyone, enough to get us through the night. I also told everyone I'd give them a $1000 bonus for helping out. That set a cheerful tone, and everyone excitedly joined in. Unlike Kat and Heidi, I didn't tell the others what the dots represented, just what I wanted them to do with the dots. The pizza arrived, and beer was available, so everyone had a bite to eat before the sun went down and was ready to get to work once the dots started moving.

Some dots came awake and started moving the instant the sun was down, while others didn't start moving until it was fully dark outside. I was also interested to note that the auras changed as the vampires awoke. They became more vibrant in color, going from a muted tone to a noticeably brighter red. Because of that, I learned that not all vampires woke up simultaneously. I had figured they would all become fully active the minute the sun dipped below the horizon, but that wasn't the case.

I wasn't sure what that might mean, did some wake sooner because they were more powerful? Was it to do with how long they had been a vampire? Or was it just completely random? No way to know, but it might be worth investigating later.

They did start to move, and we were swamped for a bit, drawing dashed lines around the map as they traveled, trying to keep up with all of them. Each of us took a section of the map and followed the vampires in our areas. Some didn't move from their lair at all; others zipped from spot to spot, stopping only for a few minutes at a time.

After a couple of hours, things settled down a bit. I suspected because they had now fed and were no longer on the hunt. They were now going about their regular nightly routines, whatever those might be.

Some, like Tom and his friends, settled into their bar in north Houston off I-45, where I had met them last night. Others kept moving the whole night, never stopping for too long. It was fun, engaging, and a bit exhausting for my team, but by morning we had a serious mess of lines all over our map; it looked like one of those FAA maps that showed the flight plans of all the planes in the air at any given time. Only these were much messier.

I did ask my team to make a note of the dots that were located in ritzy areas of the city, as those were more likely to be powerful vampires. Likewise, I suspected the nesting ones were like that group of gangbangers I had encountered a few weeks ago, low-powered individuals banding together for safety. It was a hell of a good start, but we needed to get this computerized.

I spoke up as everyone was putting their markers away the next morning. "Okay, team, that was a fantastic job last night. You know the importance of this to me, and this was a great first step. However, we need this in a format that we can track and record. I'd like to set up a digital wall in the gaming room and have a team track the movements on the PC to be entered into a database so that we can detect patterns over time and put identities on these people. Thoughts?"

Heidi, bless her heart, spoke up immediately, "Your gaming room won't be enough, you need a dedicated space for this, and if you want this set up in the next couple of days, you need some new talent. The big conference room over on the office side would be large enough, and we could temporarily run a cable to handle the required hardware from there to the server room. Get an IT expert and a digital cartographer, like someone from one of the digital mapping companies. Lastly, you need a data scientist to handle the analytics."

She thought for a second, then added, "Oh, and a database person, that goes without saying."

I had an IT background, even if it was in security rather than data science, so I knew she was right on the money with those suggestions. The team would also need a project manager, but I was pretty sure I had already found someone for that position, and her name was Heidi.

I looked around the room for suggestions and saw none, so I grinned at Kat's niece.

"Heidi, consider yourself in charge of the project. Let's get this done. Offer the experts a 6-month contract up to $150K. As for the hardware, take the recommendation of the IT person you hire, but make that a top priority. I want to get the digital wall map up and running ASAP. The database and other stuff can come later. In the meantime, find some folks to take your place. We'll do this the manual way again tonight, but you guys don't have to join in if you don't want to. We can hire some interns to do the night shift. Offer $20/hr for that and get three groups of ten so that we don't have people working back-to-back days and being so tired they make mistakes."

Turning to Heidi's aunt, "Kat, please make that two bottles of Bourbon and ask your friend to prioritize us a second set of maps so we can do this again tonight."

Again Heidi spoke up, "That's not necessary."

She blushed, seeing all eyes turn to her, as she realized she was interrupting the boss.

"Sorry, but wouldn't it be easier to get some plexiglass sheets or thick gauge clear plastic and put it over the maps and draw on that? We can number the pieces to line up with map sections, and then we could do the same thing daily until we have the digital system up and running."

She snapped her fingers as she thought of one last thing, "Overlays. That would also make it easier to see patterns as you lay one day on top of another."

I smiled at Kat. "Damn, the apple doesn't fall far from the tree. I'm glad you brought her on board. She just saved me a $500 bottle of booze."

I chuckled, and everyone smiled at the blushing girl. I looked at my group of trusted employees and quasi-friends in the room again, "Okay, I know It's been a double shift for some of you already, so go get some rest. Please stick around for a minute for those of you who will continue to work throughout the day to make the arrangements."

CHAPTER 24
SECRET REVEALED

Ralph and Jasper departed, leaving Kat and Heidi. "Ok, you two mostly know my secret already, but I can do one thing to help and make the day easier if you'll let me."

They each nodded in turn.

I hesitated for a long moment. Did I really want to do this? So far, no one at all knew my real secret, and it felt safe that way. I certainly had that urge in the back of my brain to keep it that way.

Even so, maybe it was the loneliness, or maybe it was the fact that I found Heidi more than a little attractive... Whatever the reason, I knew I wanted to do this; Queenie's compulsion for survival be damned!

"Ok, here's the full secret, and this puts you in greater danger. Are you really sure you want to stay?" Again they nodded, mirroring each other. Neither looked to the other, and neither hesitated.

I smiled at them gently as I confessed, "I'm not a mage, exactly. I am a vampire who can use magic. As far as I know, I am completely unique. Worse, if the other supernatural critters out there knew I existed, they would do everything in their power to kill me and anyone associated with me."

That hit them like a bombshell. Kat sat heavily on the chair beside her. Heidi took it a little better.

Kat just said, "That explains some things, but I see you during the day all the time; how can you do that?"

I waggled my fingers at her mystically. "Magic. An advantage other vampires don't have, which is just one of the reasons they would want me dead. Jealousy. Other vamps can do it with magic, but mages forbid their own from performing such magic. Not to mention, enchanting magic items are so costly that even most mages find it beyond their reach to own such items."

I paused for a breath, then continued when I saw they were still raptly following my words.

"This brings me to mages. They would want me dead for the same reasons. The spell I performed last night would be beyond almost all mages, and they wouldn't be happy to know someone they had no influence over had powers beyond their own."

"Wow," Heidi said eloquently.

I grinned, "Yeah, pretty much how I felt when this all fell on me." I took my thumb and bit down on it, drawing blood. "Drinking this will refresh you and allow you to go through the day without any tiredness; it will also boost your immune system while it is inside you."

Kat hesitated and looked dubious, but Heidi immediately took my hand and sucked on my thumb. It was *way* more sensual than I expected! She licked it with her tongue and sucked for a long moment. Long enough to let me know it was absolutely intentional. She let go after a long second.

Damn!

I cleared my throat and shook off the sudden inappropriate thoughts that were flooding my brain before turning to Heidi's aunt.

"Kat?" I put my other thumb to my fang, poised to bite down.

After a long moment of indecision, she nodded, so I bit down and then presented the thumb to her. She sucked on the small wound briefly, but it was not sensual for her. It hit her after a moment, and she sighed.

"Wow, that does pack a punch, and it is fast acting. I feel like I just had a good night's sleep." She stretched as if reveling in her body's suddenly loose, relaxed feeling.

Smiling, I patted her on the back. "You two are the only ones I've trusted with this secret. You are bound not to betray me, but even so, it's not something I do lightly. Thank you."

They both smiled before turning toward the door.

Heidi turned back just before walking out and said in parting, "We've got a lot of work to do. I'll see you this afternoon in the office with a group of new hires for you to approve or reject. Be there at three."

I was impressed with how competent she was for being so young. I hadn't been anywhere near that sharp or driven to success at that age.

Hell, it wasn't until I was turned into a special snowflake vampire that I got my shit in gear, and that had as much to do with the survival compulsion that Queenie had crammed into my skull as any merit of my own. She wanted to ensure her bloodline survived, so she essentially whammied me with a spell that was transferred along with her parting message. She taught me the basics of what I needed to know and magically pushed me to survive.

I had figured that out during the last year as I got used to using my mojo in others. That plus a little self-reflection, and it wasn't hard to notice the drive to pursue my goals was not exactly typical for my past self. I didn't mind, though. I wouldn't be living in a penthouse otherwise.

Although, to be fair to myself, I'm not sure Queenie's compulsion had anything to do with me robbing $42,000,000 from a Vegas casino. On the other hand, the jury was still out on that. I had the nagging suspicion in the back of my mind that I hadn't heard the end of that. It felt too easy, and that made me nervous. A year and a half on, and I still felt like the other shoe was going to drop, and I wouldn't like it.

The one problem with spending the blood to stay awake is that I don't feel the need for sleep and can't actually get to sleep once I have paid the blood price. So now I was awake, and my people were handling everything. That left me alone with the map. I spent a couple of hours looking it over. I now knew where Tom and his two buddies had their lairs, but they hadn't done anything interesting, just spent their time at their bar the whole night and gone straight home for the day.

That wasn't helpful. However, I did look at the dots that were in high-end areas. One was in an extremely affluent neighborhood near Allen Parkway, in the place where a bunch of ambassadors had mansions. Another was in a moderately rich community between Westheimer and I-10 outside the loop. One was in the Woodlands, in a spot that required serious money, according to Mr. Pope. Still, another was in the Rice University area, where the homes are all a hundred or so years old and fancy as fuck.

There were too many for me to be sure were elders, but it seemed like every area of the city had at least one vampire, and many had more. This was going to take some effort and a whole lot of leg work on my part. I would have to spend nights on the phone with my crew and wait for the vamps to come out of their lairs, then get images of each one, all while not being seen.

Then I would need to find a rat like Tom that I could whammy and get them to put names to the pictures. That part would be dangerous because I didn't know if a vamp would stay under compulsion or not. So if I asked a bunch of questions and they didn't stay quiet, I'd instantly become wanted. There were ways I could do it that wouldn't get me killed, but those would require me going dark-side.

I grinned suddenly; I had an idea....

I could go to another city where no vamp would know me and find one there to use compulsion on. If it didn't stick, no one would know me, and if it did persist, I could get info without endangering myself. I couldn't do it here for the risk of stirring things up, and as a known new person, I would be the first one they would suspect even if I was in disguise.

I was glad I had nearly 3500 blood right now because I didn't want to dip below 3000, and I would be burning a lot of blood at this rate.

CHAPTER 25
LUNCH AND LEARN

THAT AFTERNOON, I walked over to the office and "interviewed" the new hires. In other words, I whammied them and made sure they would be loyal and not remember anything of their work for me. They would remember doing basic data entry work on land surveys for my mining company. I spent the 15 blood, cast the scrying spell, and then turned the work over to Heidi and Kat.

"You guys are going to have to work without me tonight. I've got to run an errand to get some much-needed information."

Heidi looked disappointed, which inexplicably pleased me.

After a quick discussion with my team about what to do in my absence, I was about to duck back into the private side of my home when I noticed Kat and Heidi looking like they wanted to have a word.

I wasn't in a rush, so I stepped into one of the offices, and they followed me in.

Heidi looked like she wanted to speak, but Kat touched her shoulder and said, "I just want to make sure. You aren't doing all of this so you can use it against your enemies or something, are you?"

I was taken aback. "Huh? Enemies? I don't really have any enemies at the moment."

Heidi spoke then, "It's just that, with this map... it gives you an incredible amount of power over everyone else."

She sounded worried, like the idea of an immortal vampire able to track anyone's movements concerned her.

I was honestly relieved by her concern. I could tell from her body's reactions that she was interested in me. Still, I didn't know if it was because she just liked me or if she was some supernatural groupie drawn by the allure of me being a vampire. Or hell, maybe she was just a gold digger and wanted me for my money. I could have whammied her and found out, but that would have been a violation, and I was uncomfortable with that.

The fact that she was worried that I might abuse my power was a good sign that she wasn't just some groupie and that maybe she really did like me.

That thought put me in a good mood.

"I'm not creating the map for the purpose of gaining power. I really want to live in peace and be left alone by the other vampires in the city. That said, the map will give me a lot of information, and information is power. I could use it to kill off vampires, knowing their lairs where they sleep. Even though they are vampires, that would still make me a murderer. At least in my own eyes."

I considered for a moment about how I did want to use that information.

"I will create the database of vampires, and having that knowledge will let me avoid them as much as possible. I want to live in peace and not have any conflicts. But if the worst comes, it will let me eliminate enemies who want to harm me or those I care about."

Kat seemed a little mollified by that statement but still a little concerned. Heidi seemed the same, but her heartbeat sped up when I mentioned protecting those I cared about.

They seemed willing to trust me, so I said goodbye to them and went to change.

Even though I would be going to a different city, I didn't want to look like myself. What can I say? Paranoia is a bitch, especially when backed by your creator's compulsion spell.

I changed my appearance from my usual look to that of a young black-haired girl with a delicate-looking petite figure. Someone that wouldn't seem like a threat to anyone. Yeah, I can do that, and I can do it either by way of illusion or an actual physical change, thanks to the magic. In this case, I made it a physical change since I had no idea what powers the vampires I was interrogating might have. I didn't want to run into a powerful old bastard who could see through illusions. Still, I had no way of knowing what I might encounter, so I figured it was better to be safe than sorry.

How did I have clothes to fit a petite young woman when I'm a 5'10" tall guy? Mind your own damn business!

Seriously, though, I had planned ahead and had a closet full of various outfits to fit a wide range of options in case I needed to disguise myself. They were also throwaway items, so if someone tried to magically trace me through them, there wouldn't be much of a connection. Nothing I'd ever worn more than once. I figured that should minimize the chances of getting magically tracked.

When I was ready, I teleported to Austin near downtown and cast the weaker version of my new scrying spell, only doing a 3-mile radius. I figured I'd be able to find one near 6th Street, where all the bars and entertainment were. I used my phone's GPS map, onto which I had cast my spell. Sure enough, there were several vamps, so I picked one near one of the clubs.

Going inside, I spotted him immediately. His aura stood out among the crowd. I made my way over to him though not directly. He was a douchey-looking hipster type, except for being a vampire. He had way too much swagger, way too much "trying to look hip". His clothes were a mix of vintage and modern, suggesting he spent a lot of time on his wardrobe, and his waxed twisted mustaches were immaculately groomed. The guy had to spend an hour in front of a mirror each night to pull off that look.

I rolled my eyes so hard that I almost got a headache but continued my approach. As I got closer, I noticed he was pretty big, or maybe it was just that I wasn't used to being 5'4" tall. Still, unusual perspective aside, I thought he must be at least six feet tall and well built with the lean vampire shape I was starting to associate with my kind.

When he spotted me, he smiled with a predatory gleam in his eyes. I was walking past him when he reached out and grabbed my arm. "Hey, little girl, whatcha doing? Wanna join me for a drink?"

I pretended to hesitate to look around the room but said, "Uh, sure. I was meeting some friends, but it doesn't look like they showed."

He bought me a drink and asked me stupid questions, going through the motions so that he wouldn't look like a creeper to the people around him. I feigned interest but winced at the loud music a couple of times. I don't understand how vampires liked to hunt in clubs. Sure, they made good target-rich environments, but the noise levels had to hurt their ears as much as it was mine.

Before my drink could arrive, I looked over to him and asked, "Hey, wanna get out of here and go somewhere a little quieter, like maybe a restaurant or something? This music is giving me a headache."

He laughed in delight at not having to use his mojo on me. He escorted me outside, holding onto my arm possessively the whole way. However, he pretended to be doing it in a gentlemanly fashion.

Once outside, he led me straight to a dark alley saying, "My bike is down here parked at the back; you don't mind riding a motorcycle, do you?"

I grinned back. "I love bikes!"

He laughed again, and I swear there was a hint of maniacal villain in it.

Once we got to the back, he pushed me against a wall and was just about to whammy me, but I hit him with my mojo first.

Since he was a vampire of unknown strength, I pushed as hard as I could with my will. I could feel the mojo kick in flex, my power washing over him as he drowned in my eyes.

"Be silent and still. I want to ask you some questions, and you will answer me honestly. Do you understand?"

His face went slack, and his hand fell away as his eyes glazed over.

I knew immediately that I had gone overboard with the power I had put into that. *Wow, this guy is even weaker than Tom.*

I didn't waste any time marveling over the difference in our power levels and instead dove right into my questions.

"Does vampire compulsion last when done on another vampire?"

I hoped it would. If so, then I would be golden. If not, I was prepared to give a lame excuse that I was new and flee or bullshit him if it seemed like he would buy it.

Hipster Vamp replied woodenly, "Yes, but only if the difference in their power is wide enough."

Not the best answer, but I could work with that. "Is our power difference wide enough that my commands to you will stick? If so, how long will they stick?"

He still had a totally slack expression. So I was guessing that I was significantly more powerful than he was. If he were faking, he was a damned good actor.

"Yes, your commands to me will stick. I do not know how long. I hear it can take a hundred years or more for someone to get powerful enough to break their master's compulsion."

Bingo! Now we are talking. "Ok, I command you not to remember this conversation or even meeting me. Now, tell me about vampire society, as if I were a brand new vamp that had just been turned and didn't know anything."

I was still maintaining the mojo, not letting it drop.

He began with the same blank expression, "Vampires have existed for thousands of years. At least as far back as the Roman Empire, probably further. Some elders from that time are still around. They made other vamps, and then those vamps made others until you get down to ones like us. We're at the bottom of the food chain. We have to do what the elders say, or they kill or use compulsion on us."

He was rattling on with his answer, not showing any signs of stopping, which was great.

"Any vampire who gets created must serve their creator for as long as they are under their master's compulsion. Once a vampire is strong enough to break their maker's hold, then they are considered adults, able to do what they want. But from what I hear, even the older vamps that break free of their makers still serve an elder.

"It's customary for new vampires to test each other's will. If one is significantly weaker than the other, they get claimed and end up serving them. That's why many vampires only try to break free from their creator once they believe they are strong enough to fend off other vamps. Better the devil you know than getting claimed by some evil prick that would treat you worse."

That was some unfortunate shit right there. It meant every time I met another vamp, there would be a contest of wills to see who was stronger. I'd either end up on top or someone else's bitch.

"Does that mean every city has a top vampire who controls everyone else? What happens if two vampires face off and neither is stronger than the other?"

It was creepy, but the guy continued to answer like a robot, "I hear there is usually either one vampire who rules the city, or if there are several elders all about the same power, then they share the city, dividing it up among them, each taking an area."

Well, that was something then. If I were the equal of Thaddeus, then I could demand a slice of Houston, assuming he didn't go to war with me to drive me out.

"So, how does a vampire get more powerful?"

"The longer you live, the more powerful you get." He answered in the same monotone.

"Can a vampire start more powerful than others when they are first made?"

This was a big one. If the answer was yes, then I wouldn't have to try and bullshit Thaddeus and the other elders and try to trick them into believing I was hundreds of years old.

"Yes, the more powerful the one who made you was, the more powerful you will be. If an elder that was a thousand years old made you, you might be as powerful as another vampire who was two or three hundred. That is especially true if that vampire has the protection of their maker, then they might be treated as if they were an elder themselves."

There it was! That was my ace card. I could pretend I was made by a really old vampire and that they allowed me to live in Houston because they wanted someone to watch the oil and gas industry for them. Which would also explain my business.

"Does someone have to declare who their elder is that they are claimed by?"

"No, but they would be fair game if someone challenged them and they lost. Then they could be claimed, and there would not be retribution." Hipster vamp replied.

"Ok, what other supernatural people are there?" I was curious about this.

"I've only met other vampires, but I hear there are mages, werewolves, fairies, and ghosts."

"Are there any rules about dealing with them?" Now we were getting to the rules all vamps were supposed to follow.

"Don't attack them. There is a truce between us all."

Here we go... "What rules are we supposed to follow and live by?"

Hipster blandly answered, "Never kill other vampires; only the elders are allowed to pass judgment. Never reveal that we exist to mortals. Never attack a supernatural. Obey the elders. Do not make other vampires without permission from the elders. Do not feed more than once per night. Never let a mortal remember that you are a vampire or that you fed on them. If they can't be compelled, then they must be killed. If you kill, you must make it look like a mortal killing, and do not do it in a way that would draw attention to supernaturals."

Ding, ding, ding... One of those rules didn't seem to fit my expectations.

"Why are we only allowed to feed once per night?"

Without inflection, Hipster answered, "So we do not draw attention to ourselves." But then he added, "I have also heard some vampires say that you can get stronger faster by feeding more, but I think that isn't worth the risk. It would take years to feed enough to become strong enough to notice a difference."

I considered. That might be true for a typical vampire, but one who can feed and turn the blood into gems, store them, and then burn them to fuel magic?

To do all of my enchanting and store up my blood gems, I've probably fed as much in one year as another vamp would feed in 15 years. I wonder what that was doing for me. If it was like building muscles, the more you used them, the stronger you got. I was not only feeding; I was taxing my body with magic, flexing my supernatural nature, so to speak. I'm sure that wouldn't cause me to equal an elder by any means. Still, I suspected that if I was a standard vamp, the things I had done over the last year would have made me noticeably stronger than someone who had started out at the same strength.

"Who is the oldest vampire you have heard of? And do the city elders answer to anyone above themselves?" I figured it would be good to know. I was running out of questions, though.

"Freya, in Washington DC. She's supposed to be over a thousand years old. If city elders answer to anyone, I do not know it, perhaps their own makers? There is no king or queen."

Hipster had been very helpful.

I again flexed my will, "You will go back inside and continue your hunt, and you will not remember me or that we ever spoke. When you get back inside, you will blink three times and then not remember any time passing since the moment before you saw me."

I tried something I had never done before. I spent a blood gem to strengthen my command, and I could see his eyes almost close with the wave of power that hit him. He moved immediately toward the club, completely forgetting my presence.

Now that was handy. I'd have to remember that when I met Thaddeus if it seemed like I might lose the battle of wills.

With that, I teleported back to the Tower.

CHAPTER 26

FEEDING THE DATA MONSTER

IT WAS STILL EARLY, only around 10 pm. I wasn't tired thanks to my life-challenged condition, so I cast a quick illusion of my regular self over my current cute girly appearance and walked into the conference room where the team was mapping the night's vampire movements.

Heidi walked over, and I asked, "How's the mapping going?"

"The team is working out. They are all college interns, and the ones we picked are skilled enough to handle something simple like this. I've been watching over them to make sure they are keeping up. What's your plan for tonight?" She asked, looking at me curiously.

I noticed she was dressed a bit more casually tonight, wearing blue jeans and comfortable flats with a low-cut grey blouse and a black blazer over it. It struck a good balance between being in charge and being comfortable enough to work a 16-hour shift.

I also noticed the low-cut blouse... I couldn't help it, and I was absolutely sure she did it on purpose. Thanks to my senses, I could tell her heartbeat would speed up as I got near. Heidi was interested, but I wasn't going to do something we might regret. At least not until I learned whether she was interested because I was rich as fuck, or because I was a supernatural badass (*I kid*), or because she was just attracted to me.

"I'm going to use the time tonight to find some of these dots and photograph them. I hope we can use facial recognition or an image search to find out who they are. I need to put names to them so we can start to build up dossiers."

She nodded. "Damn, that's smart. Are you sure you aren't planning to wipe them out? Just use the info to get power over them?"

I raised an eyebrow at her. "Definitely not planning to go to war. Killing them would create a power vacuum, creating a chaotic situation as new ones tried to move in and started fighting to take control. The best case scenario would be a success in wiping them out, then older, more powerful vamps from around the world would take interest and try to move in, and they would be gunning for me. I might be a unique snowflake of a vampire with my magic abilities, but I don't think I'd stand a chance if they set out to kill me."

"What's that saying? I think it was from David Mamet? 'Old age and treachery will always beat youth and exuberance?'"

I chuckled, but it was true. I might be powerful thanks to the magic, but I did not want to face off against vampires who had been crushing their enemies for hundreds of years. Queenie had been the first vampire and survived for thousands of years. Still, even she had been brought down by her less powerful descendants through cunning and ruthlessness.

"Besides, it's not my place to police the world." I smiled, "As for your second question, yes and no. I am not planning to use it against them, but if any decide to come after me, I'll use that info to hit them and destroy all those allied with them to make an example."

Heidi nodded as if that was perfectly natural.

I wasn't sure about her. I was impressed and attracted, but I needed to get to know her better.

"Ok, I'm off. Hold down the fort, and I'll be back around morning."

I was turning to go when it occurred to me, "Oh, and keep your phone on you. I'll be calling for updates on locations. I will start with the ones in rich areas that have moved away from their lairs."

She nodded. "Got it. I'll be Control."

I chuckled. Maybe that was her deal; she had watched too many action adventure movies. I turned back to the map to pick my first target. I chose the one in the Rice Village area who had moved to a restaurant. That would make it easy to get close enough to take their picture. I hoped.

I walked back to the elevator and took it downstairs, then called an Uber to drop me off near that area, then called a Lyft to take me the rest of the way.

Yeah, I'm paranoid. I wasn't taking any chances. I had my cell phone ready, and it was even tweaked to silence the shutter sound that the camera is programmed to make. With vampiric hearing, I didn't want some elder to turn straight toward me when I took their picture. I had also dropped my illusion when changing vehicles and now looked like the black-haired girl again.

My current looks were not an illusion. I had physically changed my shape to be this new person. It was a little more expensive than an illusion, but it wouldn't be seen through by someone's magic or mystical abilities. Earlier, I might have accidentally faced off against an elder, but now I was intentionally going after targets I suspected of being the old powerful ones. That meant I wanted to be doubly sure I was not identified.

The restaurant turned out to be One Fifth Gulf Coast, an upscale European cuisine eatery in a former church. I loved that about Houston; it had some quirky places, but they were some of the best. I still regretted that I could no longer eat at the Hobbit Café, which had once been my favorite when I visited Houston during my living days. I sighed, once again regretting that particular aspect of my vampiric condition.

I stood at the entrance looking around and quickly spotted my target, but I wasn't sure how to get a picture of him. He was seated in the mezzanine section talking with a couple of businessmen.

I was stymied for a moment. I could see there were no open tables up there. The hostess asked me if I wanted to put my name on the list and that the wait would be at least an hour.

"No, thanks." I replied. "I'm supposed to be meeting some people, but it looks like they are running late. I'll just step outside and see if they want to eat here or not." I turned to the door and left.

Outside I found a secluded spot and tried out some of my magic items. I turned invisible and silent. Now all I had to do was wait for the door to open, then duck inside, and make my way up to the mezzanine and take the picture without anyone bumping into me.

It turned out not to be as easy as it sounded; the dining room was crowded, and I had to time my walk up the stairs when no one was coming since that was a tight space. All the while paying attention to my target to make sure he didn't notice me through some elder ability I wasn't aware of. I got to the top of the stairs, which was quite close enough. I had a good view of him and zoomed in my phone's camera to get a good shot of his face; I took two or three as he turned his head at different times.

Seeing him from this close, I could tell his aura was more vital than those of the vampires I had met before. The color was a darker red, and the spiky part was more pronounced. I wasn't sure what that said about him, but I was willing to bet it meant he was one of the city's elders.

Physically, he was white, and I guessed he was about six feet tall when standing. He was well-built and had a strong face with intelligent grey eyes.

I was shocked to see him eating food, clearly relishing it. There was no doubt. He was chewing and swallowing each bite with great relish.

What. The. Starving. Fuck!?!

I could have been eating food for the last year and more, but I'd been subsisting entirely on blood. Good golly, damn it. I was going to *have* to figure out how that was possible. I had thought all those organs had shriveled up and become useless or something.

After a long minute of annoyed regret, I refocused on the task at hand.

Their conversation was about some business deal trading in orange futures. I got out of there and walked a few blocks away before calling Control. However, I got one other detail. The people at the table called the man Mr. Schmidt.

"Heidi, I've got pictures incoming to your phone. And label this dot as Mr. Schmidt, print out a headshot of him, and place it on his dot."

"You got it, boss." She gave me the next closest target we thought might be a likely elder.

We repeated that process the rest of the night and got another five done. Two more of them were definitely elders judging by their auras. The other three were not quite so dark or so spiky. The more I saw other vampires, the more sure I became of my guess about elder vs. not-elder.

The elders were Jacquelyn and Mrs. Theriot.

Jacquelyn was a distinguished woman, mature, but without the lines or wrinkles that would have pegged her as old, thanks to her undead condition. Mrs. Theriot, however, was a dangerous-looking Creole woman with an exaggerated New Orleans accent.

I didn't get names for everyone, and I usually only got a single name rather than first and last since I was picking them up from conversations that people were having with them. It was a start, however. If I could make this kind of progress every night, it would only take me a month to get names and pictures of everyone. However, it should take less than that since some vamps traveled in packs, and others, like Tom's crew, gathered together to hang out. I was estimating two weeks if I got lucky.

It turned out to be three weeks. Each day I cast the spell, and each night I would go out tracking the vamps, changing my appearance each day but also using invisibility and silence. I was doing my best to minimize any chance of detection or discovery.

It seemed to work.

By the time we were done, we at least had pictures of every vamp in town and names, either first or last, for about 85%. I had identified nine elders in total, including Thaddeus, whose appearance I now knew along with his lair. On that front, I was pretty sure of about 90% of the vampire's principal lairs and their typical nightly movements.

We had also upgraded the war room; we had a digital wall map now projected onto a surface. That surface was a sheet of white canvas, which I enchanted with three properties. It would be extremely durable, it would shrink to the size of a scroll that I could roll up and put into a scroll case, and most importantly, it would constantly display the whereabouts of any vampire within up to a 50-mile radius of my location. I could expand or shrink the search zone on command to match whatever scale map I used.

The map didn't have to be projected onto its surface either, you could set a paper map on top, and the glowing dots were bright enough to show through. It would automatically scale to whatever map was placed on it. Man, I loved magic. It could do almost anything you could imagine if you could afford the cost. Speaking of that, enchanting it cost a pretty big pile of gems, nearly 500. That brought me down to just above my designated comfort zone of 3000.

It was time to hunt again and replenish.

While I was doing all that spellwork and legwork, my team managed to get the system going to track the vamps. It ended up taking quite a large team. Still, they wrote a program to track the movements of the dots and convert them into map coordinates and feed that info into the database. The DBA set it up so that we could associate the dots with information, so we built dossiers on each vamp to go along with their recorded movements. They got it down to the point where all I would have to do to locate Thaddeus, for example, was query where he was likely to go tonight. It would tell me an assigned probability based on his previous known destinations and habits. It was some big data predictive next-level shit. The kind of stuff they use to suggest ads to you before you even consciously think, 'I really need a new jacket.'

However, as impressive as that was, I still knew next to nothing about these vamps. Some I didn't have anything more on than a picture of them. I could mojo someone with high-level security access and run government searches on them. Still, it was far too likely that one or more vamps would have people monitoring those kinds of systems and be alerted if someone started a massive search on all the city's vampires. That left me doing it the hard way.

I needed to find and whammy some of the younger bloodsuckers in town and ask them to fill in the blanks for me. Luckily, I didn't need to bring them to the Tower; I could just take an Ipad with files on each of the vamps with me and question them where they were. I should also note that my servers containing anything sensitive were not connected to the outside world and so could only be hacked by physically getting into the server room and directly connecting. Yep, paranoid, but in a healthy way.

I hated that I had left Thaddeus waiting so long before getting back to him the way I had told Tom I would, but this was too important, and I wanted to go into that meeting fully armed with knowing who every player in the city was and as much as I could find out about each one. Not to mention what the alliances and enmities were between them all.

CHAPTER 27
AN UNEXPECTED DATE

I DECIDED to start with Tom since I knew him.

I still didn't know how strong I was compared to other vamps. Still, I had beaten Tom in a mojo battle, so I was reasonably sure I would be stronger than he was if it came to a fight. However, there was no guarantee; I was guessing rather than working from experience.

I had the route from his lair to the bar memorized, and he traveled one stretch of road each evening that would be perfect. There were still lots of areas in the northern parts of the metroplex that were relatively undeveloped, and Tom just so happened to ride his motorcycle down a road that went through several acres of undeveloped land. On both sides of the road stood tall pine trees as thick as a wall, leaving nothing but the sky above the road free to shine down a bit of starlight and the glow of the city lights. There was no place in the metroplex that was really dark, thanks to the light pollution, and with my vampire's eyes, it was as bright as day. However, it was still a bit eerie and would have been frightening to me if I were still human.

Did I have to catch him in the middle of nowhere and scare the shit out of him? No, but I did need to catch him where there wouldn't be any witnesses, so this fit the bill. I would be able to pull his bike over into the woods, and even if other cars drove by, they'd never see us even a few yards into the treeline.

The Woodlands, Texas, were especially weird like that. They purposely concealed everything behind the pine forests. You could be driving down a road in that town and not even realize there was a shopping center or a big-ass event venue that could seat a hundred-thousand people until you saw a sign next to a break in the trees where the driveway was. This area was just outside the Woodlands but hadn't been developed yet, so it seemed doubly private.

I did the natural thing and pulled the damsel in distress trick. I was wearing an illusion of being a young blond college-aged girl, walking down that dark section of the road alone and looking lost.

If there was one thing I knew, it was that bad guys target those who look defenseless and like easy prey. So that was what I was pretending to be. I guess he'd never seen that movie about the teen vampire slayer, or he might have been more cautious.

Instead, he pulled up, letting his loud-ass cruiser-style bike with its straight pipes idle at 100 decibels as he leered at me and drawled, "What's a pretty little thing like you doing walking alone in the dark?"

I pretended to be scared, and as he leaned closer, trying to ramp up the fear factor. I shot my hand out with the speed of a striking cobra and grabbed his leather jacket.

Looking into his eyes, I hit him with my compulsion, fueled by three extra blood gems worth of power. The build-up of magic-fueled will was overwhelming this time. It was like a tidal wave crashing over his mind.

His jaw went slack, and he almost fell off his bike. Hell, I think he would have shat himself if he had been human and still had working bowels.

I didn't let the illusion drop but drawled, "Good evening Tom. Let's go over into those trees and have a nice conversation. Sound good?"

In retrospect, I may have hit him a bit too hard with the mojo because he seemed to be having trouble forming words.

Sighing, I let go of Tom and grabbed his bike so it wouldn't fall over. He did, however. I gave him a little push, and he just slumped to the ground, falling off the bike backward, his body not responding to him. I'm pretty sure his mind was basically locked down from the power of the whammy I'd hit him with.

It took a few minutes, but I got him and his bike into the woods and out of sight. With my strength, lifting him with one hand and holding him against a tree wasn't hard. I purposefully backed off with the power and asked,

"You with me, Tom? You awake?"

He blinked in surprise and looked both slack faced and confused at the same time, as if he couldn't understand what was happening to him.

Grrr... I had clearly hit him too hard.

I pulled out my Ipad and propped him up so he could stand on his own, leaning against the big pine. "Okay, I'm going to show you a series of pictures, and you are going to tell me everything you know about them, all right?"

He nodded slowly.

A couple of hours went by, but I drained him of every detail he knew of the city's vampire population. I showed him every picture and got him to spill everything. He mostly knew of Thaddeus' allies and subordinates, but he also informed a bit about the rivalries and enemies his boss was known to have.

When I was done, I burned another two blood gems making him forget the conversation ever happened and erasing any knowledge of what we discussed from his mind. From that night on, the database began to take on depth. It wasn't just people I wanted to know about either, but also any personal details, business interests, hobbies, and any scrap that might be useful, no matter how trivial. I started by targeting low-level people in the areas of town where the elders held sway figuring I would get people under their umbrella and fill in the blanks as systematically as possible.

It took another two weeks before I felt I had enough info to have an accurate org chart for each elder's organization. I knew, at least on the surface, what the basic political structure was, who hated who, and who each group typically allied with.

I finally felt almost ready to have that meeting with Thaddeus. I just wanted to top off my blood supplies so that I wouldn't have to dip below 3000 if things didn't go according to plan forcing me to go to war instead. With sufficient blood, I felt like I could wipe out a significant portion of the bloodsuckers in Houston in a week.

I went on a serious bender and drank my way across several cities for a month, accumulating forty blood gems a night, bringing me to over 4100 blood gems. I also changed up my storage method. Instead of storing the base 1000 gems in my stomach, I implanted them in small groups all over my body, cutting myself open and putting them in, then healing the wounds.

I did it all for the food. I wanted to be able to eat again, and if I burned the blood to eat and drink normal food, it would have washed the gems in my belly away. We won't discuss how I got them out of there in the first place. No, we definitely won't talk about that....

I really didn't want to go to war. I wanted Thaddeus and the other elders to welcome me to the city and let me live peacefully. I felt like I could take them in a one-on-one fight if I used magic. Still, I had yet to even begin to explore magic combat spells, which I suddenly realized I should work on in the event I ever got into a fight with a mage.

Damn, I could practically feel the compulsion dig its claws into me and push me to go start working on that right now.

Fucking Queenie and her compulsion!

CHAPTER 28
LETTING SOMEONE IN

"JEEZ, am I never going to get to just relax for a damned minute?" I said it out loud when the thought hit me.

Heidi looked over, "What's that, boss?"

She had practically moved into the office over the last two months since she was working the night shift supervising the team doing the data collection. Luckily, the system's programming was mostly automated at this point and only required one person to monitor for errors or unexpected events that might need my attention. I had given her full access to the Tower's personal quarters except for my bedroom area. She had even set herself up a bed in an unused office. I was almost at the point of telling her to return to her home and take a vacation, but she seemed to want to be here.

"Nothing, just an observation that occurred to me. I just thought of something else that would improve my survival odds, and thanks to the compulsion that my maker stuck in my head, now I am going to have to work on that next, with the same intensity that I've done all this other stuff."

I chuckled darkly. "Not that I'm really complaining; if it weren't for the compulsion, I wouldn't be where I am today."

I put a mockingly sarcastic smile on my face, but I didn't mean it. Deep down, I really was thankful for it. I was about to go head to head with a powerful vampire elder, or maybe nine of them, and I had a good chance of surviving thanks to what Queenie did to me.

She raised an eyebrow questioningly. "Your maker? You've never mentioned that before. What were they like?"

I shook my head, "Not able to talk about it directly because of the survival compulsion."

That was not strictly true; I could tell her everything if I wanted. It was just a better idea if I didn't. Heidi knowing could lead to someone else discovering my secrets if they grabbed her and used compulsion on her.

And just like that, I realized I was an idiot. I had used compulsion on her not to share my secrets, but if someone with a stronger compulsion or someone with magic got her, they might be able to get it out of her.

Heidi must have seen it on my face because she got worried. "What is it?"

"I just realized that someone with magic might be able to override my compulsion on you not to reveal my secrets."

I shook my head again, this time in resignation. "I will have to create an item to protect you from compulsion or alert me if someone tries to use magic on you. Same for your Aunt."

She looked worried. "Do you think someone might target me because I work for you?"

Nodding, I said, "Definitely. If they discover where I live and who I am, then you will most definitely be in danger. You don't just work for me; you are at the center of what I do. Every elder and probably every mage in the city would want to get the information in your head."

She looked worried at that. So far, she had been amazingly accepting of all the supernatural mess surrounding me and my life. In fact, she seemed intrigued by it, like she had discovered a secret that no one else had and was reveling in being 'in the know'. At first, her attitude had even worried me, wondering how much of her interest in me was due to my supernatural nature. However, as the days passed and I got to know her better, I realized that was only a minor part of her interest.

Right now, however, I could tell the consequences of her new knowledge were dawning on her.

I smiled reassuringly, "Don't worry, though, I will create something to protect you, and once I've reached an agreement with the elders here, you should be safe from the vampires. Once someone is 'claimed' by an elder, they are safe from other vamps so long as that vampire doesn't get into a war with one of the other groups. Kinda the same way being in the mob makes you safe... so long as no one wants to do something stupid and start a war. And we all know from movies how that works out. I'd have to go all John Wick on them."

She smirked and teased, "So what am I in this analogy, your pet human? You'd go to war with them if they killed me?"

I knew she was fishing and only partly kidding with her question. She wanted to know what I felt toward her.

"Never a pet." I smiled as I said it, but the gravity of the discussion was not lost on her.

I continued, "Remember, I offered you a chance to walk away before you got in too deep, and you chose this." I gestured toward the door, "You could still leave now if you want; I could wipe your memory of the last three months well enough that no one could get the information from you. That would likely make you as safe as you can be at this point."

She sat down heavily on the couch and focused inward on her thoughts for a long moment before looking up. She was clearly considering it, which spoke volumes to how smart she was. I was happy to see she wasn't taking this lightly.

"No. I don't want that."

There was certainty in her eyes as she looked back up at me.

"I want this, and I'm not leaving. Do what you have to do to make me so they can't get the info out of me."

She stood up then, walked over to where I was sitting at the bar, and stood right before me. She was well inside my personal space.

"You know I want to be more than just your employee. I know that you know."

She stood there nervous but expectant.

I looked deep into her eyes and felt a connection, like a jolt of electricity down my spine - I could tell from the way she had responded to me that everything she said was true. How could anyone accept who I truly am without knowing?

Without hesitation, I reached up and caressed the back of her neck before tugging her toward me for a kiss. Our lips fit together perfectly in a long and passionate embrace. I hadn't experienced it in ages, but it reminded me of how normal life used to be as I felt old human stirrings once again. The kiss was powerful yet gentle, inviting but not demanding anything from either party. When we finally pulled away, there was contentment on her face.

My throat suddenly tightened with emotions, and I had to clear it before speaking. I took her hand in mine and held it gently, wishing I could do more than just offer a few words of assurance.

"I'll do what I can. Please stay in the Tower if I'm not with you so no one can get to you. It will take a few days to create an item that will protect you, and I will need to contact someone to see if we can test whether I can protect you from magical compulsion."

She smiled at me, silently expressing her faith that I would fulfill my promise.

It was a new relationship. The first one I had been in since becoming a vampire. Hell, if I was being honest, it was the first in at least a couple years before that.

I dated off and on in high school and then in college. Even so, I hadn't had time since graduation and starting my career. On top of that, before becoming a vampire, I had my friends circle, which took up most of my free time. That group had been so close and tight that the few girls I'd gone out with since college just hadn't worked out. If my friends disapproved and she didn't fit in with them, then I stopped dating them.

It might seem crazy, but that's just how tight we were.

At this moment, it hit me pretty hard that I couldn't introduce Heidi to my friends. I had a sudden and intense sense of loss that they were no longer in my life.

Damn, Queenie! If she hadn't made me into a vampire...

But she had, and this was my life now. Heidi was an unexpected bright spot in an otherwise lonely existence.

Queenie's compulsion pushed me to jump right in and work on new magic items to protect Heidi and Kat since they knew my secrets. But the part of me that was feeling those human emotions was saying, 'not today, Satan!'

I grinned at my new girlfriend, "The whole damned world might be falling apart, but how do you feel about taking a night off and just enjoying ourselves?"

The part of me controlled by the survival whammy was twitching like a caffeine addict needing their morning cup but screw that part... at least for a day.

CHAPTER 29
RELAX A LITTLE

Heidi smiled back at me, her eyes bright with excitement. "That sounds perfect," she said, and I felt a warmth in my chest at the sound of her voice.

I knew just the place. There was a small mom&pop pizza place close enough that was perfect for a quiet night out. Of course, I couldn't eat or drink, but I could enjoy it vicariously through Heidi's reactions. I knew it was possible for a vampire to eat thanks to seeing that elder, Mr. Schmidt, stuffing his face and relishing it, but I didn't know how to make it work.

The pizzeria had a dark and cozy atmosphere with a romantic feel. I had gone there a couple times back when I was visiting the city in my human days and always thought it would be a great date night place. Even though we were really just getting to know one another, I knew enough to understand she would enjoy cheap pizza in a romantic setting rather than hundred-dollar entrées at some fancy place.

I took Heidi's hand as we walked towards the restaurant and felt the electricity between us. It was like nothing I'd ever experienced before. I'd had flings and one-night stands, but this was different. I had been younger then and not looking for serious connections.

As we walked, we talked about our favorite books, music, and movies. I could see the passion in Heidi's eyes as she spoke about the books she loved, and I realized that I had so much to learn about her.

When we arrived at the restaurant, we were seated at a cozy table in the corner. We ordered a bottle of red wine and started talking about our families. I told her about my parents and my brother, who was still alive, and she shared stories about her family.

Apparently, her mother was Kat's sister, and they did not get along well. Her mother was disappointed that Heidi was going into business the way her 'childless spinster' of a sister had. Unfortunately, Heidi was just as driven as Kat, and the chances that she would settle down and produce grandchildren anytime soon were nil.

The mention of children put a damper on the conversation, not because it was too early in our relationship to talk about things like that, but because of my vampiric state. It suddenly occurred to us what our relationship would mean for her. There were some significant negative implications to dating or falling in love with a vampire.

Unless she someday decided to become a vampire, I would have to watch her grow old and die. For her part, it meant never having a family; no kids of her own.

We sat in silence for a long moment, each contemplating our choices. Eventually, she looked up at me and smiled.

"I'm young. Plenty of time to think about serious matters later. Besides, I might tire of you and toss you aside in a month." She was grinning as she teased me with her words.

I couldn't help but chuckle and remind her, "You've been working for me for weeks already, and you've only dug in deeper at the office. Next thing you know, you'll be trying to move into my house."

"What do you mean? I already live there! I've been sleeping on that cot in the spare office long enough that my back is starting to kill me, and I'm too young to have back pains!" She stuck her tongue out at me before taking another bite of her pizza.

"I know; that's why I'm teasing you about it!" I got serious, then added, "I know it's very sudden, and I don't mean for it to come across as anything, but maybe you should move in. At least until I can get you some protection. For now, I will assign Ralph and Jasper to guard you and Kat. Still, with us being this close, the minute the other vampires find out I'm in the city, it's going get serious for the people around me, and no one is closer to me than you."

It went without saying that Heidi would be the prime target since we were having this relationship, even if it was new and not entirely defined yet.

She looked around suddenly with a worried expression on her face. "Should we be talking about this stuff openly in public?"

I grinned and pointed to my eyes. "Aura sight. There's no one in here but humans and no listening devices. As long as we don't get loud, it should be fine.

She sat forward, looking into my eyes curiously. "Is that one of your abilities? You haven't ever really said what all you can do."

I shook my head. "No. Aura sight is a spell. I learned it was possible from that mage I told you about. The one I accidentally discovered when I tried to feed from him."

"Yeah, I bet that was embarrassing!" She chuckled at the look on my face.

"Hey, I learned a lot that day, all right!" I knew she was teasing and curious about me, so I gave her the rundown on what vampires could do compared to the stories. I mentioned that I had protections from the easy methods of killing vampires, but I didn't go into detail. I really liked Heidi and trusted her, but someone could capture her and take the knowledge from her mind, which would be very bad for my health.

She was fascinated by it all, and after she had heard it all, she asked the one question that I hadn't thought of but probably should.

"So, if Queenie got killed because her children got jealous of her abilities to do magic, then will you pass on magic to anyone you make someday?"

So far, my unlife has been filled with survival and establishing myself. I hadn't even considered wanting to bring someone into this supernatural world. Queenie had given me full access to her abilities when she created me, so I could make a vampire who could also do magic. But would I?

Queenie had certainly ordered that I not pass the magic to others, that doing so would mean my death. But then she also talked in terms of cursing people *down unto the seventh generation* and all that bullshit. The truth was I didn't know. If I cared about someone enough, then I might pass it on. Only time would tell, and I shared as much with Heidi, explaining my thoughts.

I could see in her eyes that an imaginary sign had just lit up over her head saying, "Challenge Accepted." Not that she had even decided she would want to be a vampire, but I was sure now that if she did, she would want the full deal.

Conversation after that went back to more mundane topics. That led to more hand-holding and cuddling. Eventually, we returned to the Tower, and I reluctantly let her retire to her office cot to sleep.

Everything else aside, she was doing a fantastic job with the interns on mapping the vampires.

We were starting to see some distinct patterns of movement to tell their regular schedules. More importantly, we had all suspected lairs located and marked. Not that some vamps might not have bolt-holes to run to if they got spooked, but for the most part, we were developing one heck of a detailed picture.

However, the next day, it seemed that my vampire mapping spell wasn't the only mystical detection field operating in the office.

I don't think Heidi told her aunt anything, but Kat seemed to sense the change in my relationship with her niece almost as soon as she came into the office the following day. She took one look at us and raised a challenging eyebrow, and pursed her lips in thought. A short time later, she pulled me into her office for a chat.

CHAPTER 30
PROTECTION MAGIC

BEING my employee didn't affect the looks she gave me or the warnings she offered should I hurt her niece. There was even mention of staking me if it came down to it.

She was joking, but there was an edge to it that you would expect under the circumstances.

I joked back that it wouldn't work. "I'm afraid you'd have to find another way to kill me. I've got magical protections against being staked through the heart."

Without missing a beat, she snapped back, "Is that so? I assume they protect against reaching your heart through your ribs or back, but tell me... do they protect your heart if the stake reaches it by being driven up your butt all the way to the chest cavity?"

She gave me the sweetest, most evil smile I think I'd ever seen. She might not be Heidi's mother, but she might as well be a mama bear protecting her cub.

Swallowing hard, I assured her that I had no intention of hurting her niece, and just like that, things went back to business as if nothing had ever happened.

I headed out to an internet café and used an anonymous email account to message George. "George, I would like to meet with you to discuss a magic performance. Could we meet at the Indian restaurant on Richmond?" I hit send without adding a name.

From there, I went to my workshop and started considering the defensive spell that might be able to block magical compulsion. With magic, it really was all about mental focus. I contemplated exactly how I wanted the protection to work. I considered the symbolism that might enhance such a spell. Historically, the Egyptian symbol of the Ankh, or Eye of Horus, was both for protection, and the rune Algiz was a Norse rune for protection. I planned. I prepared.

Finally, I began to work.

I created a platinum ring with an iron core, set with a hematite cabochon under which the rune for protection was carved. I associated more with the Norse heritage than Egyptian, so I figured it would be more powerful. That took me most of the night, and I chose to cast the spell at dawn, the time for hope. I spent 300 blood gems on the enchantment, which would make the defense quite potent. Considering mages can only cast at a much weaker level, I hoped that would make the ring capable of stopping their attempts.

Besides the protective magic, I spelled the ring to conceal its aura and deflect notice from those who might attempt harm to the wearer. I was afraid that the ring might also erode my own compulsion on Heidi, freeing her from my commands not to share my secrets. Still, I am pretty sure she willingly would want to keep those, so it was a trade-off.

It occurred to me that having such a protective device might be a damned good idea for me as well, especially since the typical meet and greet for vampires was to test each other's will through compulsion. Whoever was able to influence the other was the winner and, therefore, the boss. I would tackle that next.

I got back to the Tower about an hour after dawn and found Heidi just finishing up the shift from monitoring the map. I brought her over to my private part of the floor and into the bedroom, giving her access. I sat with her on the sunken couch, and we cuddled, neither of us saying anything for a while, just enjoying the closeness.

After a while, I sat forward, reached into my shirt pocket, and pulled out the ring. "I made something for you."

Yes, I know how that had to look; I was giving her a ring. I had only known her for a few weeks. However, it wasn't that kind of ring, and Heidi wasn't the sort of girl to take it the wrong way.

Even so, Heidi's eyes got big looking at the ring. "Wow. You made that? With magic or by hand?"

I grinned back, "Both. I was a jeweler for a while, so I made the physical item with old fashion skills and by hand. Then I enchanted it. This should protect you from magic or vampiric compulsion. So long as you aren't the target of someone trying to alter your mind, it is just a plain old ring, but if you run into a vampire and they look deeply into your eyes, their compulsion should not work. It might be a good idea to try and pretend to be hypnotized and vulnerable and pretend to answer their questions so they don't kill you. Vampires aren't allowed to leave a living witness to what they are."

She held out her right hand and let me place it on her finger. I had guessed pretty well on size, and it fit nicely. She had delicate fingers, so a size six seemed right.

"I love it. Thank you." She reached forward and gave me a tight hug, her arms around my shoulders. She leaned back and kissed me after a moment, and it was nice but not so passionate as earlier. This was more playful and a little casual.

I looked at her, "Are you able to turn the project over to the intern tonight and leave them to it after they get started?"

She nodded. 'Why, you wanna go on a date?" She asked.

I laughed. "Not quite. I thought you might want to see my workshop and keep me company while I make myself a protection item."

I got serious, "I should have met with that elder weeks ago, but I didn't want to do it until I felt prepared. Making myself a protection item should ensure I can walk away safely."

Heidi nodded, "I'd be happy to keep you company. I want to see you enchant something. It sounds fascinating."

"I chuckled; maybe less interesting than you think, but the company would be welcome. I will be engraving mostly. The casting itself is pretty quick."

I held her hand, and we drove over to my maker space, although I cast an illusion on us and took an Uber to the café on the street next to my building. I explained what I was doing so she would know the lengths to which I regularly went to keep my secrets.

"I'm paranoid, but it is safety focused. In my case, people would be out to get me if they discover my identity."

She squeezed my hand in sympathy. "I understand, and I don't mind."

From there, I made her invisible and used my own magic item to walk the block over to my building. We entered through the back door, using magic to move the steel bar on the inside. When the door was safely barred again with us on the inside, I dropped the illusion and invisibility and showed her around my workshop.

The main floor was one big room separated into work areas for different types of work. Then I took Heidi downstairs to my jewelry shop. She was pretty amazed by everything and asked tons of questions as I took my watch off and removed one link. I placed it into the vise with a special putty to keep it from moving while I engraved.

Thanks to my strength and vampiric precision, I can engrave almost anything without needing to use a hammer on the chisels, making my cuts cleaner and more artistic. The outside was already engraved with scrollwork to match the rest of the band, but the underside was blank. I quickly carved the rune of protection around the perimeter and drilled out a space to set a hematite, which was also inscribed with the rune.

That took a couple of hours, during which we talked. I asked her about her life, where she grew up, and her experiences. It was the kind of conversation any new couple had at the start of their relationship.

When everything was ready, I took her onto the roof. I cast the spell at the moment when the sun was directly overhead, as I felt that had symbolism for me against vampires in particular. It was the moment of brightest light which seemed appropriate.

I ignited two hundred blood gems inside me, their power turning a fiery blood red as it merged with my aura. I let it glow visibly before sending the power into the link from the watch band. As always, there was an earthy feel to the power as it swelled. When it left my body, it turned metallic and gold, and the power sang as it flowed, a soft song of a million voices all whispering in unison, an indescribable harmony at the edge of hearing.

Then the air around the link was filled with metallic gold light, growing as hot as a blacksmith's forge in the space between my hands. The power shone like a dying star, swirling reds and oranges and burning. As it ended, the light filled the area with a muted heat, warming us as if we stood before a campfire.

Okay, I admit, I was playing up the effects to impress Heidi. It was always impressive, but I encouraged the magic to be more *expressive* during the process than normal.

When it was done, I took her back inside and locked up the building, securing it so it could only be entered by magic. Then, I reassembled the watch in the basement and put it back on.

I kept having these moments where I felt more secure and ready to face challenges, but then I would learn of a new threat and have to go through it all over again. I resigned myself to accepting that this would be a common theme as I lived my hopefully long and extended life. I smiled and kissed Heidi, and took her hands.

"Ready to travel by teleport?"

Her eyes got big, but then we were in the Tower between one heartbeat and the next before she could even say a word.

I chuckled, "See, it's not so bad." Then I frowned slightly, "It's not cheap, though; that little jump taking you with me cost a couple hours' worth of work getting the blood to power the magic. Cheap compared to enchanting, though."

She made a worried expression when I said that, realizing what all this magic meant. Real people whose blood was taken.

"I want to make sure you understand the cost of my existence. I have to take blood from people to fuel my magic and keep me alive. I won't hurt them. In fact, I try to help each one I take from, but that doesn't change what I am doing."

I squeezed her hand again. "I won't lie to you. I want things to be honest between us so you have no regrets later."

She let go and put her arms around me. "If you were someone else, someone who didn't care about people and not hurting them, I think it would bother me a lot. I wouldn't be able to do this. Still, I've seen enough of you that I know you would never be like the vampires in the movies, casually killing or cruelly draining people of their lives."

"Thanks, that means a lot. I worry about where all this might lead me eventually, but I try to keep my humanity."

I smiled brightly then and changed the subject. "Tell you what, I just discovered how to digest food. I can eat and drink human food again, so how about we celebrate by going out to dinner tonight?"

She grinned, "That sounds fantastic!"

CHAPTER 31

DINNER AND A RELATIONSHIP?

THAT NIGHT, we ate steak at one of Houston's most expensive steak restaurants. We had a private dining room, and it was amazing! That first bite was ecstasy, blood might taste good to me now because of being a vampire, but my taste buds came alive as I ate. I didn't look forward to what would come later. I certainly hadn't missed that during the year and a half since my undeath. But for now, this was bliss.

Heidi seemed amused, witnessing my enjoyment of the meal.

"What? I literally haven't eaten in a year and a half, and a Michelin chef prepared this. I don't think I ever had a steak this good, even when I was alive." I grinned around my next bite and made exaggerated chewing motions and *nom, nom, nom* sounds.

While the food was in front of us, I had a hard time conversing. I was too enraptured by every bite. I knew I wasn't a great date, but Heidi seemed amused and content to watch me enjoy myself. Not that she didn't eat her own share of tasty food, but it was little more than a nice treat to her.

Once I had satisfied myself, things became more like a regular date. We talked about life. She told me about her plans. She was taking a break from college before her final semester, using it to learn about business from her aunt Kat.

I couldn't help but chime in, "That's honestly pretty smart. I hired Kat to run things for me, but she was more than qualified to be a C-suite executive at a Fortune 500 company. She was introduced to me by a mutual acquaintance and seemed like a great fit. You could definitely do worse than spending a semester acting as her intern, even if you don't get some fancy resume content out of it."

She smirked and shook her head in amused denial. "You just don't know how to sell it. I am an intern to the Chief Executive Officer for Orotech Mining and Survey, a multinational Oil, Gas, and Minerals exploration firm with holdings estimated to be worth over two billion dollars."

Chuckling, she took a drink of her wine and added, "I know you aren't really trying to get rich from your company, but don't sell it short. In a few years, you'll have some of the big guys knocking down your door, wanting to buy you out."

That sounded like a wild exaggeration, and I knew for a fact that the company wasn't worth more than 50 million, and that was stretching it.

"Isn't that a bit over the top? How do you figure two billion dollars? I think the real balance sheet is more like 15 million right now."

Heidi waved her hand dismissively. "The company has claims staked in Alaska, Greenland, Canada, and somewhere in South America – I forget which country."

She gave me a serious look before continuing, "You can say those claims are worth whatever you want, but I am being realistic. Those Greenland claims alone have gemstone deposits that could be worth hundreds of millions. Will they ever get mined? Maybe or maybe not, but based on the samples that were returned and the geology of the region, you could find investors that would fund the actual setup of the operation. In the meantime, your company owns the rights to the minerals on that land. You don't have billions in the bank that you could actually spend. Still, I think it is legitimate to value your land rights over one billion. So, on paper, my time with the company will look very impressive to future employers."

She lowered her head and batted her eyelashes at me. "If you don't hire me and give me a career."

He laughed and teased, "Ah, so you are a gold digger, and only after my money! And here I thought you wanted me for my body!"

She stuck her tongue out but grinned. "Definitely your body! And the way you wolfed down that steak before and made such loud chewing noises... Soo sexy!"

I threw my napkin at her, but I knew she was kidding. We were having a wonderful time, which was a little weird to me. I had never fallen into such an easy relationship as I was with Heidi. She wasn't demanding anything of me, and I wasn't making any of her. I'm not sure what we had could even be called a relationship yet, but my intuition was telling me it wouldn't be long.

After the meal, we returned to the Tower and spent the night in my bed, cuddling and letting her fall asleep in my arms. I enjoyed the experience, although I couldn't really sleep at night.

I got up around 3 am to give Tom a ring using a burner phone I kept for anonymous calls. "Been a while, Tom. My apologies to Thaddeus that I wasn't able to get back to you before now. I needed to travel a little, but now I'm back in town and would like to meet your elder at his convenience. I'd be happy to meet him at his club if he wants, just let me know the day.

He agreed to pass on the request, and I said I would call him back the next night.

CHAPTER 32
GOOD 'OL BOYS CLUB

When I called back early the following evening, Tom said I was welcome to attend his elder at his club that evening.

He seemed nervous and was overly polite to me on the phone. I would have been confused by that before, but now I knew that was because he was unsure if the political landscape would change after tonight. If I bested his master in the contest of wills significantly, then by standard rules, he would serve me by extension because his boss would serve me. Not that I wanted responsibility for them. Even if I bested Thaddeus, I didn't want him to serve me other than to leave me to my business and not bother me.

With those thoughts, I arrived at a rather clichéd gentlemen's club. The old-school English gentlemen's club was all hardwood, leather, and cigar smoke. I was shown in by a freakin' butler wearing a long-tailed black coat and white bow tie, for goodness sake. Talk about pretentiousness. It was by willpower alone that I avoided rolling my eyes. I was sure there were cameras trained on me.

I was shown to a cozy lounge to await being summoned by the master. I was sure someone was scrambling to do a facial recognition search in order to pull up every bit of information on me they could before I was escorted to see Thaddeus. I hadn't given them a chance to figure out who I was before now, so that had to make them nervous.

About 15 minutes passed before I was finally taken to a cozy library where Thaddeus sat in a leather chair, a cigar in an ashtray next to him, curling smoke into the air. To my vampire senses, it was awful. It put me off, but then I suspected that might be intentional.

Still, I wondered about a man who would do that to himself. It had to dull his own senses unless he had somehow developed an immunity to its effects. I tried to let none of that show on my face as I smiled politely in greeting, stopping a comfortable distance away.

Thaddeus stood and looked me over and put on a long-suffering face. "Well, I have to admit, I did not expect the new elder in town to be none other than Daniel Fox, founder and owner of Orotech Mining and Survey."

He shook his head the way a principal might when looking at a student who had been brought before him for discipline.

"Some elders might find it quite rude that another has come into their home and not made greeting for well over a year."

He was being careful. He was telling me he wasn't happy with this situation but not outright declaring enmity since he did not yet know how powerful I might be. He basically knew two things, I beat his minion handily, and I had been lurking in his city for a year and a half doing who knew what? That had to worry him.

I smiled in turn, spreading my hands in a dismissing gesture, "On the contrary, I would think another way to view it would be as a show of great respect for yourself and the other elders in the city. Proof that this new resident can and will live peacefully and not disturb your interests."

It gave him a way to save face for the disrespect I had shown by not presenting myself on arrival. Still, he could interpret that as me seeking to placate him, which would indicate weakness. I, too, had shown him that I could be cautious before our relative power was known.

We were like two wolves circling one another, having accidentally met in the forest, each cautious until they determined who was stronger. In the meantime, I wasn't sure about this guy. He seemed old and stuffy, very traditional, and the sort that would maintain discipline among his underlings. On the other hand, he didn't seem aggressive or like someone who was hoping for a fight, and I took that as a good sign.

He smiled and nodded as if pleased with my answer. "Well said, Daniel. If I may call you that?" He cocked his head, "Is that your real name, or would you prefer to be called something else. I, myself, have several names that the mortal world knows me by." He was digging for information.

I grinned back, "Daniel Fox is the only one I own. You may call me Daniel, as that is what my friends call me." We were dancing in the way sword fighters did. Parry and thrust, taking each other's measure before attacking.

He smiled, and it seemed genuine for the first time. "I think I might like you, Daniel. But I'm not a man to put off the inevitable; we must determine who is stronger, so let us be about it."

He took a step closer and looked into my eyes, focusing his will on me. I felt it, and he was strong, much stronger than Tom. But I had two advantages, my new protection item prevented his compulsion from taking hold. Then there was the fact that I was created by THE original vampire, who lived thousands of years before this guy's ancestors were spawned, and she whammied me to have the will to survive.

I could feel my mind protection item bolstering my mind, but that didn't mean I could beat a multi-hundred year old vampire. I focused on my own mojo and pushed back, but it was like pushing a boulder up a mountain. I tried willing the other man to submit. It wasn't easy.

Compared to his underling, Tom, this guy was like Fort Knox compared to a cardboard box fort. I reminded myself of each and every little victory, of the things I had accomplished since becoming a vampire. I put my fears into it. I pumped everything I had into it, knowing that the only way to achieve the peace I wanted was to beat this guy.

It was the most challenging thing I'd done since becoming a vampire. An eternal minute passed before I finally felt my will slide into place, slicing through his and shutting him down. His eyes glazed over slowly, and he went slack.

I sighed, relaxing.

Well, that was a relief. I had hoped but did not expect this outcome. While I had him at my mercy, I gave the command I cared about.

"You will allow me to live in peace and not cause me any trouble. You will notify me if you learn of anyone who wishes to do me harm."

Then I released him.

The focus and intelligence came back into his eyes, followed by shock and then resignation.

"Well, it seems you are more powerful than I expected. You must either be very old, or your maker was. My own creator is nearly 1000 years old; he was made during the battle of 1066."

Even now, he was fishing for information. I raised an eyebrow, "I see. Yes, my maker is a bit older than that."

He nodded in understanding. "So, what do you want from me? Do you expect me to serve you now?"

I chuckled, "No. I don't want your service. I don't even want you to let others know what happened between us. In fact, I would appreciate it if you let people think that we fought each other to a standoff and then came to an understanding. As far as you are concerned, I am free to live in the city and mind my own business. I am to be left out of vampire politics."

There was genuine surprise in his eyes. "You really don't want anything from me?"

"No. I just want to be left in peace. My mission here is to keep an eye on the oil and gas industry and watch for anything that might intentionally upset it. Beyond that, I really just want to be left alone."

A thought occurred to me. "There is one thing, I suppose, let's consider a five-block area around the Tower to be my feeding grounds and not to be encroached on."

Thaddeus shrugged. "I will leave you in peace and spread the message you are to be left alone, that you are a powerful elder and my equal. I will let my people know that the Tower area is yours. I can't speak for the other vampires of the city, however; you will need to meet with the other elders for that and get each of their cooperation." He chuckled. "I almost wish I could see their faces when you do. None of them could best me the way you did, which means you will likely control them as well."

His face took on a dark look as something occurred to him. "Be careful of them. There are those among them who won't take kindly to being beaten. Their egos won't support not being the strongest. I think that only the fact that I was here first prevented a war between us."

I could sit and get comfortable now that I had won, but even though he seemed to be taking his own defeat well, there was no need to chance it. Although, admittedly, I was tempted to pick his brain for information that only an elder like him could provide. Still, I was more worried that I would give too much information away. Every question I asked revealed ignorance on my part, and that would build a picture of me for him to pick apart over time, and he could figure out that I wasn't really who I pretended to be. Why would the child of some ancient and powerful being not know basic things about vampire society?

No, it was better to preserve the mystique and mystery around who I was than to satisfy some curiosity.

"That will be fine. I appreciate the warning and will take steps to ensure they don't make a tragic mistake." I gestured to the door. "I will see myself out. Perhaps we can meet again in the future."

He smiled, "That would be good. I would be interested to hear more of your story; it is rare to have someone to speak with that understands the nature of our positions."

I bowed my head in acknowledgment and parting. "Be well, Thaddeus."

On leaving, I headed back to the Tower, relieved to have made it through that meeting without losing everything I had built. I wasn't exactly thrilled with having been turned into this. Still, I had to be thankful to Queenie for at least making me something that wouldn't be at the bottom of the supernatural food chain.

Still, I felt good about the evening. I now had proof that, at least in terms of vampire mojo, I was on par with the elders of a big city like Houston.

There was still one big question that I hadn't asked that needed answering. The compulsion Queenie had put on me demanded it. I needed to know if the elders had contact with the Cabal. Now that I was publicly known to be an elder and in the city, would I have an unexpected visit? Would they have expectations of me for being an elder? Or worse, would they know I was a fraud because they wouldn't have any record of my creation? Hell, did they even have such records?

If they were as powerful and pervasive as people implied, then I suspected they would, which could spell trouble.

CHAPTER 33
AN UNEXPECTED INVITATION

I VERY NEARLY GOT THE answer to the question of whether the Cabal would show up on my doorstep in the scariest way possible. Or at least, that was what I thought was happening.

Two days after meeting with Thaddeus, I received an invitation to a private restaurant. It was one that I had never heard of before and was inside an old Victorian mansion in the Heights area just northwest of Downtown. The time was set for 11 pm that night, and it was signed Davin D'Argonne.

That was not a name I was familiar with. In all my research of vampires in the city, he had not been among them. And yet, there was an ever so faint hint of blood to the paper that gave me the impression that it was related to vampire business. If that were the case, then who could this be?

My thoughts went to the Cabal since I had just been thinking of them after meeting with Thaddeus. That made me wonder if this could be a representative of that shadowy organization. If so, was he here to investigate me? I was an apparent elder who had just shown up out of the blue and had an unknown background.

That made me wary and tempted to avoid the meeting. Except I didn't back down from situations like this, not anymore. Besides, I had put so much effort into establishing a home here I didn't want to run. On the other hand, I also wanted to avoid starting a war with unknown enemies. I decided the wise move would be to go to the meeting and see what they said. It's not like I couldn't teleport somewhere on the opposite side of the globe if things went terribly.

I chuckled nervously at that thought and knocked on the nearest piece of wood to ward off bad luck.

Thanks to my storage rings, I was always armed. My enchanted katana would be handy if things went sideways.

When I arrived at the restaurant, I was greeted at the front door by a woman in a period dress, although her dress was not so poofy as to make guiding customers through the various rooms difficult. She led me upstairs to what once had been a bedroom but was now a private dining room with a single table and two chairs in the center of the room. To the side were a pair of comfortable leather seats for sitting and having a conversation.

It was an interesting concept. The woman had informed me that each of the former rooms was a private space set up for various-sized parties and invited me to join their dining club. Apparently, it was exclusive, but having been invited once granted me the right to petition for membership.

I took a seat in one of the two leather chairs, seeing that my host had not yet arrived. The hostess offered to pour me a drink, and I accepted.

Alcohol was not terribly pleasant to my sensitive vampire palate. On the other hand, it also let me taste and experience the full range of whatever a particular spirit had to offer. As a mortal, I couldn't tell you good Scotch from bad Bourbon; it was all just whisky to me.

Now, however, I could appreciate all of those tasting notes people talked about. The McAllen 18 that the server poured really did have subtle hints of spice and dried fruits, and I could definitely tell it had been aged in Sherry casks. I wasn't particularly sure I wanted to drink the stuff given how strong the alcohol was, but I could appreciate them now.

I was thinking these thoughts when the door opened and a guy, maybe seventeen or eighteen years old, walked in. Except, he had the poise and confidence of an ancient vampire rather than a teen not even out of high school. He also wore a custom-tailored suit. I didn't recognize the brand, but I could tell it probably cost more than your average car.

I stood and nodded politely. "Davin D'Argonne?"

The vampire smiled in acknowledgment. "Thank you for meeting me. I only visit Houston occasionally, but I wanted to speak with you while in town."

He shook my hand, human-style, and his skin was smooth and cool to the touch, like my own, but there was power in his grip. It wasn't a contest of strength or intimidation; he wasn't trying to show his strength. However, I could tell he was stronger than any vamp I had encountered. I was glad he didn't seem hostile, and I hoped he wasn't a Cabal agent about to confront me about my mysterious background.

I gestured to the seat opposite the one I had picked. "I'm not sure what this is about, but this is an interesting choice of restaurant."

After he sat, he sighed heavily. "It belongs to my daughter, Mara."

I nodded politely, but I could tell there was something troubling him when he mentioned his daughter. There was a sadness or hopelessness to his tone.

I ventured a glance at him using my aura sight and was not shocked to see that his aura was significantly stronger and more vibrant than Thaddeus'. From what I had learned, the Houston elder was around 400 years old. If I was judging things correctly, this vampire was probably twice that or more.

I suddenly felt like it would be a terribly bad idea to test my will against his. I had the magic item that would protect me from domination. Still, I was pretty sure I could not win against Davin D'Argonne without using magic. He would know immediately that I was cheating.

Waiting for him to speak seemed like the prudent thing to do, and he soon got to the point. "Not that I wouldn't mind dining with you, but I did ask you here for a purpose, and if you don't mind, I'd like to satisfy my curiosity before we relax."

Uh, oh. Was he about to try to mojo me?

He became very serious as he began his questioning. "You arrived in this city in September of the previous year, correct?"

My stomach sank. Thaddeus and the other vampires of the city probably didn't know that, although they could deduce it if their investigators looked at the correct paperwork for when my company started business or if they discovered the property I owned and checked with the county registrar. Still, I didn't think it would be a good idea to lie to this man.

"That's right. I don't recall the exact date I arrived, but it was definitely in September. It's been almost two years."

Davin nodded as if he expected that answer. "Have you seen this woman?"

He pulled out a smartphone from his pocket and showed me a picture. The girl in the image stood around 5'6", and despite the picture being taken at night, the lights showed that she had long auburn hair that fell around her shoulders in waves. She was beautiful and had an amused smirk on her face, as if she had just heard something funny right as the picture was snapped.

She wasn't someone I would forget.

"I'm sorry, but I've never seen her before. Is that your daughter?"

"Yes." The man sighed deeply as if he had hoped very much to receive a different answer. "Your arrival in the city is merely coincidental, then. As close as I can tell, she disappeared at the beginning of June of that year, on the 6th. When I heard that you came to the city at around the same time..."

Now I understood what was happening. This wasn't some Cabal interview. It was a father whose child had gone missing looking for answers. I wished I could help him and said as much.

Davin looked sad but resigned. "I will continue my search then. I drop by every couple of months to check up on her restaurant and follow up on any new leads there might be."

I was a little afraid to ask, fearful of angering such a powerful elder, but I couldn't help myself.

"Do you know how it happened? Was she kidnapped, or do you have any suspects? I would be happy to help if I am able."

For a long moment, Davin looked at me as if he were trying to decide something important. Finally, he nodded, a decision having been made.

"She seems to have disappeared from her bed. Her door was bolted and could not be entered from the outside. Her assistant is sure she entered and locked the door before retiring for the day. The assistant grew worried when Mara didn't come out the next day or respond to knocks."

"The assistant contacted me three days later, and I came immediately to check on Mara. She was simply gone. No evidence of forced entry or that anyone exited the room. I would suspect mages, but I have ways of checking, and there was no evidence of magic being used to gain entry. Needless to say, my daughter is not able to do magic."

It was odd for him to add that last comment. Did he suspect something about me, or was that just Queenie's compulsion-based paranoia rearing its ugly head?

Davin shook his head sadly, "In any case, thank you for your offer. I do not believe there is anything you can do. However, if you do learn of anything, I would appreciate you contacting me. As a new elder in the city, I am sure you will be particularly suited to hearing things as you get settled in."

He handed me a business card that had a lion on one side and an email address on the other; no name or anything else.

He made to leave, but just as he was about to step through the door, he turned back to me and casually said, "You are covered in magic items... Few, even among the most powerful of modern vampires, could amass such a trove of artifacts. That makes me quite curious about who your sire is to have given you so much."

I froze like a deer in headlights.

How could I even respond to that? For that matter, how could he see them? He was the oldest vampire I had met. Did he have some ability that I needed to be aware of, or did he have something like my aura detection magic item?

Luckily, he didn't seem to expect a response from me and just gave me an amused smile.

"Perhaps we can discuss that next time I am in town, but for now, please do keep your ears open for any mention of my dear Mara."

Before my brain could catch up to the surprise revelation, he had gone.

Note to self: develop a spell to hide your magic items better!

I was scheduled to start meeting with the other elders of the city, and now I was paranoid there might be ones among them with similar abilities to detect my magic items.

CHAPTER 34
JURY OF MY PEERS

I WASN'T able to come up with something to hide my magic items on such short notice, and I wasn't about to meet with a bunch of unknown and possibly hostile elders without them. That meant I just had to brave it.

The other thing I had hoped to solve hadn't been addressed either.

I had no way of answering the Cabal question at this point. Still, perhaps, if I could dominate one of the other elders by a large enough margin, then I could ask. I doubted that would be possible, however. The test against Thaddeus' willpower hadn't been so easy that I'd feel confident exposing my own ignorance and then commanding him to forget.

The next night, I called and asked Thaddeus to broker an introduction for me to Jaquelyn, the next elder on my list. When I saw her, she struck me as being one of the most normal of them all. Thaddeus was helpful in confirming my observation. Having her on my side would make it 2 of 9.

I met her that night at the Museum of Natural History, where she was hosting a charity event. As before, she was elegant in her appearance and dressed as a sophisticated socialite, but she had a bearing that suggested she was a woman who was comfortable with who she was and sure of herself.

She greeted me with a smile that said no matter what was about to happen; it wouldn't change her. She excused herself from a guest, saying she needed to speak to a new donor, then nodded toward a side door. I followed her through to find a room with a table for tallying the donation pledges. She showed me all the hospitality expected from a well-mannered Southern lady, or in her case, an English noblewoman.

"Mr. Fox, I presume; I am Jacquelyn Fitzroy. Welcome to Houston. I trust the city has been kind to you so far?"

I bowed politely and smiled warmly. "It has indeed. Thank you for the welcome. May I call you Jacquelyn, or would you prefer Lady Fitzroy?"

She smiled, seeing that I was being polite and observing the niceties.

"Jacquelyn is fine." Gesturing around the room, "I apologize that I do not have more comfortable surroundings to greet you, but Thaddeus suggested we meet sooner rather than later."

I frowned slightly, "Then let me apologize in turn. I did not mean for our mutual friend to rush the meeting. Nonetheless, we are here, so I appreciate you taking time away from your event to meet me. I won't keep you long. I just wanted to introduce myself. Please let me donate to your cause while I am here as well."

I could tell she was warming to me, seeing that I was making an effort. "Thank you, that would be most kind."

Then she frowned, "I detest these things, but there is no avoiding the unpleasant necessity of the testing."

I shrugged, "That is up to you. I tested myself against Thaddeus, and he found me a suitable addition to the ranks of the city's elders. I do not feel compelled to test myself against you if you find it unpleasant. All I wish is to live peacefully and unbothered in the city."

She raised a delicate eyebrow. "That's quite refreshing, but I am afraid I am not prepared to cede some of the best shopping in the city. I understand from Thaddeus you wish to claim a five-block radius around the Tower."

"That need not be an obstacle; you may shop and feed there if you wish. I simply want to keep out the others from the area I make my home. If you were to inform your followers that the area is mine, that is all I ask."

I was hoping to have at least one meeting in which I could simply make an ally without having to dominate them.

She cocked her head in consideration. "Very well. I know my relative strength compared to Thaddeus, and I prefer avoiding the unpleasantness of testing. I will ensure my vassals do not enter your domain. In return, you may feed in my area of the city. This would be acceptable as it effectively changes nothing for me other than restricting my vassals."

The rest of the meeting was more pleasantries and careful politeness. I did make a $100k donation to Jaquelyn's museum renovation project, and we parted official allies. Though neither of us trusted the other, it was a start.

Each meeting that followed went somewhere between those two. I did have to test my strength against five of the others and beat them all, compelling them to leave me in peace and stay out of my section of the city.

I did keep looking for an opportunity to bring up the Cabal since these were the most likely vampires to actually know them or have ties to them. Over the course of the eight meetings, I never got my answer, and even the mention of the Cabal was met with nervousness and a quick change of subject.

The one time I tried to bring them up a second time, the elder declared the interview over but hastily proclaimed that she knew their rules and would not break them. As if I were somehow testing her and suggesting she was disloyal.

It didn't give me any concrete information. Still, it did tell me that even powerful vampires who ruled part of a major city like Houston would quake at the mention of that organization's name.

I had spent so long building this home that I did not want to lose it all due to some shadowy group and breaking rules I didn't even know existed.

Again I put aside thoughts of the Cabal, for now, unable to learn more. Unfortunately, two elder meetings hadn't gone so smoothly.

CHAPTER 35

SO MUCH FOR THE EASY ONES

THE ONLY TWO that were difficult were Mr. Schmidt and Mrs. Theriot. Schmidt required both compulsion and convincing that I was not someone to be fucked with. He seemed prideful and slippery, such that I worried he would find some loophole in my compulsion to cause me trouble. I convinced him by naming off every one of his lieutenants and sub-lieutenants and telling him where they were at that exact moment.

"If I find myself with any headache, you will be the first I look to. If necessary, I will destroy your organization down to the last man and do it in a single night of knives. You will only survive long enough to realize everything you've built has been obliterated. Do we understand one another?"

He gave me a reluctant and grudging bow. "As you say, Elder Fox. What is it you wish from my organization?"

"Nothing so long as you respect my territory and avoid causing me difficulties. Our interests do not overlap, so I am content to let you continue as before. Do not give me cause to regret that decision."

He seemed surprised to get off so lightly and bowed again in the way a Nazi officer might to a superior, all sharp and precise. I really did not have a good impression of him. That bow wasn't the only thing about him that screamed Nazi, and I don't just mean he was a bad person. I mean, I think he really was a German officer in WW2. I wasn't sure what part of the Third Reich he belonged to, but I was betting the SS.

Honestly, I wanted to put him down, but I didn't want to upset the balance in the city and cause a power vacuum that could start a war. Also, I wasn't a murderer. Maybe he was reformed from his old days...

I doubted that, but I would keep an eye on him, and he might end up fatally dead some night in the future.

I didn't really like the idea of becoming some kind of supernatural policeman, keeping order among the vampires. My whole goal had been to move to this city and quietly blend in and exist peacefully. I didn't want to bother anyone or be bothered. Then I met a former Nazi vampire elder or the rapist thugs that worked for Mrs. Theriot.

Which, by the way, now made much more sense. Thinking back to that little misadventure, the assholes had talked about sending a message to *Jackie* from Theriot. I was 99% sure that *Jackie* was elder Jaquelyn, who had been the most agreeable and human of all the vampires I'd met so far. Even if Theriot's thugs hadn't been vampires torturing a human woman, I would still be inclined to support Jaquelyn just because she seemed decent. She was spending her unlife running charity events to support art and history museums.

Needless to say, I didn't walk into the meeting with Mrs. Theriot with an unbiased attitude. That's not to say I didn't reserve judgment. I had hoped she would turn out to be all right. Maybe she and the other elder had some personal feud. Not that such a thing would have justified what Theriot had ordered done to a mortal.

Still, I wanted things to turn out better for no reason other than because I wanted to live in peace and not get involved any further than I already had.

Sadly, that wasn't to be. From the moment I walked into the neutral meeting spot, she struck me as off. We were supposed to come alone; that was how these meetings were supposed to go. However, she had two followers with her. One was a man, and the other a woman, but both looked like... I don't know what they looked like.

They wore scant clothing and fawned on Theriot like they were crack addicts, and she was their next fix. It was disturbing the way they behaved, both subservient and manic at the same time. Worst of all, they wore collars with silver chains attached.

If this had been anyone else, I would have thought it was just some weird bondage fetish thing, but not with this vampire holding their leashes. They didn't quite have the glassy look of someone being actively dominated with vampiric *mojo*, but it wasn't far off. And that was the other thing about this. Those were vampires, not mortals. I knew from experience that you could whammy a vampire and put them under compulsion, but to use that ability to make people behave like that?

I strongly suspected that those two had not chosen their current lifestyle willingly. I was also 100% sure that Theriot had brought them here as a psychological ploy to intimidate me and not so subtly tell me what my fate would be if I crossed her.

I wasn't going to be scared of such blatant tactics. Besides, I had my handy magic item that would prevent my mind from being dominated.

Theriot tried to strut around for a bit and made a show of dismissing her pets before she slithered over to where I waited impatiently. Neither of us spoke but looked warily at one another for a moment before getting down to business. We each pitted our wills against the other in a contest that went on several times as long as any other battle of mojo I had had before. No matter how hard I pushed, I could not break through. I even spent three blood gems to empower the mojo with magic, and it still failed.

I was not able to dominate her, but it wasn't a matter of her will. I detected magic on her; she had an item preventing domination, just as I did. We circled one another as we spoke.

"Ssso you come into de city and seek to take partsss of it from me." She spoke in a sibilant way, in her thick New Orleans accent. It was as if a Cajun was speaking parseltongue.

Like Schmidt, this woman rubbed me the wrong way. Something about her screamed that I could trust her as far as I could trust an alligator to guard a wounded chicken.

"I want nothing from you but to be left in peace and that you and your people avoid my territory. I have met with all the other elders, and they support my claim."

I wasn't sure what to do. This woman clearly had mage backing. Her aura was pure vampire, so the magic could not have been her own. I just wanted to be left alone, exactly as I said. Still, she was the type that would perceive any weakness as an opportunity to attack, so I went on the offensive first.

"That bauble you have is very impressive. Would you care to take it off and try your will against mine again? Congratulations on finding a witch or mage to make it for you, by the way."

I was surprised that the accusation alone didn't provoke her to attack immediately. If it got out that she had such a thing, I doubted she would survive long. Every elder in the city would go after her if they knew.

She grinned, but it wasn't a pleasant one. "I tink not. Does you believe I am a fool?"

I laughed darkly. "Not even a little bit. But I sense ill intent from you. Tell me, how would the other elders feel if they knew you had magic protecting your will from their testing? I wonder if they might decide to challenge you a second time?"

Her eyes narrowed. "You threaten me?"

"Openly, but I doubt you appreciate that. You seem to be the knife-in-the-back kind. I'm just pointing out that if I sense any negative action directed at me or mine or your people enter my territory, your position in the city will not survive long."

My smile had no friendliness in it. "We can live in peace together, or you can fall. Your choice. The only reason I don't kill you right now is the chaos it would cause. I would be forced to step in and take action, and that's not why I came to this city. If you wish to take off that magic trinket, I will gladly pit my will against yours and settle this the traditional way."

She hissed at me. Literally hissed!

"I will not. Very well, den, you keep out of my sssight and I will ssstay out of yoursss."

Every 'S' she spoke was drawn out like she was exaggerating it on purpose. That might work on others to make them afraid, thinking she was some kind of voodoo snake woman, but it made me laugh in her face.

Unfortunately, she was not a laughing matter; she was the most dangerous person I had met in the city. I suspected she was weaker than the other elders, maybe even a fraud about her elder status. Otherwise, why use the willpower protection item? Still, I felt a definite sense of danger from her.

I vowed to keep a close eye on her from now on and find out her source of magic. If she could get a mage to cast protection for her, she might be able to get them to cast offensively against my people or me. That galvanized my decision to work on offensive magic and prepare to face a mage in a fight. I didn't want to become a vampiric enforcer putting down the bad ones, but she might force me to do it.

I replied, "Done. The bargain is struck. We will avoid each other's domains. See that you do not break that agreement." I did not want to kill her, but I was prepared to drop her right there if she hesitated to agree.

"Done."

She hissed again and backed out the door, not turning her back on me. Her two pets slinked after her like lost puppies or addicts needing the source of their addiction.

Melodramatic much? I thought.

I returned that night to the Tower and informed Heidi to have the teams concentrate on getting info on Theriot and Schmidt.

I had a bad feeling about Theriot even before meeting her, thanks to that encounter with her thugs. Now, however, I was sure. She was bad news, and the city would definitely be better off without someone like that. My gut was telling me she was a threat that needed to be eliminated. Still, I hesitated, not wanting to cause chaos in the city. My desire to live quietly and not get involved was being sorely tempted.

I would have to see what I could do to protect myself and my people from reprisals.

CHAPTER 36

A VAMPIRE, A MAGE, AND A RABBI WALK INTO A AR...

A FEW DAYS LATER, my mage acquaintance finally responded to my email. It said simply, "Thursday 8 pm."

Well, at least he was available. In the meantime, I created a spell I thought might shield me from magic attacks just to be safe and another against fire. It was hard to figure that out since I had no one to test it with. If only George were someone I could trust, but at this point, I couldn't trust any mage.

Thursday evening, I cast a spell to give me truth sense and disguised my aura as that of a pure vampire since I now knew what those should look like. I hoped George hadn't cast any kind of aura sight on me last time, or he'd know something was different. I may have been the first vamp he'd seen, so he might not know what a vampire aura was supposed to look like.

I arrived and had my two bodyguards sitting in a van in the parking lot with sniper rifles just in case I gave the signal, or they saw shit go down.

My first mild surprise was that George was not alone. He had an older man with him that reminded me for all the world like an old Jewish rabbi. He seemed to be that sort of scholarly gentleman that loved to argue over fine details of scripture. I don't know why; that was just my impression. Maybe it was the sleeveless sweater with a shirt and tie beneath and the glasses perched on his nose. Whatever it was, I didn't sense immediate danger from him, just cautious interest.

I should add that he definitely had the aura of a mage, and sitting next to George, I could tell he was stronger. The aura was more vibrant and deeper in color.

Looking to my mage acquaintance, "Good evening George, thank you for coming." Turning to his friend, I nodded respectfully and added, "You may call me Rev; how should I address you, sir?"

The older man smiled slightly and said to George, "This one has good manners for a bloodsucker."

To me, he said, "Thank you, Rev; please call me Simon." His words were not exactly polite, but he didn't seem to be intending them to be rude.

Looking at George again, I said, "I hope you have been well. I've been swamped getting to know the others of my kind in the city. They seem likely to let me live in peace."

"That's good, I guess." George seemed to be uncertain about how to proceed. With his master, or teacher, or whatever sitting beside him, he was far less open.

Simon spoke up and got straight to the point. "Our kind do not usually mix. Though it is not strictly forbidden, it is not encouraged. While I appreciate that you seem well-mannered and that George assured me that you were young and had not brought harm to any mortals, I am hesitant to meet with you. I would not choose to do so nor allow my apprentice to do so. We will go unless you have a compelling reason to ask for this meeting."

I nodded sadly. "I am sorry you feel that way. I mean you and your kind no harm and wish we could be on more cordial terms. However, I will respect your wishes and not contact either of you without what I might consider sufficient cause. That said, I discovered something that I thought you might want to know."

A bushy eyebrow shot up on the older man's face. "Oh?"

"One of the vampire elders in this city has an enchanted item that allows her to resist mental compulsion. I don't wish to harm this woman...."

I sighed, knowing they would see through that lie, and amended, "I do not wish to attack this elder, I would prefer to live in peace with everyone, but I fear she will cause me trouble. And I remembered what George said about it being forbidden for mages to work with vampires and create enchanted items for them. That being the case, I thought it might be prudent to inform you so that you can investigate if you wish. The woman in question goes by the name Mrs. Theriot, a Creole with a New Orleans accent, and of all the vampires I have met, she strikes me as the most dangerous."

Simon frowned and shook his head. "Mages will not take action against this vampire elder nor take her enchantment from her no matter how she acquired it. We will not do your dirty work for you. If you wish to deal with her, I suggest you do it yourself."

I sighed, seeing that he was misinterpreting my intentions.

"I assume you have truth-sense active like George said he did during our first meeting. So please judge what I am about to say in light of that fact."

I leaned forward, not threateningly, and spoke, "I could wipe Mrs. Theriot away and her entire organization. I do not need anyone to *do my dirty work*. I do not need anything from you in that respect. I am informing you as a courtesy that she has had dealings with a mage who has performed an enchant for her, which I was told is forbidden. That concerns you. I would like to see her cut off from that source of magic, but I do not need you to do that for me. If I take action against her, it will create a power vacuum that would destabilize the city's vampires as other elders and their minions attempt to seize her territories, which might well generate a conflict. I do not want things to get messy."

Simon sat back, digesting all of that. I had spoken every word truthfully, meaning he had to reevaluate me. I had just let him know that I was powerful enough to take out a vampire elder and all her minions in no uncertain terms.

"Young George here led me to believe you were newly transformed into one of your kind. How is it that you can do what you say?" He was skeptical but curious.

"There are two ways a vampire can become powerful. Survive for hundreds of years; the older they become, the stronger. Or be turned by a very old vampire who has lived for hundreds of years. I have only been this for less than two years, but my maker was hundreds of years older than Mrs. Theriot's, meaning I have the power to do what I said."

I smiled at George and added, "I did not know my own strength when George and I met last year. I had never met another vampire at that point."

This time both Simon's eyebrows tried to chase his receding hairline up his forehead. "I see. Thank you for your honesty."

He was definitely more wary of me now that he knew I was not some weak, freshly turned kid. "In that case, we will look into what you said."

He stood up and gestured for his apprentice to do the same. "Good evening, Rev."

That hadn't gone at all the way I had hoped. When I had initially emailed George, it was because I hoped to test whether or not my anti-magic spell would work. Sadly, that had been before the meeting with Schmidt and Theriot.

If I can't get their help, I'll need to do it on my own. Time to prepare....

CHAPTER 37

CALM BEFORE THE STORM

I DID MORE than pawn off my task on the mages. I had originally wanted George to test Heidi's ring for me. Still, he just was too wary and not friendly enough now for me to trust him, so I had chosen to give them the info about my rival instead, knowing that if they did discover someone in their midst working for a vampire, it would put them slightly into my debt.

I followed that up by doing my own search. I cast a new scrying spell to locate mage auras but kept it contained specifically to Mrs. Theriot's territory to see if any mages were living near her. Sure enough, there was more than one mage aura, but one, in particular, was located in a building owned by Theriot. I knew that had to be it, but I was worried about a confrontation, not knowing what it would be like to face off against a mage.

Worse, I was sure she would be warned against me and prepared. But I couldn't know what the situation was. Did this mage willingly participate in making my vampire rival more powerful, or was it because the old bloodsucker had some kind of leverage against the mage? I found that hard to believe; if the mage was powerful enough to make an enchanted item, then they would be powerful enough to teleport anywhere out of reach. Best to assume a willing accomplice but keep an open mind.

So how to approach this? Should I leave it to the mages or go there myself?

I had my shield against physical attacks and my mental shield, but if I could make a shield against magic, I would be pretty invulnerable, or I hoped I would. Heck, I didn't need a magic shield to be a permanent item; I just needed to know *how* to cast a shield spell that would block magic. It was a catch-22. I couldn't make the one without knowing the other, and I couldn't know that without facing the mage.

I was deep in this thought when Heidi woke up for the morning. She sat up in bed and got that look on her face that said, 'I know something is wrong.'

"Ok, spill it. What's got you brooding?"

She grinned and added, "Not that you don't look sexy and all mysterious when you brood." She ran her hands through her hair, trying to arrange herself.

I told her my conundrum, outlining the current situation and how I had not told the mages about her ring after all.

She chuckled at me. "You are too close to the problem to see the obvious."

Grinning, she gestured at the world outside the windows. "There are more mages in this world, Horatio, than are dreamt of in your tiny city."

I slapped myself on the forehead in a heartfelt facepalm. I was so wrapped up in this being a Houston problem that I didn't even think about looking outside my backyard for answers.

"Just cast one of your scrying spells in a different city where the mages don't know who you are, and approach one at a time until you find one willing to be reasonable. You could even disguise yourself to hide that you are a vampire, and they would probably be more receptive."

I pulled her over to me and wrapped her in a big hug.

"You are a genius!" Then I kissed her, but she pulled away quickly.

"I've got morning breath; you don't want to do that right now." She hit my arm playfully. "But later, maybe...." She left unsaid what she wanted.

I grinned but then teased, "Sorry, love, but I'll be too busy off in some other city carrying out your evil plan to give in to your womanly wiles."

"Womanly wiles, indeed!" She pushed me onto my back and straddled me.

"I'll show you womanly wiles!" She was moving her hips in a very suggestive way that suddenly reminded me what it was like to be alive and all thought of leaving up and left.

A couple of hours later, we both showered and got dressed.

That had been the most fun I had had since my death, and I have to say, being a vampire made sex so much better. I could read Heidi's body and its reactions so well with my heightened senses; it was almost like I could read her mind. I don't want to brag or anything, but I definitely rocked her world. Ok yeah, I'm bragging, but damn it, I have the right. I had never been even remotely that good in life. I just hadn't had the equipment, so to speak, to do what I had just done. Not that it hadn't been equally fun for me.

She pushed me out the bathroom door. "Ok, go get 'em. I need to recover after that, so you get out of here for a while, and I'm going to get breakfast."

I was just about to burn the blood to teleport when I thought of something I had meant to ask.

I gave Heidi a serious look, "We haven't talked about it, but how is your aunt reacting to us getting together? Kat is not someone I want to be pissed off at me." I chuckled, "She threatened to stake me in a very unpleasant way..."

Heidi looked surprised at my question for a second, then gave me a small smile.

"Honestly, she's fine with it. She knows I chased you and made the first moves. If it had been the other way around, she would probably have given you more than a threatening ultimatum about treating me right and not breaking my heart. Plus, since you told us your secret, she's been kinda quiet, trying to process the fact that all the things that go bump in the night are real. It's a lot to take in."

Reaching her arm out the door, she smacked me on the ass. "Now get out of here so I can dress and go get breakfast!"

Grinning, I teleported to Beaumont, a town about a hundred miles east of Houston. I had spent time there as a kid visiting relatives. It was big enough to have at least a couple of mages but not so big that I would need help finding a good spot to talk with them.

On arriving, I opened my tablet and pulled up a map of the city, then cast the mage scrying spell. I have to say, I was really digging this mixture of technology and magic. It was seriously enhancing my abilities!

Sure enough, there were several mages, which I thought was a little odd given the city's small size; they only had a little over 100,000 people, maybe twice that if you added all the surrounding towns nearby. I would have to look around other cities and compare numbers to be sure. For all I knew, perhaps there were more mages out there than I had realized.

Focusing on the task at hand, I searched the map for one that might be in an accessible location to approach. I didn't want to go knocking on some poor mage's front door after all. Nothing says *threat* like confronting someone in their own home, and I did not want to seem threatening when I was here to seek their help.

Luckily, one was conveniently sitting in a coffee shop downtown on the corner of Crocket and Park, which would make them easy to approach. I quickly altered my aura to that of a kami and activated the aura sense, spidey sense, and truth sense spells before taking an Uber to where they were. By choosing an unusual aura, that was obviously not mortal but also not mage or vampire, I hoped it would spark their interest and not automatically set up an antagonistic relationship. I had never heard of any kami or mage having hostile relations, so I hoped that meant they would accept me as not being a threat. I also altered my appearance to seem very Keanu-like.

The coffee shop was on the ground floor of an old building and had an industrial vibe. Still, despite that, it was cozy and had the welcoming atmosphere that any good local hangout has. There was lots of concrete and old brick but with warm wood accents and comfy leather chairs and couches. I walked up to the counter, conversed politely with the barista, and ordered the house special: a Costa Rican brand I had never heard of. I took a sip, nodded, and complimented the woman on its flavor. She barely noticed as she had moved on to her next customer.

It was mid-morning now, so the shop wasn't too busy, having already passed their morning rush as people headed to work. Now that I had coffee in hand, I looked around for the mage but didn't see them. I double-checked the tablet map, and it still showed the blue dot right here in the building. Then I noticed a set of stairs against one wall, its entrance half concealed by a decorative column on which hung old black and white pictures of the downtown in the early part of the previous century. There was even a copy of the famous image of the first oil gusher, Spindletop, from which the coffee shop took its name.

I took my time enjoying the exploration of this place; there was no need to rush. When I made my way upstairs, I could see several seating areas for people to enjoy their coffee, and only a couple of the seats were occupied. The mage sat at a table in the corner by a window with a view of the street below.

I walked over casually and gestured to the chair opposite her. With the room practically empty, it was obvious that choosing that seat meant I wanted to talk. She looked me over with interest but no recognition. Then she really looked and drew back as if startled. She quickly looked around to see if anyone else was there, assessing the danger.

Hesitantly and quietly, she asked, "Um, what are you?"

CHAPTER 38
IT AIN'T EASY BEING GREEN!

I LOOKED her over as well; she seemed young but not immature. She had long, straight blonde hair and a bit of a long nose on a thin, angular face. Still, it worked for her rather than being unattractive and gave her character. Her aura showed that she was middling in strength unless she was hiding her power.

After a long second, to give her a chance to relax, I answered, "You can call me a kami."

She blinked in surprise and then came to grips with the unexpected revelation. If she was good and intelligent, she would have truth sense or something like it running when meeting a new supernatural. "Kami, as in Japanese spirit?"

I smiled and nodded. "You've heard of kami then? Not all Westerners know the kami even exist."

I was being meticulous not to say something that was a direct lie. I hadn't said I *was* a kami, only that she could call me one. Nor did I confirm that I was one but redirected her question.

She nodded slowly. "What can I do for you, Kami?" She said it as if it were a name, which was a relief since I didn't want to give her a false name, and certainly not my real one.

"Kami... I like that. Yes, please call me that. May I know how to address you?" I grinned, showing I was not offended.

"Call me Mary." She waited to see what else I would say.

I answered her previous question. "I saw you were here, so I thought I would introduce myself and ask for a favor. I hope you don't mind, and I would happily compensate you for your time. Call it a consulting fee if you'd like." I smiled hopefully.

Her brows drew down in a slight frown. "That depends on the favor. What would a kami need with a mage?"

"I wouldn't say that a kami needs anything from a mage, but I am curious. I've never had a mage cast a spell at me, and I am wondering what it is like. Is there anything you could cast at me that wouldn't damage me or do me harm?"

She blinked in astonishment. "That is the strangest request I think I've ever been given."

She squinted at me as if trying to divine my reason for asking, although I felt or saw no magic used. "Why would you want such a thing?

I chuckled. "Let's say that where I live, there is a mage who may not have my best interests at heart. I have never met them; I only know they exist and that they are allied with someone who does wish me harm. I do not want to harm the mage and will not do so unless I feel my safety depends on it. However, I also don't want to be surprised to find myself turned into a toad or something."

She nodded in understanding. "So you want another mage to cast a spell on you to see whether or not it will have an effect."

She seemed to consider the request. "Okay, I don't need any money, so there is no need for a *fee* but let's say that you will owe me a small *favor* if I ever need one. Agreed?"

"Sure, although needless to say, it can't be a favor that will harm me or those I care about." I raised an eyebrow in challenge.

Mary thought for a second before agreeing. "Besides, now you've got me curious about what will happen."

She grinned. "I'll turn your hand green; that won't harm you but is a spell that would directly affect your body. That okay?"

"As long as you can change it back. It's not easy being green, ya know."

She groaned but then giggled at my Kermit quote. She looked over at the one other patron of the coffee shop that was upstairs.

"Just one sec." She muttered some quiet words under her breath and cast a spell, but it was directed at the area around us rather than at me.

I was fascinated; it was my first time seeing a spell cast that way. The one time George had made his hands blaze with fire to threaten me, I was too busy being threatened by fire to observe his aura and watch what he was doing. Not to mention that I hadn't even known about looking at auras then.

I could see the energy concentrate in Mary's aura and focus on her hands before being pushed outward, forming a sphere around us.

"Ooh, what was that?" I was eager and curious.

Mary looked at me in consideration. "You could see me casting?"

I frowned, "Well, yeah, you did it right in front of me. How could I not see it?"

She sighed, "No, I mean could you *see* it?"

"Ah, I see what you mean, pun intended." My grin at the chance to make that pun obvious.

"But to answer you: I guess so? I can sense your aura and can feel you push power out of yourself into an area around us. Still, I don't know that I can *see* what you are doing the same way you can see another mage cast a spell because I don't know what it is like for you."

"Hmm... I guess that's acceptable. There isn't really any rule against a mage casting spells in front of other supernaturals." She seemed to make up her mind.

I asked, "That implies there are rules about other things? Should I be concerned? I won't get you in trouble with my favor, will I?"

She shook her head, "No, but we are forbidden to aid certain supernaturals that are considered dangerous. I've never heard of any rules about kami, though. Maybe if there are mages in Japan, they might have rules. Still, honestly, I've never heard of a kami visiting the US before, although I guess it must happen sometimes. That spell I cast was a protective barrier to keep anyone outside it from noticing what we are doing."

Smiling in relief, I gestured with my hand that I was ready.

Mary looked at my hand, concentrated, and spoke a rhyme, "Magic in the air, don't be mean, turn this man's hand the color green!"

I could see and sense the power as it swelled and directed its influence on me. My hand turned green as if it had been painted for St. Patrick's Day. I had felt the change and had the urge to resist, but suppressed that desire. I looked at it for a long moment before glancing back at Mary.

"Okay, please put it back."

Laughing, she said, "Sorry, one favor only!"

I could tell she was just teasing, and I waved my green hand at her in a fist. "Do not vex me, witch, or I might call on mysterious kami powers to turn you green!"

We both laughed at that, then she smiled and said, "Don't worry, it will wear off in about a minute. I wasn't sure how difficult that would be, so I made it a short-duration effect."

"Thank you." I was pleased that this interaction was going so much better than the ones with the other mages. Of course, Mary didn't know I was a vampire and, worse, a blood mage. I was sure it would be going much differently if she knew my true nature. That made me sad that I had to hide what I was to be allowed to live.

"No problem." She was clearly amused.

"Would you mind doing it one more time once this wears off so I can see if I can stop it?" This was the big test and the most significant risk. She might not have ever met a kami, but if she recognized that I was using blood magic, things could get really ugly, really fast. I would have to be prepared to teleport or attack if necessary.

Mary simply said, "Okay, but be careful. If things get out of control and that guy over there sees something, we'll both be in trouble. I've never been good with memory charms, so I'd have to call someone in to clean up our mess."

I bowed my head solemnly, "I will try, but this is completely new to me; give me a minute to prepare myself and focus."

While she did, I put my will towards nullifying the power she would send at me, but that didn't feel right. I couldn't envision a way to do that exactly. Now that I had seen her cast a couple of times, the best I could come up with would be to have the power blocked from reaching me as if it was water splashing off of an invisible shield, deflecting it off in another direction. When I felt comfortable with that, I signaled my readiness.

As I saw her gather the power and begin to push, I burned a blood gem to create a barrier between us that would send the power off to my right. She was casting a low-powered spell, so I made my shield correspondingly weak, and it held, although I could feel it being pushed back toward me. The energy ricocheted off and hit the window next to me, giving it a green tint as if it were stained glass.

Mary's eyes widened, and she exclaimed, "Holy crap, you did it! That was like a mage would do, but your power felt different, not as clean somehow, if that makes any sense. Still, it felt just as strong as I would expect from any mage, maybe a little more so."

She clearly seemed puzzled but not alarmed. "*Earthy* somehow, but not like Wiccan *earth mother* type stuff, but...." She trailed off at a loss for words.

I hoped that meant I hadn't given myself away. She clearly recognized that my power worked similarly to hers but had a different source, as it were. I decided to go for broke. If I cast again, she would see it more clearly anyway. Time for some bullshit or at least some serious misdirection.

"You know how kami are spirits of a place or thing, right? They each draw their power from whatever empowered them in the first place. A river spirit would probably feel *watery* to you." I hesitated momentarily before continuing, "What if I was empowered by the blood spilled as the result of an ancient battle." I hurried to add, "That doesn't make me evil or anything, just explaining why my power might feel that way to you."

Again, I danced really close to the line of not telling a lie.

That seemed to satisfy her.

"Oh, I get it! That was why it seemed earthy and dark, and now that you mention it, I can sense the coppery sort of residue that must come from the blood. That makes total sense now!"

I grinned. I had just pulled that out of my ass, but it fit the explanation. I'm an fucking Aes Sedai, bitches! Watch me bend the truth over and paint a picture that has no resemblance to the actual situation, but without ever speaking a single lie.

"I'm super relieved that it's at least possible to deflect a mage spell; now I feel more confident that I can meet this mage and make sure they don't mean to hurt me."

Mary looked concerned with what I said.

"Hey now, don't be so hasty. The spell I cast was about as gentle as possible, a one on a 10-point scale. If the mage wants to hurt you, they won't be hitting you with anything that weak. They will probably go with a four or a five, or even more if they feel you are a big threat to them. Definitely more if they mean to do you harm and have time to prepare. The casting could be unstoppable if they spent a month preparing a ritual. I don't want to worry you, but I want you to be realistic."

That put things in a much more negative light.

I hadn't considered that, but Mrs. Theriot had had weeks to know I was moving through the city, challenging the other elders. It might already be too late if she had told her witch to start preparing a ritual. On the other hand, I didn't feel like that was very likely. She wouldn't have had any reason to suspect I would recognize her magic talisman that protected her mind. That meant I had only become a real threat to her a few days ago.

That was still too long. It was scary for a witch to have that much time to prepare a ritual to attack me. I might be in real trouble if she cast at me before I could neutralize her.

Realizing I'd been silent too long, I said, "That's all kinds of scary!"

I needed to get out of there fast, go straight in, and confront the mage. If they were doing a ritual, I could stop it. If not, then I would be as prepared as I could be, thanks to this meeting.

"Mary, I need to go, but thank you for your help. Here is my card. Call this number if you ever need me, and I'll do you that favor I owe."

She seemed stunned that her words had had such an effect. "It's okay. I'm sure the mage isn't doing a ritual to kill you. I just wanted to make sure you didn't take them lightly. A powerful magic wielder can be very formidable."

I bowed to her Japanese style and then hurried away. I needed to get far enough from her that she wouldn't sense me teleport.

CHAPTER 39
DING, DONG...

I CALLED for a ride and took it to the other side of town, then got out and teleported when the coast was clear. I went straight to the building where the mage was and appeared on the curb outside. I masked my aura entirely and cast a powerful deflection spell before walking around its exterior. It was an old two-story brick structure that had once been a feed store a hundred years ago, so said the concrete sign embedded in the front façade.

The doors would probably be warded, and the building likely had a basement, given the windows along the ground that I could see on the side. I could see a faint aura of magic on the windows as well. I doubted the spells were permanent, but a ward could be set, and it would last for weeks or even months if cast powerfully enough. These seemed strong, and I didn't know what they would do. That only left one avenue of approach, so I leaped; it was only twenty or twenty-five feet tall. I was able to grab the stone at the top and vault over to land lightly.

The roof had a deck and a door that was not warded. I was surprised, but then powerful wards would likely be draining for a mortal mage to perform. I could sense power of a more mundane sort as I looked closely.

The door had an alarm. Well fuck.

I stood there and thought. If it didn't have magic on it, then I could use magic to get around it. I cast a scrying spell of a different sort, and suddenly, I could see within. That was all I needed; I teleported.

The hallway at the top of the stairs was dark, and there was a smell of incense in the air, but it was faint, as if it was coming from downstairs or the basement. To my vampiric eyes, it was as bright as day, and I carefully made my way down, walking near the outsides where the steps were less likely to creak under my weight.

Being a vampire had some advantages, and I was able to make it down into the building without making noise. I had to thank Queenie for this. I was no burglar or spy in my mortal life, so I didn't have any particular skill. I just had the advantages of my vampire senses and dexterity. I could hear that a floorboard was about to flex and make noise, and I had the speed and ability to react fast enough to avoid it. Of course, if another vampire were present, I'm sure they could have heard me feeling my way around, but I doubted any mortal could have.

The first floor was set up like a stereotypical psychic business, with a store containing herbs and "magic" ingredients at the front. It looked as if it had seen better days, like it had once been well cared for but had fallen into disrepair. I could make out a faded and peeling sign painted in the front window that read "Mistress Almathea's Readings and More". There was nothing particularly disturbing about the front area other than how neglected it seemed.

In the back, through a beaded curtain, waited a cliché of a room. It was set up for Tarot readings and seances, all velvet and candles; there was even a crystal ball sitting in the middle of the table. Up until this point, it could have been any psychic shop anywhere.

Then things got dark.

Against the back wall, near a door leading to stairs going down, there was an altar with a basin for blood sacrifices of small animals. Their bones still decorated its surface, and the rotting bits of flesh still attached gave off a stench to my vampiric nose that even the heavy incense couldn't mask.

That was not good. If this was a voodoo witch using blood sacrifice, she (or he) might be formidable. The stairs down to the basement were through a doorway just to the right of the altar. Luckily it was open, so I continued my stealthy movement downstairs. With my hearing, I could make out chanting, and the incense was much stronger now, but it couldn't mask the scent of blood.

Human blood.

This was bad. Really bad!

If they were sacrificing humans, they could cast magics well beyond what a mortal mage could muster. If they were doing it as part of a ritual, then they were likely performing extremely powerful magic.

Worse, I had no idea how close they might be to completion. If I knew it was coming, I could block it, burn a thousand blood gems, and cast a shield the witch would never penetrate, but there was no way to know when it would hit, so no way to ward against it.

I had a choice. I could run and try to defend against whatever they were trying to do, or I could confront the witch and stop her ritual. Either way posed dangers, but in the end, I just wasn't the kind of person who could walk away and passively wait for an enemy to strike.

I removed my blades from their storage space, proceeded to the basement, and stopped at the bottom, shocked at what I saw.

There was a stone altar in the center of the floor with a man tied to metal rings set in the stone. He was bleeding from his wrist slowly. My second shock was that I recognized him... it was Ralph, one of my bodyguards. They were striking at me and using his association with me to strengthen the spell they were casting. I was furious, and any doubt in my mind about sparing Theriot's mage was gone, blown away like a mobile home before a hurricane.

That was when I caught my first sight of the witch. She knelt before the altar bathing her hands in Ralph's blood, anointing her face and head with it. Like her master, she was a Creole too, but where Theriot's aura was red like any vampire, this witch was the darkest blue I could imagine. It was like the sky at midnight, and where George, Simon, and Mary had all been wispy and ethereal, this aura was wraith-like, with tendrils, and it sent chills up my undead spine. I didn't need to be told, "This means evil."

The woman's eyes opened, and she stared into me, eyes as black as her soul, no whites at all.

"You should not have come. Your death would have been quick and painless." Unlike her pretentious mistress, there was no snakey pretend cajun accent. However, there was a hollow echo when she spoke, as if her words resonated in a deep cavern.

That was it. I needed to end this and obliterate Theriot's organization. I stepped forward, ready to cast another shield in a split second.

As fast as I was, even with my vampiric speed, I wasn't fast enough.

She was already holding her power, ready to cast. Cold tendrils of inky blackness wrapped my legs and chest holding me in place. It was a shock. I had not expected her to be able to react so quickly. Now I was bound and unable to attack or run away. I still had my magic, so not all hope was lost, but from the strength of the bonds, I knew I'd never be able to break loose through force alone.

"You might be mighty among the vampires, but you are nothing before my blood magic. Did you think you could just walk into my home and slay me?"

She seemed to be in a monologuing mood, so I would indulge her to give myself time to think.

"Yes, actually, I did. I knew Theriot would order her pet mage to attack me, but I didn't expect you to be so powerful. Tell me, why would you choose to serve someone as weak and false as she is? You could have a real master if you chose."

There, that should wind her up. Don't get me wrong, I was scared shitless, this hag was scary as fuck, but I wouldn't go down without a fight, and I wanted to know what the situation really was.

She literally snarled, "Serve her? Is that what you think? She is merely a tool for me to operate in this city without drawing the notice of those weak-bellied magicians that have the nerve to call themselves mages."

The bands of shadow around me tightened with her wrath, squeezing me, and my enhanced bones began to grind together.

I let out a groan but didn't reply. The pain was intense but not yet so hard it would do me real damage.

"Those mages will soon learn who the real master of this city is. They shy away from the tools of real power." She gestured, and Ralph convulsed, blood from his wrist spraying the witch in the face.

"What..." I wheezed out, "What does that mean? What tools?"

She cackled maniacally.

If she weren't so scary and this situation so dangerous, I would have laughed at her theatrics. Of course, that would have required that I could get enough air into my lungs to laugh.

"Blood! Blood is the ultimate power. With it, I can cast spells far beyond what those weaklings know! They might as well be children to me. They forbid it because they fear the mortals, but they will learn... yes, they will learn soon what real fear is."

I grasped at straws as I wheezed out, "But what about the Cabal? Aren't you worried about them?"

Honestly, I barely knew anything about that shadowy organization. I had only heard its name a few times, but it struck me that if they were the boogeymen of the supernatural world, then maybe she would be afraid of them.

She seemed to sober for a split second, then steeled herself and sneered. "They might scare the others, but not me. Not anymore. They gather mana and horde it. Every little drop that accumulates, and they don't share any of it with the rest of us. They do it all for their stupid dragon god. As if he were real!" She scoffed at the idea.

"He was probably some stone age barbarian that gathered a following and made a cult out of it."

Spittle was flying from her mouth as she ranted, and I was honestly more scared now. She sounded insane. One strong flex of her inky magic tendrils, and I would be a headless corpse.

She continued, but in an introspective way, no longer ranting. "I haven't feared them and their punishments since I touched real power. A power that makes even this blood magic pale in comparison. It was just a stupid reading for a teenage girl. I barely had any magic in those days, just enough to light a candle or create an unexpected cold draft in the air to fool the gullible into believing my readings. Then I saw the boy's eyes...."

Mistress Almathea's solid black eyes turned pale as she remembered, and I felt the bonds loosen just a hair.

"Thousands of years and uncounted lives hid behind those eyes. I thought my soul would be lost staring into them, pulled away by the magic that surrounded him. When my power accidentally touched against him, it triggered something. My psychic abilities, which had never been more than a whisper, flared to life in that instant, and I knew... I knew I could never be satisfied with the crumbs of power the Cabal allow the rest of the sheep. That's why I turned to blood magic. I may never regain the spark I felt that day, but I will... not... be...held back!"

Her words and intensity built to a shout at the end. No more half-intelligible ranting; now she was focused.

I wanted to know more, but I could see in her expression that she was done playing the Bond villain as she looked at me. She was going to end this.

"Now you will die." She reached for a sacrificial dagger that lay before her on the ground.

She could end me just by squeezing with those wraith-like tendrils, but she wanted my death to power something even bigger.

I couldn't wait any longer; I spent blood.

If she wanted to know what power really looked like, I would show her!

I burned it by the tens, then by the dozens, 100... 200... 300...

The power swelled to the point of being palpable. The dark tendrils holding me dispersed like fog before a tornado. I shoved them away from myself and then ripped them from her, tearing out the power she held.

She screamed in agony and dropped the knife.

"You want to see real power?" Now it was my voice that sounded like it was echoing up out of the abyss.

I stepped closer to her.

She looked up from the floor where she had fallen, her eyes normal now and full of shock and fear.

"You were right, blood is powerful, but you are reaching into a tiny pond thinking you control the sea. Worse, taking the blood with pain and death was unnecessary; it didn't have to be done like that. That evil is all you. It is your sick jealousy and desire for power."

My voice was resonating now with everything around us. No longer simply sound, it was a palpable force.

"Now feel the ocean..."

I used the power in a way I never had before. I didn't cast a spell; there was no chanting or gestures. I felt like I was connected to everything and I was vibrating in tune with the universe.

I simply willed what I wanted, and it happened.

I burned her out of existence!

I channeled fire into a sphere around her, not letting the heat escape but pouring it in, focusing it back on itself.

She had just enough time to register her fate before she was turned to ash. Then even the dust was obliterated, leaving nothing but emptiness.

My mind was finding it hard to focus with so much power in me. I used an infinitesimal fraction of the power, channeled it into Ralph to heal his body and mind, and then sent him to the Tower.

Then I released the fire to consume this building but denied it the power to burn me. I wanted to see with my own eyes that nothing was left of this hellish place that the witch had created. I rose as the fires began devouring the building, floating through the inferno. I move through the air and forward toward the front of what had been the property.

My thoughts were becoming hard to hold onto now, but I felt rather than saw that it wasn't finished yet.

I flowed out of the flames untouched to see Mrs. Theriot standing on the curb dumbfounded as the witch's place of power collapsed in on itself; the fire so intense paint was peeling off road signs half a block away. Her eyes grew wide as she registered my presence, then fear dominated her as she realized that I was immune to the flame and that this was my doing.

She fell to her knees, "Please, no!" Her fake accent was abandoned.

I didn't know what my visage must look like to inspire such a reaction, but it pleased me at that moment. The monster within was in the driver's seat. My own thoughts were distant.

Theriot was responsible for that attack on Jaquelyn's mortal descendant. I knew she was a terrible person, but I wanted to be sure. I reached into her mind, and her plans and actions were laid out before me in all their horrific detail. What I had known barely touched the surface of how bad she was. If she had had her way, the city would be in flames, and she would stand over the ashes ruling it all.

This creature was responsible for a great deal of death and suffering, planning even worse, and it was in my power to stop it.

Distantly and with great effort, I tried to consider options. I had so much power flowing through me, barely restrained. I could use that power to dominate her will and turn her into the Mother Teresa of vampires. She would spend centuries, maybe millennia doing good deeds before she became strong enough to overcome the compulsion and return to her vile ways.

Even in this state, with hellfire flames surrounding me, I shuddered at the thought as a chill went down my spine.

That was a line I wouldn't cross.

It was one thing to kill someone and end their life. It was another to permanently violate their will and make them act against their fundamental nature. One of the reasons I despised Theriot was that she employed serial rapists like those first vampires I had encountered in this town. I wouldn't become like her, violating those who crossed me. Better a clean, quick end. I was already going to have to live with myself over these deaths. Being an executioner was cleaner than imprisoning her in her mind for hundreds or thousands of years.

I hated being put in this position that I had never wanted to be in. I had just wanted to live in peace and be left alone. Then a memory of something I had read came back to me.

"It is better to be a warrior in a garden than a gardener in a war."

I would do what I had to do because it was in my power to do it. I would do it because this place I had chosen to be my home would be better and safer as a result. And I would pay the price that it cost me to do it, whether to my soul or my future in the city.

All that was going through my thoughts in seconds as I looked at her trembling form. When I spoke, my voice seemed to echo out of the depths of hell. The strange sonic resonance of it evidence of the strain I felt holding so much power in check. It felt like it wanted to be free, to run wild, but I knew that was just because I had unleashed far too much to hold.

"You may have been a tool in the witch's hands, but you were a willing tool, and you used her borrowed power to do horrible things to innocent people. For that, you deserve death."

There was still so much power flooding my body, almost overpowering my mind to be holding this much. I needed to channel it before it was too late, and it consumed me as well.

"*Burn*," I intoned with the finality of death incarnate.

Flames like hellfire rose from beneath her in a pillar of incandescent heat a hundred feet high, erasing her from existence as thoroughly as I had done with her master.

A part of my mind knew I was lighting a beacon of magic so bright that every mage in the city had to see it, maybe every mage in a thousand miles, but I couldn't help it. Not even my vampire body was meant to channel so much power, and I could feel my regeneration struggling and failing to keep up with the damage that merely holding the energy was causing. The fires I was creating were satisfying, and they were helping, but they weren't using enough of the power to save me.

I moved. I took a step, and I was on the rocky crags of an island off the coast of New Zealand, uninhabited and so far from civilization that it was unlikely to be detected.

These thoughts were fleeting and hard to hold onto.

I channeled the flame into the stone, burning out a tunnel deep into the rock, hollowing out a space big enough to fit several houses. That was helping, the magic was diminishing, but I needed to do more...

I channeled my creative nature to shape the stone into a home, adding floors, and smoothing walls.

Yes! This was helping. The power was slowly reducing.

I melted the stone of the hillside letting it cascade down and cover the entrance, sealing me within. I erased the tunnel by melting the rock around it and solidifying it. I shot beams of energy outward, making small holes for air, and drilled downward, enlarging this hidden lair even more, adding two more floors below the surface.

Finally, the power was subsiding to a survivable level.

I would like to say I stood there looking at what I had created with the leftover power as if I were Hephaestus, God of the Forge. Unfortunately, the truth was that as the last of the energy flowed out of me, I dropped to the floor like a rag doll, unable to even move.

If I had been smart, I would have used that power to find each of Mrs. Theriot's minions and burn them out of existence, but I hadn't been. I was barely in control of myself at that point. I was lucky I managed to get to this uninhabited place and use up the rest of the energy before it destroyed me.

Always in the past, I had used massive amounts of power to do creative acts of enchantment, sending the power directly out of myself and channeling it into a spell, making it permanent and spending it immediately. I had never tried to *hold* the power and wield it the way I had that day.

I hoped I never had to do that again!

The power may have made me invincible for that short time, but it was almost my end as well.

CHAPTER 40

CLEANING UP AFTER MYSELF

When I awoke at sundown, I understood that it had been daytime on this side of the world. When my power had run dry, I had tumbled into oblivion just as any vampire would at dawn. Luckily I had plenty of magic still bound up in blood gems inside me and in my storage rings. It was so dark inside the mountain that I could barely see my hand in front of my face, even with my vampiric vision.

I burned first one gem to energize and nourish my body, then another to light the space around me.

I was horrified.

In the light, I could see that what I had created was not quite what I had remembered. I had a vague recollection of forming this place with the intention of making it a safe retreat in the event I needed to flee sometime in the future. I had thought I was making a four-level home inside the rock. Rather than being straight and smooth, the walls flowed and dripped, like something out of a Dali painting. The floors were level and smooth, but that was all I could say about the place. It was a little disturbing that my subconscious made this Geigeresque monstrosity.

It wasn't beyond repair, and it had been a good idea, so I would have to come back sometime and renovate, smoothing out the creepy vibe the melting rock had left.

When I returned to the Tower, Heidi threw herself onto me and squeezed me almost as hard as the shadow tendrils had the night before.

She was nearly in tears when she asked, "What happened? You left yesterday, and then just after sundown Ralph appeared in the Tower out of nowhere and said he couldn't remember anything from the last two days."

She pulled back away and looked me in the face. "Then there was that fire at one of Mrs. Theriot's buildings last night just before she arrived then she disappeared off the map. But then you never called or came home. I was worried you had died in that fire along with her!"

She squeezed me into another hug, not wanting to let go.

I smiled at her and took her hand. "I nearly did, but not because of the vampire or her witch. I almost took in too much magic to handle and destroyed myself."

I was about to sit on the couch when I noticed Heidi wrinkle her nose. That, in turn, made me realize that I smelled horrible. Like dirt and fire, and it was strong enough to make her human nose rebel; it must be extreme indeed. I sighed and led her toward the bathroom instead.

"Okay, I take the hint. I stink. Let's talk while I take a quick shower."

I stripped off the clothes and dropped them in the laundry on the way to the oversized glass-walled shower. Heidi wolf-whistled me as I got naked but then became serious again.

She seemed unsure about how to feel as she spoke, "You know those two vamps you told me about, the ones Theriot had collared? They were in that car when you destroyed her. The second you disappeared off the map, they took off. I don't know where they went, but they headed east on I-10 and drove like bats out of hell all the way to the edge of the city until they got out of range of your scrying spell.

I thought for a minute about that before answering.

"I think they were being held against their will, dominated either by Theriot's mojo or maybe some magic cast on them by the witch. When those two died, it must have destroyed the control and freed them. Hopefully, they can find peace somewhere after what they must have been through."

Heidi looked pale at that and empathetic towards the victims. It made me warm to her even more; she had a good heart.

As I showered, I told her what had happened since I had left the previous morning. I didn't leave anything out, from meeting Mary and learning how to deflect spells to the unexpected confrontation and the results.

"I hadn't known it then, but so long as she didn't catch me off guard, she couldn't have hurt me. She did surprise me, though, and caught me in magical bindings, and if she hadn't gone all Bond villain and gloated, she could easily have killed me. She thought she was holding so much magic power that I couldn't escape."

I paused briefly in my lathering to give Heidi a sober look. "Now that I've tried to hold that much mana and wield it, I can understand how drunk on the power she must have felt. She was only holding a fraction of what I could do, but it was so much more than a normal mage could wield, and I got it. She wasn't really overconfident; she just didn't know that there could be bigger fish swimming in the waters. She thought she was the shark when she was really just a minnow. Which makes me wonder if there are whales out there that would make me seem like a small fish by comparison."

I chuckled darkly, then added, "One lesson I'm going to try and take from this is that I should never monologue. Even if I feel unbeatable, I will not give my opponents a chance to harm me; I will strike immediately and without warning."

I became serious once again as I concluded, "If she had done that, I would not be here right now."

Heidi did not look happy to hear that, but I was not going to shield her from the truth. I almost died yesterday, and I needed to remember it.

For her part, she was out of her mind with worry the whole time because she didn't know what was happening and whether I was alive or dead. It was a legitimate concern and one I figured I ought to address with some new magic items when I got the chance.

There was one last question before we let that drop. She asked, "So, I understand that with everything happening, you couldn't stop to call me in the middle of it just to reassure me. I don't expect you to, either. But after the fight, why did you teleport all the way around the world instead of coming back here. Maybe I could have helped?"

It was a legitimate question and one I didn't want to just flippantly answer, so I gave it some thought.

"A couple reasons. In that moment, I wasn't fully in control of myself. I held so much power that it made it hard for me to think straight. Right then, I was at the point of losing control. Although I didn't think of it consciously at the time, I didn't come back here for fear I might hurt you and everyone else in the Tower. I was like a nuke on a hair trigger: one bad jostle, and it could have gone off. And I do mean a nuke. With that much power, I could have destroyed the entire city and left it a crater in the ground if I had misused it."

Her eyes got big, "Damn." It was all she said, but I could tell she understood. That was one of the things I really liked about her. She trusted me even when I told her something hard to accept.

When I was clean and dry, I dressed in comfortable clothes, but ones that I would not mind destroying. My outfit from yesterday would have to be destroyed as well. I didn't want to keep anything that could be magically traced back to me that tied me to the scene. I was sure the city's mages would be investigating the fire.

To be safe, I incinerated them on the way out of the bathroom but used my magic to make sure the smell and smoke were disposed of elsewhere. After getting ready, I also added a trench coat and hoodie to my outfit. I would also be destroying these clothes later, but I didn't want to deal with blood getting on me if I could help it.

Heidi was talkative while I dressed, asking more questions and commenting on my story. Still, I was already focused on what I needed to do.

Mrs. Theriot's minions were still out there. They were the absolute scum and villainy of the world. Her organization was filled with murderers, rapists, and those who reveled in preying on the weak and innocent. I had confirmed that from her mind in that eternal instant before I passed judgment on her. I still wasn't sure how I had accomplished that. A lot of what I had done the previous day while holding all of that power was hazy and a little vague now, like remembering a dream. Not that every other vampire in the city was a saint, but I knew most of the other elders wouldn't condone such behavior from their people. Not that the other elders necessarily cared, but they knew it would destabilize the city and bring chaos which would not be good for their own existence.

I needed to do this. Better to be a warrior when I needed to be one. The garden couldn't grow if I let it be choked by weeds like her followers.

"Heidi, today I need to eliminate the rest of Theriot's minions. I want to do it before they realize what happened and decide to flee the city or before other vamps in the city claim them. I don't want anything left of her organization after today. At least nothing supernatural...."

Heidi was one of the flowers in my little garden, and I didn't want her to be affected by this, but at the same time, I needed her to know what this life I was living entailed.

I explained what I had learned from Theriot's mind, confirming what I had previously suspected. That she and her blood mage master were building an organization of the worst scum in order to eventually destabilize the city so they could take over. I spared her the gory details but made sure she understood the world she was living in now. I also wanted her to know that the bloodbath I was about to cause wasn't something I chose to do lightly.

She had a grim expression on her face when I finished, but she seemed resolved. "Okay, let's go to the map room and see where they are. Will you do it while they sleep?"

I nodded thoughtfully, "Damn straight. Most of them literally won't know what hit them. They don't deserve to face me in a straight fight like this were some movie, and I won't risk my life when I don't have to."

We checked the map, and I plotted my course.

This might be a grim and necessary task, but I wasn't going to risk this being tied to me. The other elders might suspect, but they wouldn't be able to prove anything.

Before I teleported to that area of the city, I changed my appearance with an illusion. I looked like a young girl, complete with a school girl outfit, plaid miniskirt, white shirt, and pig tails. If they woke, let them die feeling like they had gotten killed by a teenage girl. It would be ironic and fitting.

Beneath the illusion, I was covered almost head to toe so I wouldn't get all bloody, but they wouldn't see that, and neither would any cameras. To all outward appearances, Buffy flew in from Sunnydale and she was pissed.

I won't bore you with the details, but I hunted the gang members, the rapists, drug dealers, vampiric pimps, and all other manner of scum Theriot had created or claimed. I didn't leave a single one alive by sunset. If I had been caught on camera and anyone cared to check the footage, it really would look like the Slayer had come to town and cleaned house on the East side.

When it was all done, I teleported to a secluded spot on Galveston Island and burned my clothes, then took spares out of my ring before returning to the Tower. I also used a quick spell to ensure no blood was on my clothes or blades. No traces remained, magical or mundane.

When I got back, Heidi was there in my bedroom waiting. She had known when the last dot had disappeared from the map and knew I would return soon.

She looked at me, frowning. "You know, it's almost creepy for you to look like that. I don't think I'd be attracted to you as a teenage girl." She stuck out her tongue.

I laughed and dropped the illusion. "Aww, come on, are you telling me you never experimented in college?"

I teased her, and she threw a pillow at my head in response.

I gracefully caught it and dropped it on the couch.

"That's better. I like men. And specifically, I like you, so keep it that way when we are together," she shot back.

She got serious, "I want to know if you are okay. What you did today... that had to be hard."

I could tell she wanted to ensure I was emotionally fine after all the killing, but I didn't want to deal with that yet. I needed to not think about it right then.

I gave a quick nod to her last statement, and I could see in her eyes that she was worried. Instead of talking about it, I ignored that conversation in favor of something else.

I said, "Fine. Let's go eat out tonight. It would be smart to be seen in public after the day I just had. There will be some questions in the minds of the city elders, and if they see me calm and unphased by what happened yesterday and today, it will make them question whether I had anything to do with it or not. They have to know Theriot and I did not part on good terms, and now she and her entire organization are dead in the span of two days. I suspect if Schmidt had had any ideas of challenging me, they would be put to rest now."

She grinned, "Let's do Italian tonight." She stopped in her tracks and then looked at me seriously, a little worried. "Garlic doesn't hurt you, does it?"

I just laughed. "I love garlic."

She sighed in relief, "Good, I might have had to break up with you over that." She grinned and put her arm through mine.

CHAPTER 41
UNGRATEFUL MAGES

OVER THE NEXT WEEK, I was approached by several elders asking whether I wanted to claim Mrs. Theriot's territory. I politely declined but neither confirmed nor denied that I had been the one to wipe her out. I did acknowledge that she had threatened me and that we hadn't seen eye to eye but left it at that. Let them draw their own conclusions.

I did suggest it would not be wise for the elders to get into a conflict over claiming her territory and hoped that it wouldn't come to that. They agreed, but I doubted that they would heed that particular advice. Still, hopefully, they wouldn't allow their tussle to spill into the open such that the mortals took notice.

They weren't the only ones who contacted me. Three days after the event, I received an email from George asking to meet at the restaurant for dinner. When I arrived, both he and his teacher Simon were present. Simon seemed stiff and uncomfortable but still dressed the same old way, all except for the cap.

He addressed me as I sat down. "It seems something very powerful happened in the city and involved a mage. Would you happen to know anything about that?" It was a fairly open-ended question and not a terribly polite greeting.

So I countered, "And a good evening to you too, Simon. I hope you are well, and you, George. How have you been?"

Simon frowned slightly but nodded, acknowledging the point. "Fine. You seem healthy, or at least unchanged."

I smiled and answered his question, conscious that they would both be truth-sensing me. "Yes, I do know something about it. It seems that the mage I asked you to look into was involved."

The older man paled slightly. "What happened? The entire mage community sensed a massive expenditure of power. A whole building was consumed in flames that burned so hot that not even the brick was left behind. The mortals are explaining it away as a fire due to improperly stored chemicals left over from when it was a feed store. Seems it started in the basement, although there is so little left of the property, I can't imagine they can honestly tell."

I shrugged and said, "I confronted the mage I spoke to you about. It turns out Mistress Almathea was not a minion of the Vampire elder after all but was the master. She was performing a blood sacrifice ritual, which had been going on for days."

George looked like he wanted to throw up but was holding it together. Hearing that one of their own was doing something so taboo must be hard to accept. He seemed to be the idealistic type and probably felt that no mage would stoop to such things.

"Her aim was to strike directly at me. She had my bodyguard tied to an altar and was bleeding him out when I arrived. I interrupted her ritual, and she lost control of her magic. I spirited my friend out of there and barely escaped without being destroyed by the magic myself."

I added, "I did see that the Vampire elder arrived just as I was leaving, but she was not quick enough to escape the flames."

Every word was true. Just not even close to what actually happened. Let the mages draw their own conclusions from my words.

Simon sat back and seemed to deflate. "I didn't really believe you before. Oh, I knew you thought you were telling the truth, but I didn't want to believe one of ours would stoop to working for a vampire or helping one."

He looked up and asked without real hope, "And you are absolutely sure she was using blood sacrifice to fuel her magic?" He glanced sideways at his apprentice, clearly worried about how this news would affect the young mage.

I nodded. "Absolutely sure. She gloated over the fact. It seems she had some serious disdain for the mages of the city. She said you were weak for fearing to grasp the true power that came from blood magic."

He turned to his apprentice, "And you see where that led her. This is why we teach against such practices and punish those who commit them so thoroughly."

He turned back to me.

"There is no law among the mages taken more seriously than that against the use of Blood Sacrifice. If you had not interrupted her ritual, we would have discovered and dealt with her ourselves. I assure you she would not have gotten off so easily as simple destruction."

He looked at his apprentice and added, "You will remember this all of your days, but you will speak of it to no one but me, do you understand?"

"Yes." George looked like he would have preferred living his life, never having heard this tale.

Simon focused on me again, and he expressed a little anger and frustration as he said, "I wish you had not interfered. Had we caught her, we would have made such an example of her that children for generations would have spoken her name as a cautionary tale. Instead, we will have to keep this a secret. A quick death is not enough punishment for one such as her, and we would not want our young to think they could get away so easily."

Damn, that was hardcore!

I replied, "If I hadn't acted when I did, she would have completed that ritual, and I would be dead, and you would have a witch on your hands wielding magic as dark as her soul and with the backing of a powerful vampire elder. Everyone in the city would have feared her after that. Maybe you would have made an example of her, but at what cost? How many of your lives would have been lost in the effort? Likely the Cabal would have gotten involved."

I added that last, hoping Simon would react and reveal something about the mysterious group that I didn't know.

The old mage was not mollified, but he did acknowledge my point. "Still, it is good that *they* did not become aware of this. The city would become an unpleasant place to be for a time. Even so, I cannot be satisfied with what has happened. I will have to convene a conclave and tell the others that the witch was doing ritual magic to attack you and lost control of it. If any of them investigate, they may realize there was too much magic involved to be anything but a major ritual. That sort of thing would take months to perform. It is a thin excuse and won't stand up if someone pokes at it."

He was clearly displeased and worried. "If that happens, we may yet have the Cabal poking into our business, and none of us wants that!"

I frowned. I wouldn't have nearly died if Simon and his mage community had heeded my warning.

"That is not my concern. I warned you of the witch out of courtesy. I would have happily let you do your thing. Still, when I learned she might be casting against me directly, I had to act and investigate immediately, or I would have died."

It was clear from my tone that I was deadly serious, "Had I been half an hour later in arriving, my friend would be dead, and so would I. She was at the culmination of her sacrifice as I arrived and was ready to cut his throat."

Simon sighed resignedly. "I cannot disagree, you did what you had to do, and I would have done the same in your place. Nonetheless, I hope very much that our paths do not cross again."

I shook my head sadly, "I wish that you did not have such a loathing for me and that we could be on cordial terms, but I will not contact you again unless I feel it is something you should know."

"If we were, that would surely draw the Cabal down on us. These meetings have already been a risk."

The mages stood, and Simon made to brush the dirt off his hands, in the universal sign that he was done with this. George looked a little embarrassed by the situation but was not about to show any sign of disagreeing with his master. He gave me a very slight nod of his head as he turned to go. Perhaps there was hope for the younger mage, but only time would tell.

CHAPTER 42

YOU CAN'T GO HOME AGAIN

Where did that leave me? I had accomplished pretty much all my goals. I had an incredible home and a beautiful girlfriend. The city's vampires were leaving me alone, the mages didn't want anything to do with me, and I had all the magic and defenses I could want, right?

Sure, there were still things to do... I had that nightmarish lair off the coast of New Zealand that needed to be redone and built out. There was more I could do to make my Tower home safe from attack, and there were always more enchanting projects I could undertake. Still, those weren't drives; they were just projects. Queenie's fierce compulsion that she had placed in me to survive and reach a point of safety was finally satisfied.

It had been nearly two years since my death, and I had not yet gone to see my family. I had wanted to desperately after my death and worried how they would have taken it, but Queenie's compulsion on me hadn't allowed it, both for my own sake and theirs. But now? I thought it was finally time.

There were a lot of emotions and baggage locked away, and I was looking forward to dealing with it finally. I hoped my friends and family wouldn't hate me for putting them through my "death". Regardless, I had to see them, even if only to assure myself that they were fine and that they were moving on with their lives.

I told Heidi I needed to go for a bit and take care of something. She tried to get me to tell her out of worry that I would go do something dangerous, but I assured her that was not the case. I just needed to see some people and pay off some debts. She reluctantly let me go and kissed me fiercely before I left.

Once I teleported, I changed my appearance to not look like Daniel Fox so no one would connect my new identity to my mortal family. That would undo any safety I had managed to provide them.

I walked through my parent's neighborhood and was unpleasantly surprised to find a stranger watering their lawn. I looked at him hard, using regular vision and magic to ensure he was just a normal guy.

That only took a second, but when I was satisfied, I paused on the sidewalk and asked, "Hi, do the Hurleys still live here?"

The grumpy-looking older man frowned at me as if I were bothering him, "What? Uh, no, I've lived here for the last year or so. The old owners moved to Vegas or something, I don't know."

I looked at the man; he seemed to have a standard mortal aura, so I approached a little closer and focused my will on him.

"Tell me everything you know about what happened to the couple who lived here."

His face went slack, the perpetual frown dissolving into a blank expression. "They sold me the house after their kid died. I heard from my realtor that they moved to Vegas. Some casino gave them a house out there, something to do with their kid's death or something; compensation, I guess."

Vert ta ferk?!? No casino should have any connection to my death!

As far as the authorities were concerned, I had died trying to prevent a burglary gone wrong at the AirBnB where I was staying at the time. Before my death, I hadn't made it to any casino, so there shouldn't be any connection.

Could the casino I robbed have somehow connected the random death of a visitor there for a convention to what I had taken? I had ditched everything I owned from my old life. I made sure I didn't take anything with me... except for the storage card out of my phone with my family pictures on it. Still, even that had been destroyed a couple of days later.

I thought furiously for a moment, but no, even with magic, there shouldn't be any way they could know the card was missing from the phone. I realized I had been standing there for too long looking at this guy.

"Uh, thanks. I live a few blocks over and used to talk to the couple who lived here sometimes on my walks. I was just curious. You will forget I asked about the old owners, and we just talked about how annoying the homeowners association is."

I turned and kept walking down the street. I was glad I hadn't come here looking like my new self. If they had taken my parents to lure me back to Vegas, they might be watching this neighborhood to see if someone would come by looking for them.

I was torn. On the one hand, I had somehow screwed up. When I robbed the casino and faked my death, something about that must have either tipped them off or made them suspicious. Or hell, maybe they had supernatural Sherlock Holmes investigate the scene and put together the clues that I hadn't really died. Regardless, they had taken my parents.

A sudden chill went down my spine. Had they taken anyone else? My brother and his children, or my friends?

Fury was building in my heart. I might have stolen from them, but it was just money. Money that was insured even. This was people. People I cared about!

I wanted to start burning blood gems by the dozens and storm in there and use the power to tear the casino down around them and force them to return my parents. I knew it was a bad idea. I knew there were a hundred reasons that wouldn't work.

Still, mana was beginning to build inside me when my phone rang....

Thank you for reading Vampire's Heir 1: Book Six of the Greymantle Chronicles! I hope you enjoyed this novel.

If you have enjoyed the book please leave a review. It helps tremendously and enables these books to get noticed by other potential readers.

Be sure to visit JDavidBaxter.com or the Greymantle Chronicles website. There you can sign up and gain access to exclusive content, excerpts from upcoming books, maps, artwork, and stay up to dates on what is happening with the series and the author.

AFTERWORD

A NOTE TO THE READER ABOUT UPCOMING GREYMANTLE STORIES:

I wanted to take a moment to give a glimpse into the series and what is planned next.

Books One to Five was a story arc focused on Nate Marche. This set of books tells a complete story about that protagonist and can be read as a standalone series.

However, Nate and the story of the Greymantle Chronicles does not end there!

There is a larger story that incorporates several other characters and reveals deeper secrets and plots that go beyond what was revealed in the opening five books.

Vampire's Heir 1, which you have just finished, begins a story focused on Daniel Fox. I am planning three books in this set. The events of which will include Nate and his sister Els.

Els will also have her own series, which is planned to be three books. Her story will begin with her training in the Healers Guild and her adventures will uncover unexpected new enemies. I do not want to tease too much regarding the story for fear of spoilers. However, like Daniel's story, Els' tale will tie in with the larger story arc involving all of the characters.

Lastly, another series will be based around the other half of Darian's soul. It is also planned to be three books. Note that I reserve the right to change the number of books in each story as it evolves. Some of these may end up being longer or shorter than three books.

Due to the nature of these stories being connected to one another, I will be releasing them in an order that will not spoil one story with details revealed in another character's adventures as much as possible. I listed Vampire's Heir 1 as Book Six in the overall series for this reason. The plan is to release Els' Book One next as that makes most sense to the continuity.

You can visit jdavidbaxter.com or GreymantleChronicles.com to check for more information about current plans and release schedules.

Thank you again for reading the novels of the Greymantle Chronicles series; I hope they bring much entertainment!

ABOUT THE AUTHOR

David would say his career path has been strange and varied; from falling off horses for a living as a Renaissance Festival Jouster to managing teams and projects at Fortune 500 companies. He graduated with a degree in English and earned teaching certifications in English, History, and Professional Pedagogy. Most recently, he was an editor on the Stargate Roleplaying Game core book produced by Wyvern Games. He is also co-founder of Silver Paw Publishing, a firm dedicated to helping new authors navigate the world of self-publishing.

ALSO BY J DAVID BAXTER

THE GREYMANTLE CHRONICLES:

Guardsman: Book One

Mage: Book Two

Swordmaster: Book Three

Defender: Book Four

Dragonlord: Book Five

SHOW YOUR SUPPORT!

If you have enjoyed the Greymantle Chronicles so far and would like to show your support, there are many ways in which you can do so.

Tell a friend!

At the end of each book, I mention that one of the best ways you can support me is to leave reviews and share what you like about the stories with other readers. Whether simply clicking some stars or explaining what you liked, all the good reviews help retailers know that a book or series is worth carrying. It is especially beneficial with Amazon, as their algorithm factors reviews into whether it chooses to present a book to other readers.

Ask your local library or independent bookstore to carry the books.

Drop by my Facebook page or website and leave a comment or drop me a note. facebook.com/jdavidbaxterauthor or jdavidbaxter.com

---

Check me out on Ko-fi if you'd like to drop something in the digital tip jar:

www.ko-fi.com/jdavidbaxter

Any and all support is greatly appreciated!

Made in United States
North Haven, CT
09 June 2024

53415818R00166